MW01193817

THIS KIND OF TROUBLE

THIS KIND OF TROUBLE

A NOVEL

Tochi Eze

An imprint of Penguin Random House LLC
1745 Broadway, New York, NY 10019
penguinrandomhouse.com

Book design by Laura K. Corless

LIBRARY OF CONGRESS CATALOGING-IN-PUBLICATION DATA

Names: Eze, Tochi author
Title: This kind of trouble: a novel / Tochi Eze.
Description: New York: Tiny Reparations Books, Penguin Random House, 2025.
Identifiers: LCCN 2024055115 (print) | LCCN 2024055116 (ebook) |
ISBN 9780593475102 hardcover | ISBN 9780593475126 ebook
Subjects: LCGFT: Novels
Classification: LCC PR9387.9.E9375 T45 2025 (print) |
LCC PR9387.9.E9375 (ebook)
LC record available at https://lccn.loc.gov/2024055115
LC ebook record available at https://lccn.loc.gov/2024055116

ISBN 9798217176908 (export)

Printed in the United States of America
1st Printing

Title page art: flame wave pattern © Galyna_P/Shutterstock.com

The authorized representative in the EU for product safety and compliance is Penguin Random House Ireland, Morrison Chambers, 32 Nassau Street, Dublin D02 YH68, Ireland, https://eu-contact.penguin.ie.

The child will not share the guilt of the parent,
nor will the parent share the guilt of the child.

—EZEKIEL 18:20

Families are everyone's first war.

—TOLA ABRAHAM ROTIMI,
"We Need to Talk About Snails," 2017

THIS KIND OF TROUBLE

1

Benjamin

Atlanta, 2005

Benjamin sat across from the bank officer. There was a small square window inches below the ceiling so that the afternoon sunrays slanted through the opening and fell on his face. The room reminded him of his own office in Ikoyi; the humidity, the feeling of old leather against his back, the smell of tobacco that filtered in from the entrance, as though time had frozen into a capsule. It occurred to him—while the bank officer sifted through his files—that a man should be entitled to the troubles of his making; no more, no less. Yet, it seemed his own troubles began with his father. The poor chap had been born into a quarrel that made him an orphan. And if not his father, then who? Perhaps it began with Benjamin himself those forty or so years ago when he'd moved to Lagos, that city damp with heat, aflame with postindependence ambition, unconscious of its chaos. No. He shook off the thought before it could settle. There was something else. Someone else. The conclusion was both familiar and inevitable, for his troubles, indeed, began with Margaret.

Of course his nostalgia could have been the effect of the phone call from the night before. He'd woken up this morning and wondered if he'd dreamed it—if her voice, after these many years, could have stayed the same. He was not a sentimental man. Even in the old days, he had not given himself to the usual productions of romance—flowers, walking a woman to the salon, complimenting her dress and shoes, her nails, those long cosmetic talons. It was not his style. He'd loved his women the way his father had told him to: like a bird, one had to hover and watch; affection was a matter of practicality.

The bank officer was forty-two years old, named Mark Troshinsky, after his Russian grandfather. His patrilineal family had moved to the United States in 1952; they were veterans, having fought in the Vietnam War. They bled for this country, the bank officer said, his eyes falling briefly on the small American flag on his desk. Last year, the bank officer continued, he'd had a health scare; he did not say what it was, and Benjamin did not ask. After the scare, he was thinking about early retirement. He wanted to spend time on the important things, he said. Benjamin nodded to indicate that he was listening, but his mind was now fully turned to Margaret. You must know what you are getting into, Benjamin's father had told him. However, as Benjamin would learn, there comes a time when a father's advice is cast away and the heart devises its own reasons. And when that time came for Benjamin, he followed an old cliché and fell for the great love of his life. Now he shifted slightly on his seat, an attempt to pull himself back to the present, to the bank officer's words. If it was a different day, if his mind was not crowded by the events of yesterday—by that phone call—Benjamin would have said something to the banker about the illusion of retirement. He knew firsthand that the only true retirement was death, and that the absence of work did not mean the absence of anxieties, both old and new.

The bank officer had been to Europe, Thailand, and, more recently, Brazil—an avid traveler, proud of his worldliness. He pulled out a picture from the wallet in his breast pocket and showed Benjamin—the banker standing with two tanned teenagers, his daughters, Benjamin presumed, all three of them draped with red and black shawls. Benjamin smiled at the picture and asked about a painting that hung across his desk, performing, in his own way, that polite American curiosity. When Benjamin had first moved to the United States, he thought it absurd that he could learn intimate details of people's lives so casually—in train and bus stations. He still found it affecting that Americans could be so open and friendly yet stubbornly private, generous with their stories but highly suspicious of any interest in their affairs. He smiled at the banker, then decided to offer his own gesture of a life. He shared how he, too, had traveled quite a bit, that he was originally from England, where he had his early education, that he had lived in Nigeria, and Ghana, then gone back to London before moving to the United States to attend graduate school.

"I have always wanted to go to Africa," the bank officer said. He opened his drawer to pull out stacks of paper, spreading three pages on the polished desk.

"Is that right?" Benjamin replied. "I myself am Nigerian," he added after a pause.

"I see—" the bank officer said, eyeing Benjamin. There was silence. Papers shuffled. A nudge to Benjamin to sign documents. Then the bank officer warmed up again as he put the papers away.

"I suppose if we dig far enough, we'd all find a little of Africa in us," the officer said, smiling.

Benjamin had come to enjoy watching the surprise, then confusion on people's faces whenever he said that he was Nigerian. His skin was the same pale pigment of most white men, his hazel eyes tinted toward green when he stood in the sun. It was a confusion that he, too, had carried as a boy. His father's skin had been light enough, and so Benjamin had never questioned how much paler his mother was when she stood next to his father, or the way his father's hair coiled around his head. Benjamin was nine years old when he learned about the difference between his father and mother, and he'd only discovered it when one of the boys in his catechism class asked, "How is it that your mother married a negro?" Benjamin had not said anything in response, but later that night, just before dinner, he'd stood beside his father, rolled up his dust-stained sleeves, then placed his hand against his old man's. It was the first time he saw the contrast, shocked that all this time he'd never noticed.

"You are dark," Benjamin said to his father. Not a question, a simple acknowledgment.

"It appears so," his father answered, then continued simply, "Go clean up before your mother's cooking grows cold."

Benjamin left the bank wishing he could have a cigarette, but he had not smoked in twelve years. He stood under the blue awning and watched a bird perch on a tree. His mind again returned to the events of yesterday—the call. It was a simple exchange, no longer than five seconds. Maybe six. But it was enough to send him back to Lagos, the city and the people he once called home. His father's connection to a small Nigerian village was almost mythical, a strange family story Benjamin often recounted to pretty women in his university days. But where his father's myth ended, his own life began. He'd had it all—a home. A wife. A child. His own child. Benjamin had two other marriages after that time in Nigeria, neither of which resulted in children. He had even, out of pity, entertained accusations of impotency by his second wife and their family clinician, a small weight to carry because Benjamin knew it to be undeniably false; he was capable of fatherhood, if only in a biological sense. It is true that he'd left Margaret, left his child, left the country—but leaving was not a crime. If there was one thing that he had learned as a man, it was this: all commitments are negotiable—with two legs and a good enough reason, one could always find the door. He told himself year after year that there'd been no other choice, that he'd had to remove himself from that specific situation as one might crawl out from under the weight of a stone pressing down on one's neck. Leaving was a game of survival, and he, Benjamin Fletcher, was good at surviving. He'd survived cancer at forty-seven, a motorbike accident at fifty-nine, a heart attack at sixty-one. Now, at sixty-seven, it seemed like the only demand life threw at him was to survive the consequences of the past.

2

The Kinsmen

Umumilo, 1905

The virgins of Umumilo were pregnant, and no one knew who was responsible. It began when Okolo's new bride, Adaora, showed up at her husband's bedchamber on the night they were wed. After the traditional wine-carrying ceremony, when the guests and dancers and masquerades had retired, and the village had fallen asleep to the rhythm of toads croaking at the swamp, Adaora quietly followed the senior wife, who ushered her into Okolo's hut. The young virgin's palms were sweaty, and her husband paced about in his bedchamber, slightly inebriated—both their thoughts fastened to the night and its expectations. Having married four women and been with three others, Okolo had a keen eye for a young virgin's body—the way it felt under his weight, the glistening skin, softened with youth and shea oil. Despite his experience, Okolo was nervous. He would try to slow things down this time, he thought, not breathe too heavily, wipe the drool from his mouth. He would use his wrapper to hide the sight of his member, something he considered only after his second bride fainted when he revealed himself. He was manly and eager and alive with his want. He was ready. But when Adaora unknotted her wrapper to reveal her swollen stomach, turgid on her slender waist, Okolo's blood drained from him.

Then Nneka happened. She had just seen her first blood four months earlier, small and scrawny child that she was. Her breasts, about the size of Udara seeds, were hardly noticeable enough to draw any kind of attention, much less from a man. Yet, one Nkwo market day, in the full glare of the roasted corn sellers, Nneka stooped suddenly in front of her mother's kiosk and began to vomit. She squeezed her face as though she had tasted bitter leaf, and held her stomach, screaming "nne muo"—my mother. By the time the midwives of Umumilo confirmed their suspicion, the news had spread two villages away, reaching other traders from Umugama and Umuchu.

Both Adaora and Nneka swore on their lives that no man had spread their legs apart—especially since Okolo had refused to go near Adaora the moment he realized she was with child. Both girls cried, vowing that they would stand before their God, Agwu, and swear to their purity; they would pierce their skin with the blade of the dibia—Agwu's priest—until the shrine was soaked with blood. If they were guilty, may the spirit of Agwu strike them down in their sleep. May their names be wiped from history, may their mothers be inconsolable, and may the earth refuse to swallow their bodies until vultures swooped down and fed off their wasting flesh. They stood at the village square and made their vows, their desperate pleas mingling with the embittered cries of the villagers.

It was not until Priscilla also went in the way of mothers that the village elders came together to discuss the matter. Priscilla was Okolo's youngest sister, the last child of his father's third wife, living under Okolo's own roof. Okolo had taken her in when nobody else would, after she had walked from her father's compound at the other end of the village, her raffia bag on her head, her face caked with dried tears.

Their father had sent her packing after he denounced her for abandoning the ancient ways of worship endeared to their people. You see, Priscilla had refused to learn farming or trading. Unlike other young virgins, she showed no real interest in housework, nor did she demonstrate any special talent with bead making or cloth weaving. Instead, she chose to serve at the white man's church and pray in their strange ways. The day she came home and said her name was no longer Achalugo but was now Priscilla, a foreign name befitting a foreign God, her aged father, an avowed servant of Agwu, went into his house and brought out his cutlass. He swore that no child of his would forsake the ancient and pure ways of worship. So Priscilla went to live with Okolo, sleeping in the room of his deceased second wife and grudgingly helping with housework and childcare.

It is true that three times in a market week, Priscilla would tie her clean wrapper and rub shea oil on her face, then begin the long trek to the white man's church, smiling and singing under her breath, waving to the villagers. A full yam season had barely passed since the church building was constructed, but her command of the white man's tongue was becoming clearer and sharper. "Bless you," she would chant when she walked by the butcher's corner. "Good morning, my home people," she would continue, smiling as she walked past Uchu River. The villagers happily greeted her back, mimicking her words, throwing them at her with laughter. "Goo-doo murneen o, nne," the women replied. It is also true that Priscilla had turned down the hands of many men who sought her for marriage, claiming that she was a changed woman, baptized in the Uchu River and desirous to spend the rest of her life in service to the church. She had already circled eighteen new yam seasons, ripe enough to be wed two seasons ago. But her brother Okolo did not think anything of it. If she wanted to reject the fierce, strong men of Umumilo, men who would lay their lives down first to protect their women, men whose harvests of yam and corn were renowned in all Amanasa—if she wanted to forsake them for a God who had neither gone into the evil forest and come out alive, nor fought the great wars in ancient times, it was of no concern to him. Agwu was what Okolo knew, it was what his father knew, and it was what his sons would know. He decreed it so every time he broke kola or poured palm wine to the earth—an offering to the ancestors. The white man's God was gentle and soft and, according to Priscilla, allowed himself to be killed. An affectionate God, she'd said, but Okolo knew that affection was the sentiment of women. Besides, such a temperament was not common among the white God's servants. Still, Okolo considered himself a fair man, and extending some of this consideration to his sister's happiness, he let it all pass. He allowed her to continue to visit her white man's church and acquire the new God's name for her, a name he struggled furiously to pronounce.

Three market weeks had passed since the disgrace with Adaora. Having reclaimed his bride price from her parents, Okolo had also begun to get back the shape of his life, convinced that Adaora must have soiled herself with one of the local wrestlers. He was sitting in front of his obi, the space where he received his guests, cleaning out his mouth with his chewing sticks and collecting the evening breeze, when Priscilla returned from church. She looked her usual plum self. The hem of her wrapper was speckled with sand and dust, but her waist beads still shimmied and her eyes were bright with happiness. She whistled silently past Okolo, stopping to greet him, then made to retire to the tent. But Okolo did not miss that silent swell of life—the smell, the shape of a child coming together.

"What is this you have done?" Okolo charged at her. "Eh? What is this you have done?" He raised his hands to hold the back of his head, his mouth twisted in anger.

Priscilla, startled, stepped back as he approached her. "How do you mean, brother? To what do you refer?"

"Don't play the fool, you harlot! Who put this child inside of you? Tell me now and we will see if his blood does not soak the banks of Uchu. What is this you have done, eh, Piri-shila?"

But Priscilla would not say. Unlike Adaora and Nneka, she refused to mention the name of Agwu. Instead, she insisted she would talk only to Father Patrick, the servant of the white man's God. When the council chiefs summoned her to Agwu's shrine the next day, they pleaded with her not to bring further shame to her household, since her brother was still seething from a recent disgrace; they urged her to reveal the source of the life growing inside her, but she responded, "Only God knows."

▼▲▼

"My people, it is only a short time before a drizzle becomes a heavy downpour; let us not suppose that there is any matter more urgent than this," Okolo declared decisively to the village council. The village chiefs had come together at a council member's house for their monthly meeting, despite the fact that this particular council member was the father of Adaora, the recently disgraced virgin.

"A goat that begins the long trek to the barn does not turn around halfway to find drinking water," one of the men announced, ignoring Okolo. "We came here to deliberate on the school situation. Should we not at least get that pressing issue out of the way first?"

"My man! Shut your mouth before Agwu strikes it for you. I know it is because your wife has failed to give you a child that you do not understand the weight of seeing our daughters squandered before our very eyes," Okolo replied, springing forward in a show of threat.

A full market week had passed since he discovered his sister's pregnancy. Spurred by this double disgrace—a soiled bride and now a soiled sister—he vowed that he would resolve the mystery of the pregnancies in the village. Although he had joined the villagers in their rage against Adaora and Nneka, agreeing with the community that both women swear before Agwu, he was a bit more hesitant now that his sister was involved. Agwu's justice did not leave room for mercy. Was it not the other day that a snake snuck into a villager's room and wound itself around his neck, killing the man before he awoke? The affected villager had sworn before Agwu that he was not responsible for the fire that plundered the local corn harvest, even though two witnesses saw him do it. The thought that such a fierce judgment could come upon Priscilla unsettled Okolo, although the foolish girl continued to feign ignorance. If she confessed, she would live—she would be shunned from society, but at least she would have her life, Okolo thought.

"Our daughters are being soiled. What more do we need to provoke us to action?" Okolo said, his voice softer, an attempt to reason with the men.

"Ee," the men chorused their agreement across the room.

"I am just saying," Okolo's detractor continued, "there is no need to prioritize one grievance over the other. Yes, your wife and sister are taken with child. That does not mean we should downplay the urgency of the day. The whole of Umumilo and the traditions of our ancestors are at risk of corruption if we don't resolve the school situation," the man said as he stamped his right foot to the ground, his way of announcing that he was primed for a quarrel.

Indeed, when the council had set the agenda for the meeting four market weeks ago, there was only one matter of interest—the white man's project. Christ-the-King School was about to be erected by Father Patrick and his people. You see, the white man's ways had quietly begun to infiltrate their forgotten village, and the men had watched from their farms and their huts, first with a kind of distracted skepticism, then with an embittered impatience that grew to frustration, and finally—fear. When the kinsfolk initially complained about all the changes that were happening in so short a time, their council head, Mazi Thomas, had told them to be patient. It was this same Mazi Thomas, a son of the soil, who two seasons ago had returned from his explorative sojourn in the southwest and declared that prosperity had searched the earth and decided it was time for the people of Umumilo to feel its hand. He talked about the indigenes of the southern province who had long embraced this new governing partnership with the foreigners, a partnership that resulted in so many improvements it was as though the Gods had decided to make their home with men. The people of Umumilo widened their eyes with interest as he shared his tales in the market square. Then they began to imagine what prosperity would look like. It is true that they already had their farms and their harvests. Their women were the most beautiful, their festivals renowned across the villages. The ancestors were pleased with them and the waters of Uchu had never gone dry. Yet, Thomas spoke about roads that were as smooth as the back of a clay pot, about homes that were as tall as Boko, the village giant. So the villagers went to sleep and dreamed of themselves living in huts that stood in the sky. Some of the men contended that they were happy already, that they had everything they needed, but others believed in betterment and cried that prosperity must be allowed to enter. Besides, they reasoned, why fight this progress? Why fight change? Had their fathers before them not tried and failed? Only recently, the Anglo-Aro War had been fought, the spiritual center of the Igbo people set ablaze, their key leaders arrested and hanged, like mere chickens. Prosperity was already forcing its way through the hinterlands, and it was only a matter of time before it reached them. Their village, Umumilo, being such a small community in the backwaters of Amanasa, had been—up until that moment—shrouded from the white man's gaze, so that while other villages were razed and infiltrated, they had remained untouched. It was not until Thomas returned with his talks about prosperity that the villagers opened themselves to change.

When prosperity finally arrived, it came in the shape of an old man with a small brown cross held tightly to his chest and a set of beads that hung loosely around his wrist. His skin, to the eyes of his observers, was as pale as the morning cloud, and his eyes were a deep green tint, like the blades of the mango leaves. He came with a troop of young men from Lagos, and after recruiting a few hands from the village, they started to build. Soon enough, life in the village appeared to continue as usual. The children stopped making songs about the white man's skin. Farming season resumed. The virgins danced around the village square. Young men brought drinks to families to indicate marriage interests. Indeed, all was well in Umumilo until Father Patrick walked into the market and encouraged the women to come in through the church doors to meet the living God.

The first time Priscilla went to the church in Umumilo, the congregation consisted of Father Patrick, his troop from Lagos, the village vagabond, and Derek, who had arrived in the village from Ireland. "Aya-rand," Priscilla repeated as Father Patrick attempted an introduction. Derek was a promising young lad who had just finished secondary school and had been thinking of joining the seminary. Derek's aunt was Father Patrick's cousin, and she was convinced that mission work in this part of the world would dissuade him from any romantic notions that would lead him to squander his youth. Father Patrick joked, "We'll see if he still wants to become a priest after his time here." Priscilla did not understand a word she heard. What she grasped was "Aya-rand" and the way Derek reached out to graze her fingers. She'd stepped back at his gesture, confused by his forthrightness. "That's all right," Father Patrick said, turning toward the boy. "He means to say hello." So Derek tried again, bowing his head lightly while he reached for Priscilla's hand. Priscilla told herself that the foreigners could sing, although their songs were not nearly as good as the ones the villagers danced to during the Anya masquerade festivals. Still, they were good. She also told herself that she would learn how to read like them. The troop from Lagos were just like her, yet they could interpret the white man's books. So she went back to the church again. And again. In the course of her visits, she was baptized and chased from her father's home.

One Sunday, during mass, Derek reached out for Priscilla's hand and refused to let go. It is true that, with the ceremonial sign of peace, the white man insisted you reach out and touch someone, that you hold their palm in your hands and wish them well. And it is true that Derek and Father Patrick made it a duty to touch everybody, including the village vagabond, whom the entire community provided for but whom no one dared touch. But when Derek reached for Priscilla and refused to let go until Father Patrick resumed his homily, she could have sworn on the grave of her dead mother that there was tenderness in his eyes. At the next church service, nothing happened. But at the one after, just as Priscilla was about to leave, Derek's voice rang behind her.

"Hello, Yallugo," Derek called, attempting to address her by her native name.

Startled by his voice, Priscilla turned, noticing how tall he was now that she saw him under the light of the sun. She blurted the first thing that came to her.

"I want to English," she said, as she pointed to the hymn book that Derek had tucked under his arm.

"Oh." Derek chuckled shyly. "Ohhh," he said again as her intentions dawned on him.

"I'll teach you, then. I'll teach you English," he responded. And so Priscilla had begun to learn English from Derek. They sat together first on the hard wood bench at the far back of the church, then by the coconut tree behind the parish building. Derek would then walk her back halfway to Okolo's hut, through the deserted pathway of Ubam's farm.

On one such day, when Priscilla reached the church, Derek was nowhere in sight. During mass, Priscilla found herself peering at the door, as though it might swing open any moment and let Derek in. After the service, she continued to sit on the bench, watching Father Patrick, waiting for some kind of explanation. But there was nothing. When Derek resurfaced two Sundays after, she turned away during the sign of peace. After mass, he followed her out of the church, stuttering half greetings and explanations. He'd had to travel to get some documents for Father Patrick, he explained, but she ignored him, and they both walked in silence. When they arrived at the spot where Derek would usually turn back, Priscilla hesitated and Derek stood, unmoving. Then he reached out, took her hand while searching her face, and raised it to his mouth.

3

Margaret

Lagos, 2005

The first time Margaret came to Arina Estate, in July of '95, the air smelled of rusted metal and heat, and noise from its neighbor, a slum built out of cheap wood and aluminum sheets, carried into the compounds. The slum was a small, dense settlement for the poor and unhoused that stood on water like a modern-day miracle, a sharp contrast to Arina Estate itself, which appeared caked into the earth's fist. Margaret would see on that first day that the estate was a gated community with forty twin duplexes, fifteen adjoining flats, a mosque, a sports room, two water fountains—the water glistening under the sun like colored crystals—and one Christian center layered over three acres of land. The estate's roads were made of faded pink and gray cement blocks fitted neatly into one another, as smooth as polished marble.

On that first day on the estate, Margaret had her retirement check tucked in the pages of her Bible, the Bible tucked snugly in her black leather purse, her small ringed hands with their rumpled aging skin gripping the purse, ready to claim this new life that she would build.

She'd had to meet with the estate's administration officer, a man of stork build whose ears perked up whenever he saw a person of upward social standing; he introduced himself to her as Mr. Efe Benson, enunciating the "mister" as though he'd been christened with it. He'd been waiting in his office when Margaret was ushered in by a security officer. Behind his desk, there was a seven-foot banner inscribed with the phrase WELCOME TO PARADISE. On the banner was the image of Efe Benson wearing a brown French suit, smiling a big smile, his teeth polished, evenly shaped, his beard full and trimmed, every strand of mustache in place. Even his eyes seemed to carry a certain air of authority. Margaret examined the banner, then Mr. Benson, amused by the contrast—real life dulling out the sharp edges of the image. Benson looked, to Margaret's eyes, stunted in his big executive chair, his roughened facial skin nothing to compare with the glossy sharpness of the picture. She thought it was a shame to have the banner placed right beside him, where the difference was as clear as bright afternoon and a somber evening. Such a man, Margaret considered, was clearly interested in appearances, a man who wanted to be seen and regarded with respect even though his confidence was rehearsed in front of a mirror. She'd known people like him for decades, had worked with them early in her career, at the communications ministry and then at the oil company. They flourished under flattery, needed to have their importance felt, and insisted on the performance of power and control. As Margaret continued to regard Benson, she thought to make a comment about his office, but she found the kitschy decor a little more than wanting. Then she thought to try for a joke, but her humor rarely came out as soft as she intended, so she dismissed this idea too. As she considered what to say in that short fraction of time in which they were introduced, Mr. Benson reached forward quickly, bumping his stomach against the desk, and offered her his hand.

It was Margaret's lawyer who put her in contact with this Benson man, convinced that the property was a good fit for Margaret, a safe investment to ride out postretirement life. But Margaret had been more concerned about the street thugs in the area and about how open and visible the estate seemed, seeing that it was sitting neatly between a slum market and an expressway. She'd shared some of her security concerns with the lawyer, and they had argued a small argument, but in the end, Margaret knew that she would come look at the place; after all, the barrister was very good at his job, and she was too much of a professional herself to dismiss the opinion of another expert. In truth, the estate was not beautiful to Margaret's eyes, although the designers were reaching for the quaint texture of London town houses. The duplexes sprawled and were painted peach, brown, cream, white, black—as varied as the people who lived in them. Still, there seemed to be a certain anonymizing quality to it, a stillness in its air—it seemed like a place Margaret could go to hide, erect new boundaries. If you'd asked her, she'd shrug and say there was just a rightness to it. So Margaret made the decision. She would stay in this Arina Estate. Mr. Benson and her lawyer had discussed her interest in her absence; they both knew that money was not a problem for her, that although she was recently retired, she had spent the better part of two decades making plans for a time like this, plans that only a career in the oil and gas industry could provide. She had a string of properties and other investments, most of which were managed by her lawyer. But this interest was different, personal. She wanted a place she could start afresh. It was all supposed to be done and settled. And so it was much to Margaret's surprise to hear Benson declare to her that a young family had just, the night before, indicated interest too. That they were ready to pay. He gulped from his bottle of water, ignoring the glass cup on the table, then cleared his throat before looking at Margaret's application again. "I see you want to pay at once—full payment," he'd said. Margaret smiled.

"Okay, madam, everything looks in order," Benson continued. "Let me just put this on file for you—the property association, they will discuss sometime next week," he went on. "We just purchased three more acres of land from the market; our people want to turn it into a small park for children. You know that this our estate, eh, it is very family-driven," he said, not waiting for a response. "If you have some time now, I can show you around?" he then offered, pushing his chair back as he spoke, the tour a concluded matter in his mind.

"What about the young couple?" Margaret asked. There was no point wasting her time if it was not certain that she would get the property. She'd felt insulted by the turn of the conversation and had already decided to speak to Benson's superiors once she left his office—this was often the trick to getting things done. It was, to Margaret, a constant consolation, knowing that the world was structured this way, that everyone was accountable to someone, especially the people who made a show of presenting power. When she asked about the young couple, Mr. Benson settled back in his seat and scribbled on a piece of paper. He rattled absent-mindedly about the process of application, how many people were interested, how Margaret's application had become a strong contender because of her lawyer. Margaret looked at the clock hanging adjacent to Benson's desk as she considered how much longer she could tolerate the meeting. Then she saw them. The creatures. Their teeth, that familiar glare, the sly stroke of the hour hand as if it was holding a secret. Margaret had not seen them in a few months now, and since they were constantly shifting, she had not seen them in this form in a couple years. It was in that moment, looking at the clock, that Margaret knew unequivocally, undeniably that the creatures were on their watch. Margaret turned her face back to Benson, knowing that he did not see them but that they saw him, that he had somehow opened a crack through which they floated into the room; knowing, above all, from a lifetime of seeing, that she was not to say anything about her heightened vision. Besides, there was still the younger couple contending for her property, or to her mind, Benson's ploy to get more money from her. But she had already made the trip to the estate and concluded she might as well go on the tour with him.

They walked along pavements, strolling past shrubs, orchids, yellow and purple hibiscus, peace lilies, water fountains, the tactless inelegance of the buildings. When they had nearly rounded the estate, Benson pointed to the church east of where they stood; then he eyed Margaret and asked when Mr. Okolo would join them.

"I am not married," Margaret said. "Okolo is my maiden name."

By this time, Margaret was already distracted, her attention pulled away by the movement of the creatures at the church entrance. Over there by the gate, the creatures were no longer nameless, faceless. They'd become demons with scales the texture of burnt fish. Still, it was not a problem because although she had seen them, they had not, in fact, seen her. Or perhaps they had seen her, but they had not recognized her from before.

After that first meeting, Benson reached out to Margaret's lawyer explaining that the estate's board were more in favor of younger couples because family values tied into the communal vision of the estate. Seeing that there was no Mr. Okolo in the picture, and that Margaret was a single woman over fifty, the board were more inclined to sell to the younger family who also wanted to buy.

"He is lying," Margaret screamed to her lawyer when she learned of this exchange.

"Madam, Benson doesn't make the final decisions; he just recommends," the lawyer responded, his voice stretched with impatience.

"Then get me the names of the board members. I shall write to them!"

In the end, Margaret did not need to write. She got the house because she could afford to. The younger family wanted a payment plan—she paid at once.

Ten years passed, and Margaret turned sixty-five. She had made her home in the estate, with the creatures, who had likewise forged their own rhythm of comings and goings. To her great surprise, Margaret had become fond of the people of Arina. She no longer flinched when they showed up at her house or when they slipped envelopes through her door inviting her to dinners and birthdays and weddings. She no longer thought they were conniving against her, whispering about her, or siphoning her letters, trying to sniff out her private details for God knows what. In the early years, she had rerouted her correspondence, spread between her lawyer and a private PO Box. Not anymore. Things had settled so smoothly that she had even accepted that the men who carried out occasional repairs had not planted anything in her duplex. There were no buried charms beneath her floors and therefore no need for the sporadic stomping of the tiles. Yes, there were still the dreams that reminded her of the other world she carried, but dreams were merely suggestions, not reality. She held this thought in her mind every morning when she yawned awake from sleep, her hands stretched out to feel the blue walls of her bedroom. It was in this natural progression of cohabitation that Margaret and the people of Arina Estate learned to laugh together. They planned community Christmas parties, attended their neighbors' weddings. And when death came through sickness or a car accident, they also grieved together. It was here, in this non-beginning of things, that Margaret stayed, contently. Until everything changed.

4

Benjamin

Lagos, 1962

The city had a swirl about it. Forceful. Almost dizzying. There was a hardness in the air—in the cement walls, on the pavements, in the way the people spoke, their different languages falling against one another on the streets. Many of them arrived from the farther states into the capital following the fever of independence. They wanted to partake in the craze of oil money, in the fire of Western education—all the promised opportunities of a new Nigeria. It was in this Lagos, in this mix of hope and hunger, that Benjamin arrived that fated February '62. It was at the Nigeria Broadcasting Corporation that he'd taken up work weeks after he arrived. And it was amid this bright chaos of change that Benjamin met his first Nigerian lover, Madam Cynthia.

They met at a cocktail party in April of that year. He was twenty-four. She was thirty-three. Benjamin had showed up at the venue wearing a green shirt tucked into gray khakis, and almost immediately he wished he'd put more effort into his appearance. The men had donned their agbadas, their bellies wide with girth; the women wore shimmering party gowns, some of them in flamboyant scarfs. There was something about the way the room hummed with highlife music, the sound of the talking drums, that made Benjamin feel uneasy. He signaled a waiter to get him wine a few minutes after scanning the room.

"Oyibo, will you not dance with me?" a voice said from behind him; it sounded coarse but confident. When he turned around, a woman held her glass to her mouth and took a sip, staining the rim of the glass with the bold red of her lipstick.

"I'm afraid I'm not very good at it," Benjamin said, taking a shy step backward.

The woman turned to wave at someone who mentioned her name—Cynthia. She was round-faced and plump, full in all the places Benjamin considered essential.

"You're not good at it, abi you don't like our music?" she teased.

"Quite the contrary, I love the music," Benjamin said eagerly. And indeed, he loved it—the music, the women, the food. Especially the food. For many weeks, after his morning shift at the broadcast network, Benjamin, along with the producers and local staff, walked to the cafeteria, where they laughed, drank beer, and smoked on the veranda, just before a meal of native jollof rice or egusi, that thick Nigerian soup made of pureed melon seeds and spices, usually served with garri or on hot white rice, the oils leaking to the sides of the plate like paint on a blank canvas. The menu showcased items like poached eggs, baked beans—an assortment of English options for Nigeria's finest, a testament to how truly intercontinental the cafeteria service was. But despite these English options, despite their representation of supposed refinement and education, Benjamin—the people noted—preferred the local dishes.

"This man you too like pepper o, see how your face red," some of his colleagues teased. "Ehn, onye ocha—white man, we must find you a Nigerian wife o," they continued, each time with a glint of approval in their eyes. They'd privately considered that there was something different about Benjamin, something rooted to the ground, familiar. They took his culinary curiosities as a compliment, feeling flattered that he'd opt for peppered stews instead of sandwiches. His interactions with them felt genuine, something that stood out from other white men; what a humble man, they whispered to one another—a foreigner with a true taste for Africa. This Benjamin, to them, was not like the others, those British officials who lingered around the vicinity with an air of authority, conducting themselves with their shoulders high as if they owned the place, their conversations an endless reference to the queen, to the proper way things were done in London. This was how Benjamin, in so short a time, had come to earn among his colleagues support, friendship, and finally the revered status of a brother.

Cynthia was an astute businesswoman, daughter to one of the wealthiest bankers in the southwest, and thanks to her father, she had connections in industry and politics. She was congenial, and as Benjamin came to learn, she was not an easy woman to turn down. So, they had danced after that first prompt, and then the evening truly opened up. Benjamin, though still somewhat shy, found his curiosity about Cynthia energizing; he knew himself well enough to admit that power was alluring, and when power was draped around a woman's body, it was the kind he'd find attractive. And so Benjamin had left the party with Cynthia that night. They had more drinks. He smoked his cigarettes, then passed out on her settee. The next morning, she fed him oranges and apples stored in her fridge and insisted he drink a bottle of water to clear his head. Then she accompanied him home. It was there, in his small Ikoyi flat, in his sparsely furnished living room, with the dull brown curtains and linoleum floors, that they had sex. It was hurried and graceless that first time, but Cynthia returned the next day and the day after, until they fell into that familiar rhythm from which most relationships emerge.

In the early weeks of their relationship, Benjamin enjoyed sharing with Cynthia details from his London life—his secondary school adventures, his aversion to cats, the latter something they had in common. He told her he was Nigerian, and she laughed and shoved him away, saying in jest, "Stop playing around." But he'd brought it up again, and again, first to explain a trip he had to take to southeast Nigeria, then to explain why it made sense that he would blend so easily with the culture.

"But you can't really claim to be Nigerian," she'd said one evening.

He was nestled against her thigh, and she was stroking his hair. He sat up immediately. "Why—why do you say that?"

"Look at you, oyibo," she teased, taking no note of his discomfort. "Who on earth would believe this story of yours?"

"You think I'm making this up?"

"That's not what I'm saying."

"All right, what are you saying?"

"I said that's not what I'm saying o."

"Tell me, then, tell me what you are saying."

"I just don't see the point, ehn, telling everybody that you are Nigerian. What do you hope to achieve from that? What is the benefit?"

"It's the truth," Benjamin retorted. A sudden fear seized him, as if her doubt rendered his mission more precarious.

"There doesn't have to be a point to saying who I am. My grandmother is from here. My father was born here." He raised his hand to his chest as he made this statement, as though by saying his father, he meant himself.

"I hear you, but what will this claim get you? What will it bring you?"

They'd argued and it was ugly. Benjamin went back to his flat mulling over Cynthia's question in spite of himself. It was foolish to let her words settle in his chest, yet there they were, following him through the hot, damp night.

▼▲▼

When Benjamin had first boarded his flight to Nigeria, his task had been simple: land in Lagos, get a local guide, plan a trip to southeast Nigeria, to his grandmother's village of Umumilo. It was not supposed to be his journey, he thought. It was a trip his father should have made, having spent his life skirting the idea. But in order to return home, one had to have people waiting, and the people his father sought were supposedly all dead. Perhaps this was what kept his old man away, the idea of returning to an empty house, a longing that catered only to graveyards and bones. Now Benjamin was here. He had come to verify the facts of his life that his father could not. And he'd come with his own arsenal of authority—letters from his father's uncle who was a Catholic missionary, the uncle's diary, which seemed to detail the strange events that transpired with his grandfather. Benjamin had always thought that history, no matter how well-documented, had the tendency to take the shape of the fantastical. So he'd come to see things for himself and perhaps, finally, to lay his father's ghost to rest.

On two occasions, Benjamin tried to return to Umumilo, the land of his father's birth, but with no success. The first time, he'd arrived at the bus station with his brown leather bag slung over his shoulder. He'd been accompanied by two of his colleagues at the broadcast network, both men much older than him though they considered him their friend, and he, theirs. In truth, they'd also been assigned to travel with him by their supervisor, because what did Benjamin really know about traveling to the east on his own? The three of them met a few minutes after five a.m., but the bus station was already full, bristling with that listless Lagos energy. There were passengers queueing outside the bus station, their eyes still heavy with sleep, many of them traders in Lagos making a trip to the east for new wares or to see their families. Benjamin and his colleagues had moved to the ticket seller, where a conversation ensued.

"Oyibo, why you wan go village?" the ticket seller had asked Benjamin. "You sure say you go fit stay that our side? No be like Lagos o," the seller continued.

He eyed Benjamin, searching his face as if he might find something interesting.

"Ah, forget o, I be village boy," Benjamin replied in the pidgin English he'd quickly picked up. Their eyes met, and both men laughed; a few observers at the booth who did not hear the exchange joined in the laughter. Then they heard a scream from outside.

"Ole ole—thief o, thief!"

Benjamin and his colleagues rushed out immediately to see if the thief had really been caught, and if so, what would happen. They were barely outside the bus station when they heard another commotion coming from inside the ticketing stand. It happened in the way of many Lagos tragedies—quickly. Benjamin turned around just in time to see a young lad jump out of the ticketing stand, holding, much to Benjamin's shock, the brown bag he'd left on the table while he tried to sort out his payment. It turned out that the initial scream had been a distraction, and Benjamin, the white foreign face in the crowd, had been the target. Naturally, the trip was aborted, now rendered futile by the appurtenances they had lost in that bag; a recorder, along with a hat that belonged to Benjamin's father. At least the diary was safe in his other bag. The second time Benjamin planned to return, he never made it to the bus station. He'd awoken from a dream he could not remember, drenched in his own sweat, with a strange feeling of sadness that seemed to take over his body. He'd looked at his watch, knowing that the bus would leave by six a.m., then he turned to the other side of his bed, his decision already made. It became his own private joke, that although he had come to resolve the mystery of his grandparents, the city had other plans for him. He was, after all, enjoying Lagos. And he was enjoying Cynthia. And he was enjoying the idea of being a little bit Nigerian, even though it seemed that the soil upon which his father was conceived was somehow avoiding him.

▼▲▼

Benjamin and Cynthia reconciled after their last argument. It was after that reconciliation that Cynthia took it upon herself to help Benjamin feel more rooted in his life in Nigeria.

"Darling, you know you can do a lot better than radio, abi? Especially with your—experience," Cynthia said to Benjamin one morning. She'd spent the night in his flat as she tended to, even though her apartment was more spacious.

By experience, Benjamin knew she meant his Britishness, the currency that being and looking foreign presented. But he did not resent her for it—he'd come to understand that Cynthia, much like him, like his father, was a person of prudence and practicality. In the universe she occupied, everything was a step toward the next thing.

"We can have you on the network, you know? TV."

He'd been lying down in his bedroom, fanning himself with a newspaper, when Cynthia walked in.

"TV?"

"Or you can start your own project?"

"My own project?"

He couldn't stop himself from echoing her, quite distracted. He sat up, reached into his pocket for a cigarette.

"I mean branching out, doing your own thing," she said.

When Cynthia offered to introduce him to one of her father's friends who was in politics, Benjamin did not resist. Her idea was for him to expand his networks along the corridors that mattered. Benjamin did not care for Cynthia's networks, and he'd had no plan to stay long term, but he'd said yes for the sake of peace. It was in this spirit of peace, in his service to his relationship to Cynthia, that he'd agreed to the fated meeting at the director's office. It was, incidentally, through Cynthia that he'd met Margaret. And it was in spite of Cynthia, and against the walls she'd carefully erected to shield their relationship, that he pursued Margaret. For years after they parted, Benjamin would sometimes wonder what became of Cynthia. When they separated, Cynthia had told him in a fit of rage that he would never be happy, but Benjamin had never been a man given to superstition, especially one sponsored by a woman's anger. Still, he was not able to completely discard his memories of Cynthia. After all, it was also through Cynthia that he'd first learned that there was something lurking and waiting inside his precious Margaret's mind.

These days, Benjamin allowed himself to think only of his daughter, Nwando. He thought about the young boy, too, his daughter's son, Chuka. The boy was fourteen, played chess and tennis, tried his hand at music as well, the piano and guitar—the sort of education his middle-class parents insisted upon because they could afford to, though it would turn out that the boy had no musical talent himself. The boy's left knee bore a dark scar, a remnant of a fall that happened when he was eight. The stone had cut deep into his skin, his small bones jutting out. Nwando recounted these details to Benjamin during their brief phone interactions. She'd also sent a family portrait in which she was standing by a pool, the boy undressed down to his underwear, fresh from a swim. Between them, his daughter's husband looked distracted but was laughing anyway, his face turned away from the camera, his hands draped around his wife and the boy. Benjamin had framed the photo and placed it on his bedside table, knowing in his heart that this was the closest he would come to having them as a family.

Benjamin had first reached out to Nwando in 1992. By then, his second marriage had long failed. He wrote a letter introducing himself, the absent father now seeking to be known, explaining how he got her address after reconnecting with an acquaintance from his time in Nigeria. It was a kind of experiment, to see how he would take to her mind, but he'd left no address for her response. He ended up not writing again for another seven years—what was the point in digging up old bones? But in 1999, when his third marriage failed, he wrote again. The letter had been brief, more casual, and this time came with a forwarding address. Nwando wrote him back. Though the tone of her letter had been formal, he'd dialed her home number, surprised that she picked up the phone directly, only on the second ring. After that, they settled into a sporadic habit of keeping in touch. They'd spoken four times in less than two years—the longest they'd ever stayed in touch.

"How is your health?" Nwando would ask during their calls. "What are you doing to keep busy?" It was a line of questioning Benjamin would have been less patient with if it'd come from someone else.

"Chuka is now in senior secondary school," she'd said in their last conversation. "He won a chess competition; do you know that he'd rather go to university in London than the US, can you imagine that?"

Benjamin could not imagine it. But he laughed, the roar of his own voice drowning out the question he wanted to ask: When will I meet him? It was thoughts like this that kept him restless many evenings. It was in fact this very thought that had, only the day before, set him on edge. In the past few days, he'd been so wrapped up in these thoughts, in his longing to connect with Chuka, that he decided he would call Nwando and ask when he could speak with the boy. It was late in Nigeria, about ten p.m. to his five p.m. More so, they had always scheduled their calls. But last evening, he'd dialed Nwando's landline anyway. His plan had been clear in his mind. He would ask her about the boy, about her plans for next summer. Perhaps they would come to the States. Benjamin had allowed the phone to ring through till the end. When no one picked up, he reminded himself that it was late, that he should try again the next day. He knew that Nwando would be upset that he was breaking their schedule, but he dialed again anyway. And then came the answer.

"Hallo?" the voice called from the receiver.

There was only one person Benjamin knew who said their *hello* as *hallo*.

"Is that you, Maggie?"

5

The Kinsmen

Umumilo, 1905

"Tell them we are ready," the priestess of Agwu said. She stood by the bank of the Uchu River and spoke to her reflection. The council chiefs of Umumilo stood behind her, their heads dropped down as the prayers demanded. The virgins—Adaora, Nneka, and Priscilla—still insisted that they did not know how they had become pregnant, so the chiefs congregated to seek clarity and judgment from their God.

"Nna anyi, I send you this message on behalf of our people. Tell our fathers on that other side that we welcome their judgment, that Umumilo has rejected this abomination. We have not condoned it—let Agwu not rest until he sends his punishment." The priestess poured hot drink into the flowing stream, then knelt to kiss the earth.

At this time, the village had become tight with tension. Things were changing faster than the elders could complain about them. First, the pregnant virgins began to show. Their stomachs and breasts—even Nneka's tiny breasts—swelled under their wrappers. Adaora could barely walk the distance to the farm. Nneka's stomach slanted her walk; she was now like a child who had swallowed a medium-sized calabash. Pricilla spent her time in church with Father Patrick and two foreign midwives who'd arrived from London. The church tried to intervene in the manner of asserting its knowledge about these things. The midwives asked the women to rest, to leave the farming to the boys. But the villagers in turn insisted the women had to show strength; they had to walk to the stream, pull the harvests from the ground, like their mothers had done before them. Childbearing was an act of courage, and to show strength one had to prepare for it. But it was not just about the birthing process, or building strength. There was a much simpler reason that the villagers resisted the midwives' orders. If the white man's God could not reveal who put the babies in the virgins, then he should not send his servants to teach them how to bring those children into the world. Father Patrick reminded the villagers that their savior had come through a virgin.

"So, Father, are you saying it is God who put these babies inside our daughters?" Thomas asked one day, his Western inclinations overcome by outrage.

Father Patrick, who walked about the village with his cross and his journal, had no answers. He said the village must show patience. That the truth comes out with time. But time was one thing the people of Umumilo no longer had, nor trusted. The white man's people, the ones that even Father Patrick had to answer to, had begun to build the school the moment the church was completed. They had showed up one day with long sticks and guns. None of them said "bless you" or went to the church. They walked through the market square and along the banks of the Uchu, pointing at trees and rocks, throwing words like "over here—oh, right, this spot. Precisely."

The men built offices for themselves, and living quarters, and there was talk about more buildings, more development. Even the young ladies could no longer dance at the village square because their section had been marked off for construction. No one expected that when the kinsmen called for a meeting to halt the changes and allow the people to familiarize themselves with the plans, there would be resistance from the white men. And no one expected that during a scuffle in the marketplace, when one of the local traders spat at the white man's shoe, the white man would raise his stick and hit the villager, breaking his nose. So coming now to Agwu's priestess was a culmination of their frustrations. With the failure of diplomacy, it was time to resort to more convincing means. Some of the villagers believed that if they could solve the pregnancies, Agwu would bless them again and the foreigners would pack up and leave their small village alone. So they continued to pray and seek out the priestess, calling for Agwu's vindication, asking him to let his judgment pass through the village like an army of locusts.

▼▲▼

Judgment arrived when no one expected. On that day, farmers farmed. Traders traded. The sculptors of Agbaji molded their clay and beat their metals till the clanging sounds were high in the air. The young men and women listened to town orators tell their fables at the market square. Then evening arrived. The market women returned home to their children. The men carried their farm tools over their shoulders and walked under the full moon to their wives. It was an ordinary day by Umumilo standards, except that Priscilla was at the church when her child began to press down on her loins, announcing its arrival.

Priscilla had moved into the parish quarters after Okolo could no longer condone the sight of her growing stomach or the abomination of her silence. Her baby was coming earlier than the midwives had suggested. Meanwhile outside the church, in the heart of the village, another young virgin was about to take in with child.

Kene, who was preparing for her wine-carrying ceremony in a fortnight, was stirred from sleep by a desire to relieve herself. She woke up to find the village vagabond, Olisa, on top of her. At her sudden stirring, Olisa's eyes widened in surprise. He immediately placed his finger over his mouth, prodding her to be quiet, his face blank, unsearchable. But Kene's scream rang through the compound, and Olisa, acting swiftly, blew out the powder on his palm that sent the virgin into a deep sleeping spell. This was a powder notorious for enchanting people, creating a haze in time and memory so that those affected did not know themselves or remember what had happened to them. It was so effective that when Kene woke up, she would not remember that anything had transpired. But one of the nearby villagers heard the scream before she passed out. And so did Thomas from the next compound. They both ran out to find Olisa trying to jump across the goat shed. Pouncing on him, they pulled him by the leg and shouted the compound awake.

"We have found him. Agwu has answered, Agwu the great one has answered. Ndi b'anyi puta puta—come out, everyone, you must all see this," they screamed, as they kicked and punched Olisa, who was now bleeding on the ground. The news traveled quickly, and the court was set up at dawn, although Kene, still sound asleep from the powder blown into her face, had yet to tell the council what had transpired.

In the morning, Adaora, the first virgin to get pregnant, kept crying at the open court with her mother. Nneka's father pushed through the crowd with his cutlass. "Let me have his head. If I don't have his head, there will be no peace in Umumilo," he cried.

Away from all the noise, Priscilla lay on a cot, surrounded by the church people and their midwives, bringing her son into the world.

By early afternoon, the events had passed through the council and a judgment had been reached. Olisa would die in a market week. He would be marked and left in the evil forest, where the Gods would then do as they pleased with him. But first, the chiefs wondered, Where was Priscilla? Did she not know that she had been vindicated? She must be called in at once to look her defiler in the eye before he is taken away. Okolo and the council chiefs, as well as some of the younger farmers and the priestess, began the long march to the church, singing songs about Agwu's righteous vindication. Their daughters who had been soiled like rotten ugwu leaves would now be avenged. They sang and trekked and sang some more. But this singing and this swelling of their pride stopped as they reached the parish, jarred by the crying sounds of a baby.

Okolo raised his hand to hold off the other villagers.

"Is that what I think it is?" he asked, his voice low and dejected. He grunted, as if to collect his thoughts, then proceeded into the hut, signaling to the villagers behind him. He found Priscilla and Father Patrick and Derek circling a baby—a baby whose skin and hair did not belong to Umumilo, a strange child colored like the light of daybreak. Derek's head rested softly on Priscilla's, his left hand over hers.

Perhaps it was the sentencing of Olisa, or more construction materials sprawled over the market square, or Christ-the-King School now nearing completion, or the realization that Priscilla, despite what she had said, had known the father of her child all along; perhaps it was all of this that propelled the events that transpired. In that moment, Okolo grunted, pushed Father Patrick to the ground, and pulled Derek out of the hut by the neck. When the council chiefs saw what Okolo had seen, when the rest of the troop peered through the entryway and found Priscilla holding a white man's baby, they screamed and spat on the ground.

It was a young farmer who found the first rock and sent it flying toward Derek.

Derek had been in Umumilo long enough to understand that a stone in the hand of an angry villager was a verdict. And so Derek charged out of the scene, making a run toward the secretariat. But it would seem—in his case—that even if legs could move with the speed of a leopard, they could not outrun a judgment. Still, he ran. And the men ran behind him. Stones flew from their hands to his head. He ran. Even after his legs were shot with pain and bleeding, after a rock hit him on his neck. He turned around to plead, and another stone met his left eye. He continued to run as the trees blurred, as his head pounded, as he heard Priscilla and their baby crying. He ran until he fell to the ground.

6

Margaret

Lagos, 2005

The incident was not entirely sudden. There was a gradual but steady buildup, invisible to the eye and therefore both alarming and unsettling in its eventual emergence. This is what happened: Months before the creatures found Margaret, that is, before Margaret understood that they now recognized her, they'd appeared to her in her sleep. In those dreams, Margaret's hair was not yet gray and thinned, and she could still roll her neck and hips as the creatures raised their canes to her back, beating her skin to blisters, prodding her to dance. Margaret would wake in the mornings drenched in her own sweat. Then she'd stretch out her hands and feel the walls, testing her sense of place, a trick she'd mastered to transition from nightmare back to real life. After the dreams, the creatures started to squeeze their way into reality, pressing through the cracks of her mind, wanting more. They were everywhere, tugging at the hem of her boubou, ogling from the window, their noses and eyes squashed against the damp transparent surface. They appeared to Margaret in the supermarket, and in her brand-new kettle, their eyes simmering beneath the boiling water. She heard them calling to her during her errands, from between the pages of her Bible, and even deep in the throes of sleep. Sometimes they were an angry mob, other times a single disapproving glare, their many faces melding into one. But it was no trouble—dreams are dreams, Margaret thought. The fact that you see something does not make it real, she'd reminded herself, the words of Dr. Mary Pryce returning to her. So she'd continued with her life, learning to go back to sleep after the dreams, just as she learned to drink her tea despite the eyes that stared back at her from inside the cup.

Before Margaret's name became the recurring whisper in Arina Estate, before her neighbors squeezed their children's shoulders, warning them to stop interacting with the strange old woman, Margaret held a thought in her mind—she would win. This was the real reason she ignored all the usual signs: the fogginess in her head, the creatures becoming bolder, louder; the medicines that she once again found numbing. This time, however, she did not fill out her diary journals. Or talk to her daughter. Or book an appointment to see the doctor. She had even very quietly, but only on occasion, taken to flushing her medicine down the kitchen sink, an experiment to see how far she could go, how much healing time alone could bring. She was confident the creatures would leave like they had done in the past; they would fold themselves up and disappear, and she, Margaret Okolo, would win. She was sure of these things because God told her so.

God himself had come into her room on a Tuesday night. The estate generator had just been turned off and the fan whirred slowly up above her as it yielded its final strength before shutting down. Outside, rain pelted the asphalt, falling on the roof before trickling down and racing into the streets. Margaret closed the curtains and turned around in time to see God walk in and sit down on her bedroom sofa, one leg crossed over the other, his two palms clasped together as though he were deep in thought: divinity in full flesh, dark-skinned with a balding hairline and a facial mole.

Just because you see a thing doesn't mean it's real, she thought to herself. Still, she'd climbed into bed, pulled the covers all the way up to her chin, the cold of the rain seeping through the thin windows. Margaret saw through the side of her eyes that the creatures, too, were in the room, their shapeless form in a heap of clothes on the floor next to the window. She stared at the clothes, then at God. When God raised his head to look back at Margaret, his face became the face of her neighbor from the green duplex down the street.

"Don't worry, you will win," God said. Nothing more. As if the announcement came on its own terms, with a self-enforcing power. Then he got up and walked out of the room with a limp.

Margaret did not see him again after that. It could have been a dream, or reality, she did not know. It could have been the God of her Bible or echoes from her ancestors, it was impossible to be sure, but she liked the way the words *you will win* tasted on her tongue. And she liked the way it prompted her to turn herself back to prayer. In fact, one hour of prayer in the mornings became three hours, then five, until Margaret was either praying or she was dying. In the evenings, she'd walk through the estate in her house boubou, binding and casting the presence of evil, even as the little creatures pulled at her gown, singing, "Look at what you've caused, old woman, naked woman, this is all your fault."

There were many things that time did not change for Margaret. Like her urge to dance, to throw her body forward and move her hips this way and that, or the itch in her lower back, or the feeling of crawling spiders on her hands, the slight tremor from slapping at them, the surprise that she had done or was capable of doing things that were not supposed to be done: living in that in-between space where she knew herself and yet was a stranger, watching her life with all its flailing performances. And then there was the relief that came with scratching, and slapping, and pulling at herself—time did not change any of this. Yet, she had wanted the sayings to be true; she wanted time to be on her side. Time to take your medicine, her daughter, Nwando, would say. Time for another checkup, Mama. Time to sleep, as though the visions in her head could read the clock and respond to some calendar markings. No, Margaret decided, time was many things, but it was mostly unforgiving. When Margaret still worked at the oil company, she'd often shared her theories on the futility of time during intimate corporate dinners, in those small women's network meetings, and, once, during the final interview for yet another secretary. The interview candidate did not return after Margaret's impassioned lecture. Therefore, when those crooked fingers returned at night, when the creatures pulled the blanket to the floor and traced their dirt-caked nails along Margaret's back, she lay still and closed her eyes—ready. After all, it had happened before. Time was merely circling its loop.

A few weeks before the incident, Margaret went to visit Nwando. It was a perfunctory visit, one she indulged reluctantly given how controlling her daughter could be. "Mama, you have to take your medicine. You cannot miss even a single day. Mama, you're sounding off; have you taken your medicine? Mama, there's nothing behind the curtain; let me fetch your medicine." However, Margaret's latest visit was lit up by the fact that her grandson, Chuka, would be home from boarding school on midterm break. Margaret was more than eager to play the dutiful grandmother and the stern supervisor peering over Chuka's homework. For him, she would be anyone, do anything. Often, she'd pretend that she was not in her sixties, and he was not in his early teens, and she'd ask him about the girls in his class, or they would play chess and watch one of those action movies he liked.

Margaret arrived on Friday evening and sat in the living room with

Nwando while she watched a telenovela on the screen. They'd both heard Nwando's husband, Nosa, drive in, the sliding entrance to the family room unlatch, and there he was, Chuka.

"You're here," Chuka shrieked when he saw his grandmother; then he threw himself on Margaret, who'd already stood up, smiling.

"My darling, come let me look at you." But the boy was already on her chest, his arms around her waist, his head pressed against her neck. Margaret touched his chin, his shoulders, feeling his head. He seemed thin to her eyes, and his face was rough and covered with pimples.

"You've grown taller o," Margaret teased. He laughed but did not let her go.

"Chuka, you won't say hello to your mother?" Nwando asked, her face in a smile.

"Hi, Mum," he said, and turned to look at Nwando, but he did not leave Margaret, and Margaret did not stop stroking his head.

"Are you eating? You're thin o. It looks like you're not eating enough," Margaret fussed.

"Grandma, the food in school is disgusting," Chuka said. He shook his head but managed to keep his smile.

"What about your allowance? Can't you buy food?"

He looked at his mother again, and then at Margaret. Then they quietly exchanged a smile.

"All right," Margaret said, understanding his silence. "I will have them increase your allowance."

Nosa walked in and dropped their bags. "That's enough, Chuka. Go take a shower. Mama will still be here when you return," his father said. The boy drew away from Margaret and leaned to give his mother a kiss on the cheek, mumbling about how he missed her.

This was how they passed that Friday evening. Nosa retired early, tired from the long drive. Nwando fell asleep in front of the television, and Chuka sat across from his grandmother, playing chess. For that evening, they were a normal family. Margaret was a doting grandparent; there were no visions, no questions strong enough to pull her away from this quiet contentment. Then she heard the phone ring. It stopped and started again moments later. She picked it up and said her hallo, and there it was again—that cycle of time, the past becoming present. After forty years, ten of which she'd spent grieving, her husband's voice remained unmistakable.

"Benni?" she'd said when she heard his question.

She'd dropped the phone back into the receiver, but she did not move from where she stood.

"It's your turn, Mama," Chuka said. He looked at her, saw her hand on the phone, then added, "Who was it?" Margaret turned her gaze to Nwando, who was asleep on the sofa and quietly snoring, her skirt raised high to expose a birthmark behind her thigh.

"Who was it?" Chuka asked again, concern in his voice. Margaret laughed. "Wrong number," she replied, then added, "I remembered something and got carried away."

Some might say that it was Benjamin's voice that frazzled Margaret. Or that it was the extended period of excitement with Chuka. Or simply that it was God, his words in Margaret's ears—*you will win.* But the following week, when Margaret returned to her duplex at Arina Estate, she began her daily prayer walks again. She'd begun these walks the year she turned fourteen and had just come out of an argument with her mother. And she'd carried the practice of walking like an instruction through the years; when things got tense, she walked. When life felt overwhelming, she walked, and when she started to see the creatures many years ago, she also knew she must walk. This time around, Margaret walked and prayed multiple times every day. She went on her walks in the afternoon after lunch. Sometimes she went as early as four a.m., before the estate awoke. The people of Arina Estate did not think it unusual that Madam Margaret walked and walked; after all, she was always within the estate; after all, she was all by herself and lonely; after all, exercise was good for the body.

Margaret had walked peacefully in the estate since that call with Benjamin, until one Saturday, while she was out as usual, quietly binding and casting the creatures, Onome, a woman who lived on the ninth street of Arina Estate, came up to her.

"Mummy Nwando," Onome called out, waving her arm in Margaret's direction, its soft flesh quivering from the effort. "Eh, ma, it's like you were praying, abi?" Onome said rather than asked. "Mummy, Mummy, pray for me too o," Onome teased further.

"Cash Madam!" Margaret called to her, a little louder than she needed to, her attempt to mask the slight annoyance she felt from having her prayers interrupted. Everybody called Onome "Cash Madam" because she'd built a multimillion-naira skin-bleaching business from the ground up.

Hearing her nickname, Onome spun her body around as if for an audience. Margaret liked the younger woman—she was upbeat in a way that was charming. Margaret admired the fact that Onome paid no mind to her critics, that she centered her joy on her business profits and the women whose lives she changed by lightening them up.

Onome wore black tights and running shoes, her legs so small and thin that Margaret wondered if her upper body felt heavy on her feet. "Did the fitness instructor just leave?" Margaret asked.

"Ah, yes o, he left about an hour ago," Onome replied. "Only three of us showed up today; you know our neighbors think they are the busiest people in Lagos; even me, I was tired, but, Mummy, you know health is wealth, so I forced myself to come out jare," Onome said and laughed.

Margaret enjoyed her disapproving tone and played along.

"Don't mind them," Margaret said, returning the laughter. "I would have joined you if not for my dried-up joints." She reached down to touch her knees and feigned pain. "See now, one of these days I will fall from exhaustion and you people will send a handsome man to carry me back to my duplex," Margaret teased. They both chuckled. And then a wind blew, and Margaret threw her hands to her neck and slapped and slapped and scratched.

"Mummy, are you okay?" Onome asked. Margaret saw a quick flicker of fear pass through Onome's eyes, or was it anger? She knew that she had to stop the conversation, return behind closed doors. But you see, there is a soft torment of nature that one cannot fight. It is in the natural order of life—to pee, to sleep, to dance—and for Margaret, to scratch the perpetual itch. The creatures had entered the scene. Now it was time to either fight or dance. She reached out again to her neck, a light pat at first, and then a slap, again and again, quick and urgent.

"Mummy, let me leave you o, I'm already late to the shop," Onome said, then hopped back to the other end of the street before briskly walking out of sight.

After that exchange with Onome, every time Margaret went on a prayer walk, she took her wooden crucifix with her. When a neighbor craned their neck from their living room window or waved at her, she raised the cross. When they attempted to start a conversation, she raised the cross. Eventually, as she'd hoped, the people of Arina Estate let her be. They carried their whispers into their cars, pointing from behind the wound-up tinted glass, saying to themselves—

See her again o. Who is she talking to?

Now, on the morning of the incident, Margaret sat on a kitchen stool in her duplex, speaking softly to Tina, the young lady who had been contracted by Nwando to clean every Tuesday and Saturday. Her job was to clean out the shelves, change the sheets, vacuum the carpets, occasionally to sit and talk with Margaret, though she was also expected to report back to Nwando. Margaret occasionally overheard Tina on the phone with her daughter, giving harmless little updates: "Mama is fine, yes, she is eating well, I think she sleeps well too. I checked the medicine cabinet; the tablets are lessening. Yes, ma, I think she is taking them." Tina had been with Margaret in this capacity for almost two years, and her presence was one of the very few things that both Margaret and Nwando agreed upon.

That morning, however, Tina came in with her face looking tired and dejected. She'd not even had the decency to put some powder on or to cover her hair while she made the eggs Margaret asked for.

"Mummy, good morning," she'd said, then marched immediately to the sink, not waiting for a response. Margaret would have none of that broodiness around her—the girl would end up dampening her own mood—so she interfered in the manner of the aged and wise, counseling from where she sat on the kitchen stool. It turned out that Tina had saved up money to go back to school but was torn by the decision of whether to invest it in her boyfriend's dreams or to watch him struggle while she pursued her plans. The young man had accused her of thinking only of herself, of not being supportive of his music career.

"There will always be a reason not to go back to school," Margaret said. "Your boyfriend today, something else tomorrow."

Tina sniffed hard, her jaw trembling from holding back tears.

"If he thinks you are not supportive today, he will still think this after you are married; he will always see your endeavors in the way that benefits him," Margaret continued. She did not understand why she had to spell out something so obvious. How could anyone place their faith in the affections of others? How did they not see that love was about self-interest? As Margaret continued to talk, she heard the creatures start to clap behind her.

"Tell her she will die," one of them hissed at Margaret. "Tell her now, tell her now, now, tell her she will die of loneliness," they chorused. "No, tell her she will die because we will sit on her chest hee hee, hee haa."

"Mummy, are you okay?" Tina interrupted.

"Of course I am," Margaret said; then she sipped her lemon water and placed her hand on Tina's shoulder. "I'm a little dizzy; let me go up and lie down."

On her way up to her bedroom, Margaret felt the sudden itch to pray. It'd been a full two hours since she sprinkled holy water in the building or smeared her face with anointed oil. The phrase *she will die* rang in her head, so she knew that she surely had to pray. The urge was so strong that her clothes felt as though they were burning, and she thought to take them off, unhook her bra, let her breasts sleep against the soft of her belly.

"Do it, do it," the creatures chanted behind her. She raised her hand to her neck and slapped twice, shaking her head to the left and to the right, waiting for their voices to fall out of her ears. When they did not, she fell into a familiar tune from her church-attending days.

She was singing in her bedroom, sprinkling holy water, shaking her head this way and that, when the doorbell rang.

"Good afternoon, Tina, is Mummy around?"

Margaret could hear the voice of her friendly neighbor Yetunde down below, and so she'd kept her boubou in place, her bra properly snapped back on, her small feet snug in her slippers, and left her room. She stood at the head of the stairs behind the door, where only Tina could see her, then signaled for her to send Yetunde off. I must pray, I must pray, I need to pray, she thought.

"Mummy is sleeping," Tina said to Yetunde. "I'll tell her you came."

Tina was just about to close the door when Yetunde's "k-kay" fell out of her mouth. It was spoken so softly that Margaret could barely hear it, but it felt knotted and hard, like a hiccup. This was when Margaret knew that Yetunde had been crying. Poor Yetunde, why is she crying? Margaret thought, then she walked down the stairs as fast as her knees would allow, calling out to Yetunde as she approached.

"Yetty dear, how are you doing?" Margaret asked.

As soon as Yetunde saw her, her eyes brightened. "Ah, Mummy, you are awake." Then Yetunde raised the back of her hand to wipe her tears.

"Ewoo, my dear, come in—come and tell me what's going on," Margaret said, brushing Tina aside and letting Yetunde in.

They were both in the living room now, and Tina had moved upstairs to clean the bedrooms and bathroom.

"Mummy, it is Ibori," Yetunde said, crying more. "He is planning to marry again."

Yetunde had been married to Ibori for five years, but their marriage was strained by the fact that they did not have a child.

"Is it serious, did he say that to you?" Margaret asked.

"Yes, Mama," Yetunde replied, then sniffed into a fold of tissue she pulled from her purse. "Mama, his people have taken a wife for him," Yetunde said. The tears started falling again.

"Oh, so it's not his choice, then. That's a good thing, it means he can still reason with his people." Margaret said, convinced that the problem had an easy solution.

Yetunde sniffed hard again, then wiped her eyes once more.

"It's not that he cannot talk to his people, Mama. It's that this girl, this wicked girl, went and got pregnant, can you imagine that, Mama?"

"Pregnant by whom?" Margaret asked, confused.

"By Ibori, Mama," Yetunde replied. Then with a matter-of-fact stare at Margaret, she added, "How can I ask them not to marry when she is carrying his child?"

"So, it's not really his people, then," Margaret said; she forced her gaze on Yetunde's face even as she could now see a snake crawling over the picture frame behind Yetunde's head.

"How do you mean, Mama?" Yetunde replied.

"Your husband was having an affair, and he got a girl pregnant," Margaret clarified, enunciating her words.

"I suppose so," Yetunde said, then looked away.

"Look, my dear, why are you punishing yourself with these tears—"

"I just don't know what to do, Mama, tell me, Mama, what should I do?" Yetunde asked.

The demons started their singing, and Margaret, feeling lightheaded, decided she needed to eat something. She walked to the kitchen to get a banana. That was when she saw the knife. It sat there on the kitchen counter—clean steel. Tina had probably forgotten it after peeling oranges, Margaret thought. Nwando would be very upset by such carelessness. Her daughter's instruction had been clear: keep all sharp objects away from Mama. Nwando had given the instruction in a low voice on Tina's first day, as though Margaret, sitting in the living room, could not hear the conversation. Margaret decided to put the knife away and made a mental note to give Tina a stern scolding. But as she picked up the knife, the sun from the kitchen window cast light on its blade, and it glittered like the finest jewelry. It would do no harm just to hold on to it, just for a short while, after which she would give it back to Tina. So, Margaret placed the knife in the pocket of her boubou, twirling in her mind like a little girl who had been given a sacred gift. She returned to the sofa with her half-eaten banana.

"What should I do, Mama?" Yetunde asked again.

This was the moment the incident happened. A cloud floated through Margaret's head, and everything was white and soft and perfect, and Yetunde was no longer Yetunde, and Margaret was no longer Margaret, and the knife moved from Margaret's pocket to her hand, the banana discarded, and then she was stabbing at Yetunde's face and hair and shoulder.

The creatures stood behind, clapping and singing, "Good, good, good."

Margaret echoed their voices. "Good, good," she sang through Yetunde's screeching and screaming.

Tina heard the screaming from upstairs and ran down. "Mummy, no, nooo."

Eventually Yetunde wrung herself out of Margaret's grip and ran to the door. Tina ran out, too, leaving the door wide-open.

Margaret continued to sing, "Good, good—Arina is good. Nwando is good. I am good. God is good." She stayed there singing until the men from the Arina security post appeared in front of her, their dark blue uniforms shadowing the bright cloud in her head.

7

Benjamin

Atlanta, 2005

It was the bread, Benjamin thought. He arched his back, trying to trace his source of unease. It was all the bread stacked in rows, he thought again—loaves and buns; brown, white, speckled with grains. He picked one off the shelf and sniffed. Stale. He shook his head; this bread did not have the burnt-vanilla scent of freshly baked goods, and any bread that was not the day's bread was no good. A couple behind him inched their cart forward, the toddler in their trolley holding his hands above his head, his small open mouth moistened with saliva while he mimicked the sounds of an airplane in the sky. The toddler's parents were young, likely still in their twenties. The woman wore brown shorts and flat slippers. The man had his hands on the trolley as he leaned close to the little boy's face. Benjamin gave a curt nod and turned away quickly when the young man acknowledged his gaze. Seconds later, the couple were laughing, cooing at their child, a life-size frame of contentment. Benjamin did not care for it. He'd long held an aversion to people who made a show of how happy they were. Once, he'd said to his ex-wife Tricia that half of this whole happiness business is pretense anyway—a needless performance. What about the other half? Tricia had asked. Even worse, he'd responded, it's absent-mindedness; it takes sustained inattention to be anything but alarmed by the state of the world. You should try being inattentive, then, Tricia had said. It might do you some good.

Benjamin looked at the couple again. The woman had dark straight hair and thick eyebrows; her lips and cheekbones seemed tight enough to make her appear serious. The man was somewhat handsome, with stork legs, brown eyes. There was a time when Benjamin would have speculated about their ethnicity. If he asked them where they came from, he was sure they'd mention someplace local, perhaps Chicago or Arizona or New York, their claim to an American identity. But was that not also another American lie—the idea that being born on the land meant that the American soil could belong to a person as much as the person belonged to it? He'd been long naturalized himself, an American in his own right, but perhaps he had the objectivity of a late arrival, since he'd come to the country at almost thirty. He did not feel American, yet he did not feel British either. His father was Nigeria-born, London-groomed; his life was European, but his hair was African. These things—where a person lived, where they came to assemble their life, where they worked or earned their living—they could mean everything. They could also mean nothing. Benjamin preferred to read the body instead, to trust it more than a certificate of birth. When Benjamin played these body-reading games, he could usually tell who had Italian roots, who was Black Caribbean and who was Black Brazilian, simply by looking at them. It was somewhat of an obsession; since he could not place himself within a fixed frame, he'd taken to placing others. It turned out that it was a skill he was particularly good at; there was no science to it, just instinct, sharp as a razor.

As the couple inched farther down the aisle, Benjamin's mind returned to the bread. Pick one already, he thought. Such a simple task, yet enormous in its demand, almost impossible. The options were endless; how on earth was he supposed to choose? When Benjamin was still married to Tricia, he'd typically pick up the first bread he found at the store, a habit that frustrated her.

"It's ciabatta bread," she'd say as a reminder, her voice falling against the closed car window as Benjamin grudgingly left for the store. Before she left him, they'd had one of their frequent arguments where she'd accused him of not getting anything right in their marriage. She'd said that he did not try, did not pay attention to anything, not even the bread. Benjamin had scoffed. He stood in the aisle now, in a near daze, thinking about Tricia, but also about Margaret and Nwando, but mostly, he thought about the bread. It seemed like this decision to buy the right type was somehow a moral one. He picked a pack of flat bread, held it against the light as though to read the label: 180 calories a serving. He felt a small tug in his chest, light and quick. Air rushed to his lungs; he sighed a deep sigh. He stared at the bread, then at his hands, the bulging green veins, the gray curls sprawled across them, seeing himself in a strange new way, as though his hand was detached and placed on a surgical table for observation. It was in that moment—holding the bread, a frown on his face—that he understood his confusion. The problem, he realized, was with choosing. It was this need to make one singular lasting choice. Benjamin had never done anything singularly in his life. He believed in having a plan B. And then a plan C. It was what he had told a young protégé who wanted to join the army. *What are your options?* he asked the boy. *A decision is not a decision unless there are options.*

Up until two days before, when Benjamin made the unexpected call to Nigeria, Margaret had existed like a faint echo in the background of his life. He'd asked Nwando about her just once, during one of their conversations.

"And how is your mother?"

To which Nwando had replied, "She's okay."

He'd been grateful for the hurried change in subject, and grateful still that Nwando, likewise, skirted her mother in their conversations. Yet here he was, after hearing her voice, panicking over bread.

▽△▽

Benjamin and Cynthia arrived at the director's office sometime before two p.m. From the hallway, he could hear the faint sounds of children laughing on the streets, done with school for the day. Cynthia asked Ben, as she called him then, to wait at reception. She'd have a chat with the director first, lay the groundwork for their meeting, then she'd come get him. Left to himself, Benjamin realized that he'd brought neither a magazine nor a newspaper to read and therefore was not sure what to do with this time. He reached into his pockets, pulled his hands out, empty. He raked his fingers through his hair. Finally, he walked toward the window and lit up his cigarette.

"Mister man, you cannot smoke here."

Benjamin turned lazily; he was not used to such direct address.

"I beg your pardon?" he replied.

"No need to. This is an office and a no-smoking area; please put this off until you are out of the premises," the woman continued, matter-of-fact.

Benjamin found himself unusually upset, the feeling instant and overpowering. Who was she to be so rude? He'd looked at her for a long three seconds, and then the lights came on. She was short, with soft facial features, but her voice was the clear steel of an adult.

"I apologize," Benjamin heard himself saying, the anger lifting from him.

He took the cigarette from his mouth and stubbed it on the windowsill. "All better now?" He smiled.

"I will find someone to clean that up," she said, and walked out of the area.

It was well over an hour before she returned. Benjamin was seated now, his legs crossed, his hands resting on his thighs. From his position, he noticed the dress she wore, a sun-colored linen gown with green flower patterns. Her legs were firm, almost thick; they were slightly curved, inches away from being considered bowlegs. Still, Benjamin thought she was surprisingly shapely for a woman her size, small but curvy. He wondered if she was married.

"Mr. Fletcher? You are Benjamin Fletcher?"

"Yes."

"The director will see you now. Follow me, please," she said.

Benjamin found Cynthia in the director's office holding a glass of wine; she smiled charmingly at him. Benjamin followed her hand gesture and took the seat beside her.

"So, Chief," Cynthia began, "this is the brilliant friend I spoke to you about." She placed her palm over Benjamin's on the chair.

"Is he just your friend?" the director replied, his eyes laughing.

"Whatever you call him," Cynthia said, enjoying the tease. Her hand moved lower and rested on Benjamin's thigh. At this gesture, Benjamin felt an instinct to look out for the woman from the hall, though she was not in the room. When, minutes later, she brought them soft drinks, and when her hands rested briefly on the table as she set down the glassware, Benjamin found himself relieved—there'd been no ring on her finger.

The director was a small man, but what he lacked in physical stature, he made up for with rambunctious laughter. He laughed at something Cynthia had said, and the room filled up, his small, boyish face deepened with lines. Eager to be done with the meeting, Benjamin preoccupied himself by looking around the room, while the director and Cynthia talked. From the corner of his eyes, Benjamin could trace the woman's outline as she scribbled notes in shorthand; he could smell her powder, a mix of musk and rose petals; he sensed her bored detachment, the way she stiffened when she asked the director to repeat a statement.

"So, oyibo, I hear you are one of us, is it true?" the director asked, then fell into another flirtatious bout of laughter with Cynthia. Benjamin chuckled, not minding the humor at his expense. They discussed briefly Benjamin's journalism degree, a few projects he could run for the director, then they got up, shook hands, and left.

The meeting had gone very well to Benjamin's mind, though he was still not sure how he could fit himself into the director's political projects. So, naturally, Benjamin was surprised at the turn of the conversation when they returned to Cynthia's car.

"How could you disrespect me like that?" Cynthia asked.

"What do you mean?"

"We'll talk about it later," she hissed, eyeing the driver, who watched her through the rearview mirror.

Benjamin could not place what the problem was, and he had never seen this side of Cynthia. He leaned over to her, smoothing his hands down her thigh, letting his hair brush against her ear.

"What is it, love? I'm sorry; help me make it right?"

Even as he said the words, he could not believe they were his. What they shared, this mutual exchange of bodies and time, had it become serious?

"You kept looking at her—that girl—the secretary, the one taking notes."

"What?"

"Why would you embarrass me like that?"

"What are you talking about?" Benjamin said. "I wasn't looking at anyone; you and Chief had my full attention."

After a brief pause, Benjamin continued. "I heard all of it, darling; do you want me to repeat everything we talked about?"

"Don't play your small-boy games with me," Cynthia retorted, holding back tears. "You men are all the same; eventually you look for someone your own age."

It was the first time their age difference growled out loud. They continued the journey in silence. The silence continued into the night, when he returned to her apartment after work. It persisted through their lovemaking—the thoughtless groping and pinching of skin and folds.

Although Benjamin did not admit this to himself, he'd carried the image of the woman out of the director's office that day, recasting her in his mind like an actress in a scene. In two instances, she'd interrupted the dictation to correct a fact. Both times, his ears perked up at her voice. The attraction was a surprise, but was it that strange? After all, it was just curiosity, he thought after Cynthia's accusation. So what if she intrigued him? He told himself to relish the private thoughts, to enjoy the contours of those memories—eventually his mind would shake it off.

He almost succeeded. He went back to his routine, to being himself with Cynthia, the ever-present, amiable lover. Until Cynthia came bursting into the kitchen one Sunday afternoon, three weeks after the meeting, and asked Benjamin to stop by the post office the next day. He'd have to phone the director's office early in the morning.

"What for?" Benjamin had asked.

"To schedule an appointment."

"Why don't you ring him?"

"You are not serious. So you want me to do everything, abi?"

"Very well, what should I say when I ring?"

"Honey, this is a rare opportunity. Please take this seriously." Then she added, beaming, "They are expecting your call. Just say Cynthia's friend from London—they'll give you the next available appointment."

Benjamin did not call on Monday, and he did not call on Tuesday. Much in the general manner of his life, he was biding his time, waiting for this idea offered to him to become somewhat familiar, like something pulled from his own imagination. He found that he was more inclined to do something when he didn't feel like he was being propped up for it, a trait he shared with his father.

By Wednesday, as he'd finally settled into the idea, he took a taxi to the phone booth in Ikoyi and placed the call.

"Hallo."

There was no way to be certain who had picked up, no way to tell if it was the receptionist or the clerical assistant, but somehow Benjamin had instantly known that it was the woman from the hallway.

"Hallo, this is Chief Gimba's office. Who is speaking, please?" she called into the receiver again.

Benjamin said nothing. Simply waited. When she said nothing either, Benjamin dropped the phone.

Later that night, while they were seated at a dinner of boiled yams and oil-fried vegetables, Cynthia asked Benjamin if he'd booked the appointment. He'd looked up from his meal, hot soft yam still in his mouth. "I rang the office and there was no response," he said.

"Hm, that is strange o," Cynthia replied.

"Strange indeed."

▼▲▼

"Will that be all, sir?" the checkout attendant asked, smiling but not looking at Benjamin. He was a teenager, certainly not older than nineteen; scruffy hair, his teeth stained, perhaps cigarettes, coffee? There was something about the red of his hair and the freckles sprawled across his face that seemed easy, even charming.

"That will be $16.57, sir," he said, still not looking Benjamin in the face.

"Irish?" Benjamin said.

"What?" the boy answered. He looked up at Benjamin for the first time.

"Your family is of Irish descent, probably from your mother's side."

"Will that be card or cash?" the boy asked; his eyes searched the area and rested briefly on someone who appeared to be his supervisor.

"Oh, never mind me," Benjamin said. "It's a bit of a guessing game," he added, thinking he might have embarrassed the boy.

At his car, Benjamin offloaded the bread, the pickles, the batteries and beer; he carried the eggs to the passenger side of the car and placed them on the car's seat. Then he returned to the trunk, which was still open. Something was missing, he realized. He scanned the contents of the trunk again, lurching forward, his torso leaning into it. He picked up the Jamaican bun, sniffed it. From the side of his eye, he noticed a young man walking up to him with large looming strides. Benjamin closed his trunk. The last thing he wanted to do was share his bread with a hippie. Still, he could not shake the feeling: something was wrong. He thought about Margaret again in that instant. He had to speak to her again. It was childish of him to have cut the line like that, as if he had still been twenty-four. He felt the need to explain why he'd called. It occurred to him that she seemed fine on the phone; then he chided himself. What did he expect? And what was that feeling in his chest? he thought. Was it regret?

He was no longer standing by the trunk of his car. He was sitting behind the wheel, his hand raised to his stomach, an attempt to trace the nagging feeling that lingered. As he sat there, Benjamin was unaware that the young red-haired checkout attendant stared at him through the slitted blinds, that a woman in her black SUV cursed him from inside her car as she waited for him to vacate the parking spot, the air conditioner swallowing her voice as the words came out. He was unaware of the squirrel darting through the tree trunk behind his car; unaware, too, that the feeling of emptiness, that sense of forgetting something, had become a dull pain. He started his car and began his journey home, but he'd barely taken the first right turn when finally, he realized what was happening. His heart. His heart was failing him.

He slowed the car, edged it to the side of the road. Then he stopped, straightened his back, forcing air out of his lungs and through his nose and mouth. The pain was not sharp, not like that first time. But it was there still, this time as a kind of absence, a desperate and sudden losing of a part of oneself. He strained his right arm, lurching over to the side from the effort, slouching on the car seat as he pried the glove compartment open and reached for the bottle of aspirin. He had quit smoking, quit fried foods, even forced himself to take that extra glass of water every day at six a.m. He jogged three times a week, ate his vegetables. Yet, here he was, dying again.

8

The Kinsmen

Umumilo, 1905

There is a God for every occasion, spirit beings lurking in that space of timelessness, light as a chicken's feather. They sit on the clouds, on the fresh green blades of mango leaves, in the red dust of the earth, ground in by the stomping of praying men. The Gods are multitude—yet each content to stay within the jurisdiction of their powers. If a woman failed to conceive, the village dibia would direct the prayers to Ala, the life-stirring Goddess of earth who causes the ground to swell and yield fruit. If a man was called to battle, he would defer to Ikenga, God of strength and war, mighty and valorous, for indeed, there can be no victory for a fighter who does not first seek out his chi. So it went, from farmers seeking blessings on the season's harvest to young virgins in wait for husbands; the Igbos did not believe in one God or the concentration of power in one center; such an idea was an aberration in light of the fact that each person, in some small measure but by divine right, carried within them their own God.

For the people of Umumilo, Agwu was the spirit of their choosing, the God of divination and healing, known for turning dying leaves into bounteous harvests. But Agwu was a pathway, too, a bridge that connected the people to other spirits. Despite their devotion to Agwu, the people did not think it unjust to consult other Gods. However, the God behind every occasion must be known, so that it could be thanked appropriately, for thankless worshippers were considered worse than infidels. It was for this reason that on that fateful day, as young Derek bled into the ground, as sweat and tears mixed around his vacant eyes, the men of Umumilo erupted in song.

Ogbunabali a biago.
ka ya nwere nke ya—nke ya, nke ya.
Obia go, obia go, ye ya nke ya, nke ya.

"Ogbunabali," the men chanted. God of death and vengeance, known to steal his way into town at night and kill his opponents; the strange, shy God who hides himself until it is time to strike. He was considered the God of judgment, the God of respite; the one who enters the scene with a machete to slay his offenders. His punishment was capital, and by the time his hand was seen, it was already too late. Once, the stories go, Ogbunabali sent a coconut tree down, crushing an evil man beyond recognition. And once, the stories go, he snuck into the family of a wicked warrior and severed the heads of the entire household. Make no mistake, Ogbunabali would not appear unless a verdict was given and a soul was found guilty, for such a God was merely an executioner; it was the job of the people to point out the accused. It was for this reason that while young Derek lay on the ground, the smell of his death still fresh in the air, the men of Umumilo praised Ogbunabali, who did not need guns, nor English, nor patience. Ogbunabali had avenged.

As the villagers sang, they did not see the gray cloud that now hovered above them, nor did they feel the light pebbles of rain falling, already washing the bloodstains off Derek's face. The people did not think of Father Patrick, whom they had pushed aside earlier, and who had pulled himself up and run for help at the newly constructed secretariat. They did not think about Olisa, the village vagabond awaiting his own execution. They had even forgotten about Priscilla, whose tears trailed them as they chased Derek, nor did they remember Nneka and Adaora, the other impregnated virgins. They would not think of their wives or their children, only the blood of this stranger, which now seemed to be the blood of all the strangers, sinking into the red soil.

And so it went, that while the villagers stood in that scattered circle, giving thanks to Ogbunabali, a bullet from the white man's gun tore through their haze and hit Thomas. He fell to the ground at once, screaming, "Anwuola m—I am dying, they have killed me." His cry had barely left his mouth when the sound of the white man's gun thundered again. This time, two other villagers fell to the ground, without a sound, dead on the spot. Boko, the village giant, directed his rage at the white officer whom he spotted pointing the gun. The officer's eyes were squinted as he angled his shoulders and hands, as he stooped in a half squat behind a small bush, prepared to fire again. Spurred by that vision, Boko let out a loud cry, then charged toward the officer. There was a simple thought in his head as he sprang forward: Let us finish this one too; we must put away these imposters today. But Boko's thought was cut short by a bullet that pierced his chest. Still, his body kept moving forward. The officer shot again. Then again. Until Boko, the great giant of Umumilo, dropped to the ground, first with his right knee and then with the entire weight of his life.

Then the cloud lifted.

The people became themselves again. Each man turned to his left and right, as if to make a head count of who remained, who had not yet fallen to the ground. It was a young cobbler who made the first move. He picked up his footwear and took to his heels. The rest of the men followed him. They ran south, and they ran east and west, none daring to move north, where the white man stood. Their hands were raised to their heads; their wrappers hung loose, threatening to fall off their waists. As the men ran, the white officer walked toward Derek and lowered himself. When he touched the boy on the neck and saw that he was dead, he turned toward Thomas, still writhing in pain, and shot him again. This time in the face.

▼▲▼

"You do not recall the time you spent with the man?"

"Mm-hmm."

"And you say you've never had an encounter with this man?"

"Mm-hmm."

"Is that a yes or no?"

"Ee—it is a yes," Adaora responded.

The man who issued the questions was called Mr. Walter, a British consul who'd arrived at the village following the death of Derek. Mr. Walter stood at the edge of the bamboo bed where Adaora lay in her cot. Her body was soaked in sweat, though the evening was chilly, and the trees danced from the push of the winds. The interpreter, Bassey, stood at the edge of the bamboo bed, too, closer to Adaora's shoulders, where the head of her newborn rested. Mr. Walter stood behind both of them.

The room smelled of salt and sand and wet wood.

"Ask her again," Mr. Walter said to his interpreter as he gulped down the last of the palm wine in his gourd. "Ask her if she was friends with him at least. Perhaps they had a secret affair her father would disapprove of."

At that suggestion, Adaora began to cry. Her crying was so thick and profuse that it was difficult to tell her tears from her sweat. Bassey, the interpreter, glanced at her and frowned. She continued to cry, heaving louder. Ever since this child was born, she'd been at the edge of a strange sadness, as though she had woken up and newly found out she was pregnant. For nearly one market week, she had not bothered to wash herself. What was the point? She looked at the baby in her arms, his nose, his eyes that roamed, his gaze still not fixed, the soft wrinkles on his face as he fussed and squirmed. She resented every part of this newborn. But it was better to look at this child than it was to look up at the white man and his aide. Spittle drooled from the child's mouth and trickled down her arms as the child turned toward her breast, searching. Adaora winced. Her own father had not come to see her since the baby arrived; he had not come out of his chambers at all according to her mother's report. Adaora sat up to feed the baby, but Bassey stirred behind her. "Not now," he said, "when we finish." She cried some more, realizing that it was not just the shame of this bastard son that brought her such sorrow, nor was it the fact that she had lost a suitor, Mazi Okolo, the warrior she had secretly loved from the time she was a little girl. It was, instead, this tiresome questioning, this suggestion that she, Adaora the beauty, the heart and prize of the whole of Umumilo, might have secretly had an affair with Olisa—that aimless vagabond who lived without speech or thought—that deranged man. Why did this thing happen to her? She had done everything she was supposed to do. She had tended her mother's herbs, helped on the farm, entertained with kindness the gestures of men with prying eyes, men who hungered after her beauty but who did not have what it took to court her. And when the time came, she'd won Okolo's heart, an honorable man who had quietly watched her with interest; he did not speak to her until he obtained her father's consent for their marriage—this same Okolo who was now among the villagers who shunned her. It was not her who threw the stones, who killed the white boy, who put the baby into her body. It was not her who asked the soldiers to invade their village long before the boy arrived, nor was she responsible for the wars between Ndi Igbo and their European intruders at Arochukwu, or that final blow that gave the white man his confidence and led to the collapse of the Aro confederacy; why, then, was she being interrogated? She let out another sob, her hands tightening around the baby.

When Adaora and the child quieted a little, Bassey spoke again.

"So, tell us now," he said. He glanced at Mr. Walter, as if waiting for some nod of approval.

"Tell us about your love with Olisa."

Bassey made the statement in a simple manner, in his typical quiet demeanor. He was therefore startled when Adaora looked up at him and let out a loud scream. Without thinking, Bassey raised his hand to the air and brought it down on Adaora's face.

"Be quiet, or you will offend Mr. Walter," he said. His response had been instinctive, and he felt small traces of guilt afterward. "Mr. Walter is a powerful man. If we make him angry, his people will be very cross. Not just with you but with our whole village," Bassey explained in dialect.

Adaora nodded.

It was true that Walter was a no-nonsense, high-ranking British administrator dispatched from Lagos to investigate the killing of the young Derek. And it was true that his report could bear grave consequences. Already, there were rumors that the British would set up a court in the village, like they had done in Amanasa and in smaller villages across the southeastern regions. But it was not true that Bassey feared for the village. Indeed, what Bassey feared was that Adaora's scream would be perceived as a failure on his part to communicate, and this could cost him this newfound work. He would not stand for that, especially now that he had been transferred from serving the church missions in Badagry to the district commission. He'd worked hard to get here, and he would not lose this opportunity to the screaming of a woman.

After they had completed their questioning, Walter and Bassey left Adaora's hut and walked back together to the central quarters, a single-level building made of mud and stones. Inside the building, there were wooden desks and chairs, and Walter, tired from the trek, sat down on one, then pulled out his small notepad. Bassey stood beside him, unaccustomed to leaving until he was dismissed.

"The young woman, you say her name is Ado-ore?" Mr. Walter asked.

"No, sah, it is Ada-ora—'ora,' it means first daughter of the people," Bassey volunteered. He was not Igbo himself, but his mother was, and he had grown up in the regions and knew the language better than his own father's dialect.

"Yes, I suppose so," Mr. Walter replied. He lit a cigarette and inhaled deeply.

"And you say Ado-oore conceived first, before Priscilla, though Priscilla's baby came first?"

"Yes, sah, you know it, sah," Bassey responded. He worried that Mr. Walter was fixated on needless details. After a careful pause, Bassey continued. "So, the vagabond, when you take him away, sah?"

"The vagabond?"

"Yes, sah," Bassey replied, "the man that put pregnant in the village women—when you take him away, sah?"

"Look," Mr. Walter said, springing up. "Be reasonable, my man. The fact that a person says a thing does not make it so."

"That is partly true, sah, so when?"

"It's not that straightforward, my man. We have to get to the root of things," Mr. Walter remarked. Then he put out his cigarette and sat back down.

"But we see the babies, sah, and the people catch the vagabond with their hand."

"Exactly, but he has not accepted his crimes," Mr. Walter said.

"He no say anything, sah. He keep quiet because of shame."

Mr. Walter ignored this final statement, choosing instead to ruminate quietly.

When Walter first arrived in Umumilo, he'd read the reports about the priest's nephew, a young lad no more than twenty, stoned to his death. He'd been briefed on the shootings carried out to curb the villagers, the tensions that would certainly halt the development schedule. The consulate wanted a tidy cleanup. Someone with Walter's experience who could get to the root of things with minimal military interference. His presence was, therefore, a matter of expediency, since he had supervised the establishment of six court systems in the southeast and was already familiar with their native laws. When he arrived, he'd skimmed through the plans the consulate had devised to set up a local administration that networked Umumilo with five other villages; plans that itemized his role, along with the timeline in which he was to report back to his superiors. Walter knew he would deliver on the task without spilling British blood. He knew that no harm would come to his men. No waste of officers. No pillage of European lives. One boy—the young Derek—was enough. And he knew how to achieve this. From his experience, it was always cheaper, more effective, to deploy the locals in the service of the Crown rather than deploy more force. Besides, the use of force often gave the dissenters a cause to rebel—a sense of purpose. It made them feel that they had a right to defend their liberties. He had moved up through the ranks by making allies instead. He did not think himself a pacifist, more like a strategist. He was loyal to Europe, to the Crown, to the lives of his countrypeople. His current assignment was to scan the people of Umumilo, weed out the weak from the strong, understand who could be trusted by the consulate, who was hungry for power, who was open to change. And once such people were identified, he would put them in service to the Crown and leave to attend to the next project. It seemed easy enough. There was only one problem this time—the virgin pregnancies that he'd stumbled upon in the reports. The boy they called the vagabond, the perpetrator of the alleged crimes, had been sentenced to death by his people. But Walter would not bring himself to succumb to the verdict of the villagers—a summary judgment that was to be executed by who—spirits? There was, of course, also the fact of the story itself, and all the underlying questions that bothered him. How did the virgins stay asleep through the ordeal? Bassey had explained the vagabond's powder to him, a sleep potion known by many herbalists, used both as a way to treat pain and as a medium to channel spirits. But how could the villagers allow such a dangerous powder to get into the vagabond's hands? How did they not know that such a powerful potion could be used for mischief? Bassey looked at him incredulously and said, "But why anybody use it for mischief? Our people are good." Walter had humphed and quietly decided—having speculated on this alternative theory in his mind as well—that the alleged rapes were false. It was more likely that the babies were the result of affairs gone wrong. This was why he'd insisted on getting a confession out of Adaora. He needed something practical to put in his reports. An affair was more plausible than the story of this powder. His superiors would scoff if they read such an account. No. He needed something more tangible. He needed a confession.

Truth be told, it would have been easier to lock up the vagabond. Even if he did not acquiesce to the verdict of the evil forest, he could still use the boy as the first example of the Crown's court of equity. It would be evidence to the people that their traditional laws and that of the consul could align. But in order to do this, he would have to first acknowledge the crime and the alleged use of the powder. Once again, this was not an option. No, he insisted to himself. Even if the story were possible, it was not believable. And he, Walter Blackburn, did not rise through the ranks by selling fantasies.

▼▲▼

Okolo had never been a man to hide. Yet he had now taken to sneaking through the village at night, moving between bushes, aware that even in his own eyes he had become a worm, one of those detestable crawling creatures, without spine or strength. He blamed the vagabond for this. If the bastard had not violated the women, none of the events of the past few market weeks would have occurred; he would have consummated his marriage with Adaora and retained his respect among the villagers. His courtship of the young woman had been genuine, despite the two-decade age gap between them. He had chosen not to take advantage of his influence over her, chosen to do the honorable thing and ask for her hand. They met in public, chaperoned by her own brothers, by her father, by his older wives; he had considered that a joining with her was a blessing by the Gods. This was one regret he had not spoken aloud. He had lashed out about his reputation, but he did not dare to voice the disappointment he felt, or the fact that in the weeks since the death of the church boy, he had thought more and more about Adaora, wondering why he had to give up on the prospect of her completely, especially now that the truth was revealed—she had not soiled herself. This thing that happened was a thing that was done to her. After all, when a fox meets a leopard, one does not blame the fox for getting eaten. Of course, there was also his sister Priscilla, who was no fox, indeed, but who was not completely to blame, since she was clearly deceived by the white man's ways of worship. He thought about his own role in the boy's death but shook it off at once. It was not like he threw the stone himself. If he, the great

Okolo, who could kill a rabbit with two fingers, had intended to harm the boy, he would not have needed stones. No. The boy's death, it was not on him. And he would not blame the villagers either—none of them set out to kill. None of them left their homes with weapons. Their only crime was anger, and who can blame a man whose home has been invaded for getting angry?

In any case, their anger had since dissipated, and in the absence of that rage, Okolo understood now that it was time for something else. Temperance, perhaps. Even the hotheaded warrior must learn the language of diplomacy, since the real goal was to win the battle, not merely to strike a blow at one's opponent. This was the reason Okolo had swallowed his pride and his threats and was now on his way to meet with Bassey, the white man's interpreter. This was to be their third time meeting—two unlikely men holding court under the mango tree at the edge of the Uchu River. Okolo, tall and sprightly; Bassey, short and thin with eyes that bulged as though he were constantly surprised.

In their earlier meetings, Bassey wore his official khaki shorts and shirt, girded by a belt. Despite his serious demeanor—his back straight, chest pushed out, the way he stomped his foot on the ground whenever he was interrupted—Bassey still looked, to Okolo's eyes, like a lizard. Yet, despite Okolo's mistrust of him, he kept in mind an ancient wisdom of his people: it is not every serpent that one must kill; there are some you keep safeguarded in your home, which is to say that in times of trouble, you must find that enemy who is most likely to become a friend. Okolo considered that Bassey ate with the men who shot the villagers; he spoke their language, slept in their quarters; he was no friend of Okolo, but at least he could be of use to him. Like the rest of the village, Okolo knew a few things about Bassey, details that were scattered but, when pieced together, formed a logical explanation for his whereabouts and motivations. Bassey was from the Old Calabar region, but he'd grown up in the nearby village of

Amafuru—his own father served and died in the missions, and Bassey had desired nothing else but to pick up where his father had left off, to master his father's limits, since the man himself never learned to speak English. Like his father, Bassey started in the missions in Badagry, but he knew that unlike his father, he would not die there, and so he'd followed the scent of opportunity. Like Mr. Walter, he, too, had arrived shortly after the incident with Father Patrick's nephew; he did not know Father Patrick directly, but the diocese in which he served had recently recommended him to the consul, since his English was so good it was a shame to not put him to administrative work. It was therefore Bassey, newly arrived in Umumilo, who took the words of the officers to the village square after the shooting. He used a gong as a call to attention, then raised his voice, moving from one corner to the next with his message. "We come in peace—if you comply, there will be no quarrel." The announcement rang through the village as the men who'd chased Derek continued to hide out in their tents. No one knew what peace Bassey spoke of, or what he meant by "comply." Whose rules? Which new God required their cooperation? What the people understood was the fact of Thomas's death, Boko's death, the sudden haunted silence of a village grieving its strong men. They decided to remain indoors, struck with a confusing fear, determined to outwait the invaders. However, after two market weeks, the villagers returned to their stalls. It was the women who came out first, determined to brace the unknown rather than watch their children writhe from hunger. Then a few men followed, shy and hesitant, trembling all the way to their farms. There was no incident or threat, so they returned the next day, and the day after that, until one day Bassey strolled casually into their midst at the village square. He entered Nkwo market with his stick and khaki shorts, his legs skinny and hairy. He spoke in dialect and attempted to purchase some roasted corn from one of the sellers. He was about to put one in his mouth—

it was not unusual for villagers to taste the product before the transaction was concluded—but the seller slapped the cob out of his hand.

"Do you know who I am?" Bassey said in dialect. He pointed to the tray and ordered, "Pick that one for me." The seller, an aged woman, took one look at him and spat in his face.

"Chineke!" he muttered, raising his hand to wipe his face. Then he heard a voice coming from behind.

"What do you want here? Have you not done enough?" Okolo asked.

Bassey looked at the machete in Okolo's hand.

"This is a public place. Am I not allowed to move freely? Can I, too, not make purchases?" Bassey responded in his thickest native dialect, a reminder that he was more of them than of their enemies.

"Move freely? You want to move freely? Do you not know that a man who betrays his people will have no home when the sky turns dark?" Okolo asked.

"You speak of home, you speak of the dark, but how can I sleep at home when the hands of my kinsmen are stained with blood?" Bassey responded. He reached to his waist to pull up his shorts, something he did whenever he was nervous.

"Better the bloodstain of a kinsman than the feast of strangers," Okolo responded. "Or did you not learn—food that is not cooked in your mother's kitchen will sour in your belly."

Their simple exchange, dressed in the ancient proverbs of their fathers, served as an opening, the first seed of the idea that perhaps they had more to say to each other. Bassey returned to his quarters that day and stewed over Okolo's words. Indeed, when he'd first joined the commission, his intentions were clear. He would serve as a bridge, a way for the white man to acclimatize with the culture of the Igbo people—how could people transact as equals if they were speaking from two ends of the world? Language, he knew, would bring fairness, some balance.

With shared language, a person could ask for what they wanted and refuse what they did not; perhaps if his father had learned the language of his masters, he would have gone further than he did. But Bassey also often wondered whose language would be compromised to arrive at this middle. He had learned the language of the Igbo people because he had grown up there. Was it not the duty of the guest to adhere to the rules of their host? Perhaps the white men should learn the language of the Igbos, he thought then. But it became increasingly harder to tell the guest from the host. In the wake of the Aro wars, the guests were no longer guests, and their visit no longer had an end in sight. Since both native and foreigner were now stuck together, the need for integration became even more crucial. In this regard, Bassey considered himself a cultural missionary, although he had also since come to learn that there was more to translation than the exchange of words and meaning, that translation required silence too. Sometimes it required the conjuring of what was not yet there. No matter how much he sought to be the bridge, neither of the parties truly wanted to cross to the other side. He often feared he would die the death of his father, in lifelong service, but with no true measure of impact. This was the reason he opened himself to the idea proposed by Okolo—to work together, to be the inside man for both parties, to do something beyond translation, beyond language, to put his actions where his heart wanted to be.

▽ ▲ ▽

"You mean to tell me that the vagabond still lives?" Okolo asked.

"It is what I have said," Bassey responded.

"He walks about freely with your master, Mr. Walter, and the others?" Okolo stood astride in a warrior stance, his arms folded across his chest.

"Mr. Walter is not my master, but yes, it is so. They may be coming for important members of the village; you should consider visiting your mother's family for some time," Bassey warned.

"Hmm, what do they want from the villagers?" Okolo asked.

Bassey adjusted his belt, then looked up at the moon. "They want answers," he said after a short silence. The statement sounded like a question.

Okolo decided to ignore Bassey's hint to leave the village. He would face whatever was coming, even if it was death or, worse, exile. Still, nothing prepared him for his own arrest. It is true that on the morning Okolo was captured for this questioning, he had been ruminating on the information that Bassey had given. And it is true that it was Bassey himself who led the two officers who arrested him, all three of them accosting Okolo on his way to the farm. Okolo left his compound that morning thinking to himself that the sun was out in its full strength, a sign that the day held the promise of good work. But he'd found the men waiting for him as he made the turn from the butcher's corner.

"Mazi Okolo, your attention is wanted at once," Bassey said, looking away from him.

"Is that so?" Okolo responded. He eyed the men with Bassey and moved past them.

Upon Okolo's resistance, Bassey nodded to the two officers, both of whom were locals serving with the consul. They moved toward Okolo with the precision of cats—one took him by the right thigh and the other on the left. By instinct, Okolo let out a low whistle, his warring mind kicking in. He stepped back as though in a stagger and laughed. The two men approached him again, but Okolo moved quickly, wrapping his hands around one of them at the waist in a motion that was so swift it seemed like a dream. It was with just one hand that he raised the officer above the ground; he made to reach out for the other, but then he saw that the second officer had pulled out a gun. Okolo glared at Bassey, then dropped the man to the ground; he could feel sweat on his face, sand on his calves, the sun beating down on his back. He turned his gaze toward the butcher's corner, and farther down the expanse, at the slim untraveled path that led out of Umumilo.

"We must go," Bassey said in dialect. Okolo turned to him and smirked.

When they reached the white man's quarters, the men sat Okolo on a stool. A small cup of water was placed before him, as though he'd said he was thirsty. Bassey paused, then asked him if he wanted anything else; Okolo had barely responded when Mr. Walter stepped in holding his cigarette. He settled into another wooden chair, one that stood slightly elevated to the stool Okolo sat on. Okolo stared Mr. Walter in the face—man to man—he thought, let him know that we are equals.

Then Bassey came and stood beside his Mr. Walter.

"We understand that a series of crimes have happened in the village," Mr. Walter began. "We are still conducting our investigation, but we think a man of your reputation and influence will make the process more productive." Mr. Walter rubbed his hands over his face, scratching his eyes lightly, then his mustache. He took a puff of his cigarette. "We are prepared to drop all charges, but you must in turn help us too. If you do not help us, then we'd consider you complicit and you'll be sentenced immediately."

Okolo thought Bassey may have misunderstood or misinterpreted the officer's words. They wanted him, Okolo—the dancing warrior, the one who moves like a serpent and fights like a leopard—they wanted him to help them. But help them to do what?

"Have you lost your senses?" Okolo replied.

On hearing this, Mr. Walter closed his notebook. "Very well, then," he said. "Take him away. We can have this conversation when he is ready."

9

Margaret

Lagos, 2005

Margaret leaned against the beige-painted wall, her left arm resting atop the windowsill, from where she watched Nwando through the louvers. It was late afternoon, and the weather had taken a dull tone, as though rain might come. Moments earlier, she'd heard the car horn, a sign of Nwando's return. She'd moved to the window and peeled back the curtains; then she watched Nwando's driver pull into the compound, the metal gate screeching as it was opened. The driver parked, then scrambled out; he rushed to hold the passenger door open for Nwando, who in turn smiled and fussed at him, telling him not to bother, as though his gesture was not necessary, as if she did not require it. Margaret felt herself tense at the performance. It occurred to her that she did not have this ability to wear a different face for the sake of another, to appear pleasant, congenial, even when she did not feel so. For three days now, she'd carried her frown openly, letting her eyes and the turn of her mouth show her unhappiness. Her presence here, in Nwando's home, was stifling.

Still watching through the louvers, Margaret's gaze locked with Nwando's. She felt a little startled, embarrassed at suddenly being discovered. Nwando smiled. "How was your day, Mama?" she said in a half shout, waving from outside. Her face was smooth and clean, bare of makeup except for the bold red of her lipstick. Without responding, Margaret moved away from the louvers. A few minutes later, she decided to do what she'd been meaning to do all day—confront her daughter, demand her release.

"I need to get back to my home," Margaret said.

She was now standing in the hallway that connected the guest bedroom to the living room; Nwando had just come in; the sliding door was still open. She dropped her purse on the sofa, then nodded to her driver to take the other bags into the kitchen. Margaret moved to the living room and sat down.

"Did you not hear me?" she asked.

Nwando pulled out her earrings, took off her necklace. In a moment, Martina, the housekeeper, would reach for the discarded jewelry and take it where it belonged. She made to take off the last item, her wristwatch, and paused.

"When did you stop taking it?"

"Taking what?"

"You know what I mean, Mama. Your medicines."

"I need to leave; you must ask your driver to take me home."

"What home? Where exactly do you want to go back to?" Nwando hissed. Then she sighed, turned to Margaret, and continued. "This is your home too; do you not like it here?" She was smiling that smile of hers, the same one that Margaret had watched her give the driver, the one she used for Chuka sometimes; the kind of smile that masked what she really wanted to say.

"Tina was supposed to call me to refill your bottles two weeks ago; she says you've not run out yet." Nwando rummaged through her purse, searching for some mint she kept there, but she watched Margaret from the side of her eyes.

"Has anything changed?" Nwando continued. "You have to tell me if the medicines bother you."

Margaret stiffened. "And when did you become a doctor?"

"For God's sake, Mama, I'm just asking a question. I-I am trying to do the right thing."

"The right thing for who?" Margaret asked. This time she raised her voice.

"For you, for Yetunde—have you even thought about Yetunde?"

Margaret scoffed.

In truth, Margaret had not stopped thinking about Yetunde, or seeing her face like a small photo framed in her mind. How could she not, when, even now, she still felt the pulse in her hands, the tremor from holding the knife, plunging it into flesh and hair. She did not remember the entire sequence of events. If she had to explain, she would say that the lights had simply gone out; that it felt like falling asleep and walking into a dream; that she'd had a vague recollection of what was happening, but that the events that transpired were not her actions. Yet, where her mind was blurry, her hands were clear—with every tremor, every bulging vein, every wrinkled line, they seemed to suggest that they remembered what happened.

Nwando's husband stepped into the living room, interrupting Margaret's thoughts. He stopped by the table where Nwando had started to peel oranges and rested his hand on Nwando's back; their eyes locked briefly. He picked up an orange.

"How was your day, Mama?" Nosa asked, his tone carefully moderated.

He turned to smile at Margaret as he settled onto the sofa beside her. He squeezed the orange into his mouth, licked the juice, then spat the seeds into his hands.

"Fine," Margaret mumbled. Her hands were folded across her chest, her teeth biting into her bottom lip.

"That's good," Nosa said, nodding. "That's very good."

Silence.

Margaret watched him from the corner of her eyes—he'd made no effort to discard the orange seeds, and she felt a growing irritation from thinking of the seeds clumped up in his palm. If it was a different place, a different person, she'd have insisted he spill the seeds in a bin at once, but she reminded herself that such a battle at this time would be distracting. Better to face one agenda at a time. It was also possible that he was doing it just to aggravate her—holding the seeds in his palms as he sat so close to her. He wanted her to say something, she realized. She, however, chose to keep their exchanges brief. It was what they both deserved, keeping her here like this, trying to placate her as though she was a child who needed to be watched. There was of course something else on her mind. Benjamin's call. She'd been quiet about it the past few weeks. At first, she told herself it was because she was not ready to talk about him. Then she told herself she had imagined the call. Of course it was not real—how could it be? Nwando was still an infant when he left. They were strangers, both of them.

"Dinner will soon be ready," Nwando suddenly said. "About twenty minutes or so." Nwando was still standing by the dining table when she made this announcement. It did not matter that dinner was cooked by Martina, their housekeeper, or that after Nwando had peeled the oranges, Martina would rush to the table, lift the tray, then proceed to juice the oranges. Nwando liked to insert herself into these small domestic moments—announcing dinners she did not make, peeling oranges she would not juice.

"How long have you been talking to him?" Margaret asked.

"Talking to who?" Nwando replied.

"You know wh-who," Margaret stuttered. "Your father."

"My father?" Nwando asked with a nervous laugh.

"Stop that," Margaret hissed.

"How did you know about—"

"How long have you both been speaking behind me?" Margaret asked again, this time bolder.

"No one is doing anything behind you, Mama." Nwando looked at Nosa, willing him to step into the conversation.

"You have not answered my question." Margaret crossed her left leg over her right.

"Mama, I need you to calm down—" Nwando continued.

Margaret laughed as she uncrossed her legs. "So you've been feeding him information about me?"

"What—what do you mean feeding him information? This is not about you, Mama," Nwando said.

"You will not answer my question?"

"But you haven't answered mine either. I asked you a question earlier—about your medicines."

"Oho! Is this the game we're playing now? You hold back an answer because I did not answer you, akwa ya?"

"Mama, you're getting worked up," Nosa interjected. "See, dinner is ready. Martina, Martina! Where is the food now?" Nosa shouted, as though the tension in the room was a result of the delayed dinner.

"Seven months," Margaret said, ignoring Nosa. She shook her head as though surprised by the statement.

"What?"

"You were seven months old when he left us." Margaret stood up now. "Do you know what it took from me to raise an infant alone?"

"Mama, please, not now, let's eat first."

"He abandoned us. Even when the war started, he did not look back. Do you know what it means to raise a child with bombs flying over your head? Ehn?"

"Mamaaa," Nwando said in a whisper.

"Nwando, he left you. He left me and you." Margaret's voice cracked; her words became unsteady. "What kind of a man does that?" she continued, turning to Nosa. She felt her face wet, a surprise, as she had not cried in many years.

Martina emerged from the kitchen, sweating.

"Not now, Martina," Nwando said. She looked at Margaret and said, "Biko, e me cha. Let's talk about this later, biko."

"Mba," Margaret began to reply in Igbo, then stopped. "I want to talk about it now, since you have refused to release me to my home." She paused, then asked again. "How long have been talking to him?"

"It's been a few years," Nwando said, wiping her hands on her skirt. Suddenly she was a teenager again, afraid to be criticized.

Margaret opened her mouth to speak, but the words did not come out. She tried again, but the words came out low and unclear.

"I really don't want to upset you," Nwando said.

It was those words that finally stilled Margaret. Nwando had used the word *upset*, but Margaret understood what Nwando would not bring herself to say. I don't want you to have another of your episodes; I don't want you to fall apart in the middle of my tidy life. Not here, please, not where the help can see. This is what it came down to, what she had become, a fragile piece of china carefully shelved. She wanted so badly to say something, press against the thoughts that were now scrunched up in her mind, the words that were on her tongue, sharp as knives, but she could not. Benjamin had been speaking with Nwando for a few years now, and no one had bothered to tell her. After everything he'd done, life had rewarded him, the man, with a reunion. And she, the woman, the mother who stayed and raised the daughter, what did she have? She felt her face wet again. But it was not her anger that drove her to tears, though she was very angry. It was that every argument she could make against the relationship would be dismissed with platitudes—Mama is sick, they would say. Mama is not being reasonable, and that would be the end of the matter.

After the incident with Yetunde, as Margaret returned to herself and found the knife still in her hand, she'd realized that the head security officer at Arina Estate had come into her duplex with a group of men, all of them dressed in uniform. They'd stood around her tentatively, ready to swing into action though it was not clear what that action would be. At first, Margaret had not been sure what was happening; then she'd looked down and seen her hands. She'd realized, too, that she was almost naked; her boubou was piled in a heap behind the sofa, leaving her in her cream silk underskirt and brassiere. Slowly, her confusion gave way to clarity, and with her clarity came the shame. Mama is sick. The men did not say those words, but she could see it in their eyes.

Tina stood by the door, behind one of the officers.

"Tina, why did you open the door for these men?" Margaret screamed, scanning the room.

"Can't you see I'm undressed?" she continued. She moved to squat behind the sofa.

The men stared.

"All of you leave my house now," Margaret demanded from where she hunched down.

"I mean it; don't let me call the police," she threatened. Still, the men did not leave. The head security officer finally spoke—he asked that she follow them. To where? He did not say. She refused, of course. They could not abduct her from her home, she argued. They would all pay for this, she screamed. But her words meant nothing. Finally, the men lifted her off the ground and made toward the door. She was still in her shimmy and brassiere, her arguments and explanations pointless.

They had not treated her like a criminal, but they had not treated her like an innocent either. She had simply become a presence to be managed—half naked in their quarters while they waited for the building administrator, for Nwando, for Yetunde to return from the hospital.

Margaret lowered herself onto the bed, her boubou still on. She'd left the dinner table without eating. Now, as she adjusted the pillows behind her, she realized she was hungry and would have to seek out something to eat when the house went to sleep. She got up, moved toward the louvers, by habit, to scan the compound. The rain that threatened earlier had come and gone, the night speckled with moonlight and streetlights. She closed the curtain, then turned to the bed, wondering in an instant if she was alone. She squatted and peeked under the bed. And then checked the bathroom. She moved to the bed and sat again, sure that she would struggle to sleep. Was it the incident with Yetunde or was it Benjamin? Or perhaps it was just her daughter who now made her restless.

Nwando's face was a mirror of what Margaret's once was—the full, thick brows, the hairline receded by the sides. Even their bodies were shaped in the same form. Small frames, wide hips, full chests, flat buttocks; the slight slant of their legs, almost bow-shaped. The only difference was Nwando's light complexion. Otherwise, Margaret and Nwando could have been two fruits plucked from the same tree. Yet their views of the world seemed to constantly collide.

Margaret remembered her own mother, long dead, her father also gone. Both her parents had spoken to her in English as a child. Her father had been adopted by the great Okolo. And her father had gone from being the adopted child to being the most revered and loved son. It was an abomination at the time, her grandmother Ma Adaora used to say—who gives the bastard the title of a son? But it was not just that Okolo gave the boy his name; it was that Okolo had insisted on marrying Ma Adaora after it was clear that no one else in the village would come near her. He was a man of tradition, but he ignored the counsel of his people and chose instead to follow—for once—the strange machinations of his heart. As a parent, the great Okolo, who had felt the hope for European acculturation wane with his older children, insisted that Margaret's father be brought up in the ways of the white man. And it was in this tradition of acclimatizing to a Western sensibility that Margaret's parents had decided to give her the best of Western education.

Margaret's aunt, her mother's older sister, had protested this kind of exposure.

"You will fill this child with nonsensical Western mannerisms," the older woman had warned. "Suo ro ya Igbo—speak our language to her," she'd said. Margaret was a little shy of turning seven years old, already bilingual.

"How many doors has Igbo language opened? Eh, gwam?" Margaret's mother replied. "How many Njidekas do you see walking the streets of London? Or Lagos? Tell me. The most intelligent girls have English names—even the Catholic saints, all of them are English," she reasoned.

"Oho, so that is your plan, eh?" Margaret's aunt had said. "If you continue to fill her head with this nonsense, she will grow ashamed of our ways."

"You call it shame; I call it opportunity. Is English not the language of the powerful?"

This was what her mother wanted to give her. Power. The kind of power that came from aligning with the powerful.

On the other hand, what Margaret tried to bequeath to her own daughter was a sense of self that was separate from what she was taught in school. Not power, but freedom. She'd wanted Nwando to have an identity on her own terms, one in which she could choose to be neither her ancestors nor their conquerors, or she could choose to be both. More importantly, Margaret had raised Nwando to understand that she did not need societal approval to be happy. The Nigeria in which Margaret raised her daughter was accusing and impatient. It was as unpardonable to be fatherless as it was to be without a husband. So Margaret had set out to create a shield around Nwando, to show her, through the scrapes and scratches of her own wounds, that no matter how hard life bit, one could always bite back.

But Margaret's efforts, it seemed, were unfruitful. She'd watched with muted surprise as her child shape-shifted into something unrecognizable. From the time Nwando turned fourteen, she made it clear that she wanted nothing more than to have a husband, children, a big house, work that she could do at her own leisure, open a shop, perhaps to not even work at all. What was worse, in those teenage years, Nwando had incessantly asked about her father. Margaret had shared what she could, but the young Nwando was unrelenting. "Mama, did I get my height from Daddy? Mama, they say I look like those children whom the sun has bleached their eyes; was my father onye ocha? Was he light-skinned like me? Tell me about him, Mama."

Eventually, Margaret acquiesced and gave Nwando the truth about her father, the man who left them, the stranger who made all the promises in the world and then absconded. It was a grace her own parents had not given her, knowing the truth about the men in her family, the truth about her biological grandfather, whom they called the vagabond, the truth about his crimes, his curse. She had been sure that the truth of Benjamin's abandonment would do the work of prying Nwando out of her father's hands. And if that was not sufficient, then surely the weight in her voice as she narrated the man's absence would move her daughter to reason.

A knock rasped against the door. It was Nwando. She did not wait for an answer before she entered the room with a tray in her hand—yams, egg sauce so hot the heat spiraled above the stew. There was also a glass of water.

"Mama, I brought your dinner."

"I said I was not hungry."

"I know," Nwando said bitingly, and then, softer, "I thought you might want to eat it later."

"Thank you. Put it on the dresser, please," Margaret replied, suddenly feeling self-conscious. She picked up a wrapper and clutched it to her chest.

"We need to talk, Mama," Nwando said. "We can't continue to put off this talk."

"Talk if you want. I'm listening," Margaret said. She lifted her boubou from where she'd hung it on the wardrobe, then slid it over her head.

"Ahn, are you still angry? Relax, Mama," Nwando teased, touching Margaret on the arm. "Relax now," she said with a laugh.

Margaret held back her smile. "I am relaxed," she said.

"I will tell you about Daddy, Mama, but first we have to talk."

There was an endearment in the way Nwando said the word *Daddy*, thickened with her own accent. It felt private—protective. Margaret sat back down on the bed and Nwando joined her.

"Mama, you know I care for you," Nwando began. "Do you think I will ever do anything to harm you?"

"Pass me the plate. No, the whole tray—can't you see that it's hot?" Margaret said, ignoring Nwando's question.

"Yetunde called; she asked after you; she said her husband also asked after you." Nwando got up and walked to the window. "You should call them. It's been three days, Mama. It's the right thing to do."

"And who made you the police in the situation?" Margaret asked. She raised her head, staring at Nwando.

"You have to call them, Mama; tell them you are sorry. This is getting embarrassing."

"Oho, so that's what you wanted to say, akwa ya? It has come to this. I embarrass you."

"Oya sorry, I'm sorry, Mama. Hah. You need to relax o," Nwando said nervously. She returned to the bed, scooting onto the mattress so that she was now lying down. It was fascinating to Margaret, how easily Nwando could return to her preteen self, reminding Margaret of the times they used to spend on the same bed in a one-room apartment, Nwando's head against her shoulder, their breathing and sweat intertwined, the strange mother-child connection that begins in the womb.

Margaret continued to eat. She sniffed as the peppers passed her throat.

"The food is good," Margaret said as Nwando watched her eat.

"Ehn? Is it only the food that you like here?" Nwando said, smiling.

"And Chuka," Margaret added. "I like Chuka." They both laughed.

"You know he is coming home this weekend?"

"Home? Is there a holiday?" Margaret asked, distracted.

"Hm, holiday ke? When he comes you can ask him what happened o. That boy has been acting out, fighting in school; this is the third time now," Nwando explained. She sat up on the bed now, her back against the headrest, a pillow on her thigh. "Do you know he was almost expelled if not for Nosa's donations toward their interhouse sports last term? Anyway, they've asked him to go home for a week to cool off. I will give him a serious scolding when he returns."

Margaret stopped chewing. "But why is he fighting?"

"You can ask him when he comes. Drink your water, Mama," Nwando said with slight impatience.

"When did the fighting start?" Margaret asked, her voice a whisper. "Do you think he's affected?" she said, turning her head to Nwando but keeping her voice low.

"Affected by what?" Nwando asked.

"Chuka is a good boy. He does not fight. What if they have come for him like they came for me?" Margaret paused, then looked at Nwando's face as though waiting for a sign.

"What are you saying? You've started again."

"Never mind," Margaret replied.

It occurred to Margaret now that Nwando could not see what she saw. She had always known, always had a feeling that they would one day come for the boy, that they would not rest until the past had been avenged. Who exactly they were, she was not sure. Still, a mother senses these things, so how could Nwando not? Besides, the creatures had been more upset with her lately. Perhaps targeting Chuka was a way to register their displeasure. She had to protect him. If Nwando could not see the threat, then it was left to Margaret to protect the boy no matter the cost. She looked at the tray, her appetite now lost; then she picked up the glass of water.

"What is this?" Margaret asked. She was staring into the glass; there seemed to be a faint trace of chalk at the bottom.

"What is what?"

"This," Margaret repeated. She held the glass up to Nwando.

"Oh, it's just something to help you sleep."

"Are you mad?" Margaret screamed. How could Nwando have tried to slip Valium in her drink?

"Mama, you're shouting. Drink the water, please."

"Get out," Margaret said.

"I'm tired, Mama. Why are you so difficult? Why do you make this so hard?" Nwando screamed back, her voice breaking. She raised her hand to her head.

"I said get out of my room now."

"Mama, please, please just drink the medicine, you need to rest."

Margaret pushed aside the tray of food, stood up, and continued to scream: "A sim gi get out of here."

Hours after Nwando left the room, Margaret was still seething. Nwando had sworn to her that they would never go down this road again. It had been years since Margaret last carried the frustration of being forcefully put to sleep, that next-morning fogginess after waking up with limbs that felt strange and heavy. It was one thing to take the occasional sleeping pill, but it was another to be unknowingly sedated, to lose your will in that naked, blatant way—to be stripped of control.

"I do not like how sedatives make me feel," Margaret had tried to explain back then.

"But it is just sleeping medicine, Mama," Nwando had replied.

"No. It is sleep when you want to sleep. If you do not want to sleep, it can feel like dying. Remember that time in the village when I thought I would die and leave you to be snatched by the war thugs? It feels exactly like that."

It happened in 1968, during the Biafra War. At the time, Margaret had stayed in the village with her mother's elder sister, the same one who disagreed with all her English exposure as a child. Margaret and her baby, along with her grown cousins, had lived in an abandoned village kiosk. It was a season haunted by the dread of what would happen next. Some days, they would be in the backyard, eating cassava and sparse vegetables, and then they would hear the faint whisper of sprayed bullets, like muffled hiccups. Sometimes the bullets felt close enough that the ground they stood on shook. But that morning in question, Margaret had woken up to a clear sky and set off to go fetch water. It was quite a distance to the borehole, and a risky enterprise to go alone. Yet, Margaret had woken up trusting the universe. She reasoned that she could make at least one trip, fill at least one pail. And if Nwando wanted to come along, she could. She whistled to Nwando as they walked, singing and telling her stories. Nwando was two months shy of turning three, but her feet were sturdy on the ground as she tottered behind Margaret, who was carrying a huge pail of water on her head. It was on the journey home, making mindless quibbles with her young child, that she looked down and startled at the sight of a snake circling Nwando's leg. It happened in an instant. The pail of water on her head shifted as she screamed, so that she lost her balance and fell, the pail splashing water on both Margaret and Nwando. She tried to get up but could not. She tried to reach out to Nwando but could not. Then she felt herself begin to drift, as one being dragged into a very deep sleep. She tried to say Nwando's name but could not. She tried to scream, call out for help, but could not. She tried to fight the pull into the darkness, tried to keep her focus on Nwando, who was now sitting on the ground crying. She lay there, floating in and out of herself, one small stray tear climbing down her left cheek as she wondered what would happen to her child if she was gone. The snake had disappeared, but it was too late. Her body lost the fight. Not even the love she had for Nwando was enough to keep her from giving in to the darkness.

Margaret often recounted that story to Nwando in the immediate years after the war, then in the years when Nwando was off to boarding school for her A-levels. Finally, Margaret recounted it with solemn emphasis after her first hospitalization by Nwando. Nwando was nineteen then; she did not remember the earlier event, except for the accounts Margaret had shared over the years, but Nwando had seen Margaret, twice, screaming and begging not to be injected. "I won't do it again, please. See, I'm fine, look at me, please, look at me, please.

See, Nwando, tell them I won't do it again," she had cried once at the teaching hospital. Yet, both times the doctor had injected her, and she had found herself swirling, floating toward a darkness that was thickening—sometimes she felt like someone had their hands around her throat, like she was losing her grip on life. Eventually, she always came out of it, awakened in some clinic or hospital room, eyes swollen and foggy, the taste in her mouth gone, strange faces hovering above hers. After Margaret had made Nwando promise never to sedate her again, she nodded and said, "Okay, Mummy, no sleep medicine." This was why Margaret could not believe that so many years after her last episode, after her last hospitalization, Nwando would dare to slip a pill into her water. And after putting her to sleep, what next? Send her off to some institution?

Suddenly, she knew that she had to act fast. How much longer before Nwando would make her move again? How much longer before they arrived and took her away? She had to get out. She had to leave, tonight. Maybe leave the country. But she did not have her passport. Was it in Arina Estate? No, leave the city, then? She was now in a frenzy, pacing about, scratching her hair. When it was past midnight, she snuck out to the living room, where she picked up the phone and called her lawyer.

It was his wife who picked up.

"This is Margaret. Tell Francis I need to speak to him urgently. Is he there?"

"Madam Margaret, is that you?"

"It is urgent, you must get him at once. They might get me tonight."

"Madam, it's after midnight. Francis is asleep."

"You don't understand, they will try again. I can't hold them off for too long—you must get me Francis right away. Tell him it's important."

The woman sighed a long sigh. "Okay, hold on. I will see if I can wake him up."

"Hurry, it is important."

The phone went static. The house had grown silent, except for the whoosh of the air conditioner. The living room was dark, though the light from the moon rested on the curtains and bounced into the space behind the door. Margaret was also now aware that Francis may have been waiting for her call, that Nwando and Nosa could have been listening in on her. What if the woman who'd picked up Francis's call was not his wife, but a doctor? She stilled herself, clenching the phone tighter than she should have. In her mind, she could see Nwando and Nosa upstairs with their ears craning toward their bedroom phone, trying to listen, laughing at her, at her ignorance. In that moment she understood that they had probably put something in her yam, in the sauce. That extra-sharp taste? What was it? She held her neck, her chest, her stomach. She started to scratch.

10

Benjamin

Atlanta, 2005

Before Benjamin opened his eyes, he'd known where he was. Something about the smell of diluted vodka and bleach—and his aversion to hospitals from the time he watched his father die in London—echoed in his mind. If things followed their usual protocol, in the morning, a senior nurse or attending doctor would walk into his room. They'd come in smiling with their pristine white overcoats. They'd read his vitals or nod at whatever sounds rattled in his chest. Then they'd look out the window while he adjusted the thin fabric that covered his body. He would play along, feign gratitude at this gesture to his right to modesty. It was not too much of a stretch from the truth; the hospital gowns were too thin; the shape of his age-worn body—the contour of his rotund belly, the spry hairs, his softened arms—pressed against the thin fabric. After he adjusted himself, the doctor or nurse would try to confirm his next of kin, though Americans preferred the term *emergency contact.*

"Is there anyone we can call?" they'd ask.

The thought of this prompt to produce a family member sent his mind back to the time he spent at a Lagos clinic those many years ago, Margaret's hand on his head, checking his fever, smoothing his strands.

Who was his next of kin now? He struggled to remember. Benjamin had not bothered to update his emergency contact since his last divorce. He'd not even done so after his first heart attack, when they called the number listed for his second wife, and the furious woman on the phone muttered her disbelief because they had been divorced for years. His father was long dead, as was his mother. There was always his accountant, he thought, but he shook off the idea. They had a good rapport, but Benjamin always got the sense that he was being indulged; those invitations to golf, the tickets to watch baseball, all tokens to acknowledge his monthly retainership. There was perhaps Cecelia. She was fifty-eight; married with two grown children she'd adopted from Congo. They'd started their affair casually, having met on a running trail. The attraction was instant, first because, like she said, it was nice to meet another "mature" runner. By the second week, they took their chatter to a café, where they openly flirted over coffee. By the end of the third week, they were in Benjamin's bedroom fooling around like teenagers. Two months after their rendezvous began, Cecelia revealed that she was married; four months later, she announced that she was ready to leave her husband. That same weekend, Benjamin called things off. It occurred to him now that although he had been married a few times, had a number of lovers, and reconnected with his daughter, there was no one to watch him die.

To be clear, he did not mind being alone all that much—or even the idea of dying alone. What he resented was the way that this aloneness was a question, an accusation. Being alone was his own choice. When he left Margaret, he knew there was no going back. And so forward he went to Ghana and London, before finally landing in America, the land of self-reinvention—a journey that thrust him briefly into the military, and then academia. He'd inherited a small fortune from his deceased mother and lived a full life. Yet sometimes he wondered what it all meant if there was no one to witness it.

▼▲▼

The first time Benjamin kissed Margaret, they were seated in the back of a cab driving through the Lagos Island market, the sound of jazz seeping out of the radio. The taxi smelled of wet tomatoes at the brink of spoilage; residue from the previous passenger, the driver explained. It had been raining in Lagos for six days straight, and the streets were damp and soiled with dirt; the moisture rose into the air, mixing with the smell of exhaust fumes and rotten vegetables. It was a horrid but familiar smell. Benjamin tried to keep his mind on the details of the evening—the sound of jazz on the radio, the smell of ugwu leaves and squashed tomatoes and rain, the sweat from bodies touching on the streets, the texture of the city so wild and alive—Benjamin was convinced that only by keeping his mind on these details would he drown out the presence of Margaret sitting next to him. He was surprised when Margaret leaned into him first. It was a chaste touching of their lips, perhaps even something he might have shared with his mother. But Margaret was not his mother. They kissed, then Margaret giggled as she leaned back to her side of the taxi. The driver dropped her off at the director's office even though it was well after six p.m. and it was dangerous for a single woman to be unescorted in certain parts of the city. But Margaret insisted on stopping at the office first; it was a Friday, there was a report she needed to get ready by Monday, and since she had a typewriter at home, she would pick up the file where she had scribbled the director's dictations and work through the weekend. Benjamin had offered to wait for her, to ask the taxi to take her home, to see that she was safe. But she had brushed him off.

"Don't be silly, I can take care of myself. Moreover, we both know someone is waiting for you at home," she said. Her voice was not quite accusing, but it had lost its earlier warmth. It was a conversation they'd refused to have in the past week while working together on the director's documentary project; the fact that Benjamin was now living with Cynthia hovered between them, silent but heavy. In truth, when Cynthia had first suggested they move in together, Benjamin did not mind. Through this arrangement, he'd have access to Cynthia's cocktail of domestic attendants—a driver, a cook, the elderly woman who came to clean the apartment on Saturdays. He'd been with Cynthia for months now, found her maturity calming, her ambition intriguing. It was not love, but it worked, and if it worked, wasn't that enough? He found that he much preferred the ease of lying back in a relationship, of having the woman steer the wheels; he much liked the safety that Cynthia represented, the way that by being with her, he'd come to learn about himself. He even liked her sudden outbursts of rage, the insecurity she felt about their age difference, about her body—folds and folds of stomach tucked into her skirts. He'd thought her sexy in their early weeks together, thought that her shy gaze, the aversion of her eyes during lovemaking, was endearing. He'd never traced his attractions to something as arbitrary as a woman's size, and it surprised him when women made such conclusions about their weight during sex—it was the thing that mattered the least in the moment. Still, he'd enjoyed this self-consciousness about Cynthia, especially when he considered her influence in social society; sometimes he'd even played it to his advantage. There were moments in their relationship when he felt that she had chosen him the way one might pick an item from the racks of a supermarket. And that he, being chosen, being the object, had simply followed. But this did not take away from the fact that things were good between them, especially since he wasn't the type to worry about the future, to ask or consider where any of it was going.

So, when, three months earlier, Cynthia had brought up the fact that they should move in together, that he should bring his suitcases and not bother paying his rent for the next year, he did not think too much about it.

Then that first kiss with Margaret happened. As the taxi pulled away from the director's office, Benjamin had only one thought in his mind: he had to call things off with Cynthia—immediately. All his life, he had never been the one to end a relationship. It was much easier to allow the woman to decide that she was done with him; the trick was to play the rag and then be promptly discarded. There was an art to this, a protocol that made things expire of their own accord. In London, he simply did not show up to appointments; he allowed his thoughts to wander while his girlfriends were speaking, so that his replies were distracted, sometimes even cryptic. Eventually the girls flowered under the gazes of other men. Benjamin was not sure if any of that would hold with Cynthia. She was not the kind of woman given to interpretations and inferences. She would want answers, words, clarity. And then what would he say? He would have to have a strong reason for leaving. And was a faint touching of lips reason enough? His relationship with Margaret was a non-thing. It did not exist. Their interactions, up till that moment, were complex, strange, indecipherable, like a foreign language. At first, there was that cool indifference between them; her tone with him had been rigidly formal, sometimes biting, so that he told himself he had imagined the initial attraction. Then he told himself that she was one of those women who was good at hiding her feelings, because surely she was secretly attracted to him, to what he represented, a British foreigner with government connections. He'd had his first close interaction with Margaret when he had grudgingly taken Cynthia's cue and dropped the program proposal at the director's office. The work he proposed was not at all like anything he had done on the radio; the director was soon to declare his political intentions and wanted a media production that reflected his philanthropic projects, something to depict him as a man of the people. It was all about grassroots influence, he explained; he wanted to be talked about in the markets, not just in the newspapers. And so the proposal was to create a commercial montage that interviewed certain traders as the director's beneficiaries.

"A brilliant idea," Cynthia had said swooningly. "Make sure you hand it directly to either his secretary or receptionist—if it gets to the wrong hands, that's the end o," Cynthia warned.

When Benjamin got to the director's office, he was relieved to meet a different person at the reception area, a middle-aged woman who upon recognizing him grunted a good afternoon and continued typing.

"You want to drop a file?" she asked, looking at his hands after Benjamin walked toward her. "All right, please wait."

"Exactly how long?" Benjamin asked—it was not quite five minutes since he arrived.

"You say what?"

"How long do I have to wait to drop this file? The oga is expecting it; I'm told to give it directly to his secretary. That should be you, right?"

"I don't collect documents. That is Maggie's work."

"Very well, so when is Maggie going to be here?"

"I don't know."

He was frustrated. He could have turned around with the file, stomped out of the office, muttered something about how much he had been disrespected, how Nigerians were impossible, how such a thing would never happen in London. These thoughts roiled in his head, and then, just as he was going to leave, Margaret walked in, smiling.

She reached for the file in his hand with one of hers, then stretched out her other hand to shake his. "I've not had the opportunity to introduce myself. The name is Margaret," she said.

"Ah, Margaret, pleased to make your acquaintance. I'm Benjamin. I reckon you know this already."

"Matter of fact, I do," she said, then chuckled. "I see you are alone today. Your lady friend is not with you." She was bold, and in her presence, Benjamin was a stutter of words.

It happened that Margaret had been assigned to him as a personal aide for the director's project, both of them now thrust together. It was early July, the peak of the rainy season, so the sky was seldom clear. But on days it was, Benjamin stood in the heat, his trousers rolled up, his face burned red under the sun. The site was the Lagos Island market, where the producers set up props, Benjamin asked questions, and Margaret made reports, relayed instructions.

"I am going to have lunch," Benjamin announced on their second day together.

"All right," Margaret said.

"Would you like to come with me?"

Benjamin was surprised by how easily the question had come out. And by how quickly she'd agreed. Suddenly, he found himself scraping away in his mind for a fancy restaurant, wondering what she liked to eat, what she thought of the stress pimples on his face, that red blotch of burnt skin, the mud stain on his khaki trousers. They'd settled on an informal meal; he'd ordered rice and Margaret ordered a bottle of Fanta and a meat pie. They ate in silence; she brought out her file and occasionally scribbled. And then Margaret did something that Benjamin did not expect. She teased him. She said it was good to see him outside the element of work. She said he was exasperating the traders, wearying the poor old women with his honeyed accent, and then she laughed, reached out her hand, and touched his arm lightly. She then mimicked him, his sharp, shrill call of "Stop, let's take that again."

"If not that you are oyibo—a white man—those women would have chased you out of the market with brooms," she teased. Later that day, Benjamin would return home to Cynthia and compliment her salty eggs, her freshly made braids, the thighs that she had always complained about, the same thighs that he sometimes thought beautiful, wondrous even, when he was caught between them. He would stroke her cheek, draw close to her, raise his leg across her thighs, the specific way she had once mentioned she liked. And in the morning, he would rush his bath, pick his clean ironed shirt and his polished shoes, and wonder what canteen Margaret would choose for lunch. He convinced himself that nothing was happening. It was a little private dance between them, two colleagues who worked together, eating together. He told himself that it was the idea of talking to someone around his own age, a young woman who was so accomplished, so passionate about her work. She had just turned twenty-two, but unlike other women vying for the stability of marriage and family, she knew what she wanted out of life. She would leave the director's office soon, she'd revealed to him. There was a German company coming to set up an advertising agency in Lagos, and she had interviewed with them. And there was the newly established law school she hoped to get into. She wanted to do things, actual real things. He thought about himself, how Cynthia had pushed him to take the project. And he thought about the way, it seemed, there was no aspect of his life that he could touch, pin down and say, This is my own; this is what I want. He'd come to Nigeria to explore his curiosity about his lineage, his grandfather's legacy, but he seemed unable to follow through with any of that.

Finally, on the last day of the shoot, which was a Friday, they'd planned to finish earlier than scheduled, because the Muslim traders had to go pray. Benjamin and Margaret had gone to have lunch as they usually did, and one hour away became five. It was then that Benjamin mentioned his mother, his late father, the questions that had brought him to Nigeria, the unexplainable fear that halted him in his steps every time he considered going to the southeast.

"I come from a small village called Umumilo," she'd said, her face a blank stare.

"Pardon?"

She laughed. "I know, it was all I could do not to exclaim when you mentioned the name of your grandmother's village."

He reached out across the table and touched her hand.

"I have letters, journals from my great-uncle, I have to show you, you have to see them," he said excitedly. "I feel like I am talking to a real-life historical artifact."

Now, after the kiss, after dropping Margaret off, Benjamin rode back home, the taxi snaking through potholes and road congestions. He tried, in his mind, to map out the beginning of what they now shared. What was it about Margaret that was so alluring? It was not just the kiss. Now their connection to the same ancestral homeland had come to light. He frowned as he imagined his grandmother Priscilla. His great-uncle who was a priest had written a lot about Derek—his grandfather. But Priscilla was an ellipsis—incomplete, almost as though she had moved to the edge of the pages and fallen off. He leaned over the window, smelled the tomatoes and the mud and the rain, and thought about calling off the relationship with Cynthia. Surely she would understand. This was fate.

▼▲▼

"Boys will be boys," Benjamin said, wincing at the platitude. He moved the phone from his right ear to his left.

"Boys will be boys," Nwando repeated on the other end, her tone flat and resigned.

It was the third time they were speaking after his heart attack, the equivalent of two years' worth of conversation between them crammed into two weeks. Benjamin had called first, days after his discharge from the hospital, his voice still hoarse from the aftershocks of his failed heart.

"I have been in the hospital," he'd said, rushing through the statement when Nwando had offered the perfunctory "How are you?"

"A heart attack. Doctors were worried but I'm recovering just fine." Benjamin thought he heard Nwando gasp. Perhaps she was shocked; this was good.

"You shouldn't be by yourself, you know? You should have a woman, a lady friend or someone," she'd said.

The conversation then fell into a familiar routine—how is life, how is Nosa, and the boy, Chuka? It was the longest they'd spoken, too, twenty-eight minutes, trading reports about health scares and medical prognoses. Benjamin learned that this was something he shared with Nwando, an aversion to hospital rooms, the clinical politeness of medical practitioners; the sense that their bodies were falling apart, quietly waiting for an unsuspecting day to lash out. He learned that when Nwando was thirty, she had been sure she was having a stroke.

"It gets better with age," Benjamin had said to Nwando then. "This unconscious obsession with your own mortality. When you are younger, you have dreams, you look around you—at your work, your family, your people—and you realize you want your life even though it is far from perfect; somehow you just want it."

"Hmm," Nwando replied.

"When you get to my age, you worry less about dying—these things become almost inevitable. I mean, you still want your life, but you also know that it is not yours to have. There's no exact moment this shift in perspective happens, but it does."

"Hmm, I can't say I understand what you mean, Dad."

It was the first time Nwando had called him Dad. Once, she had referred to him as "my father," speaking of him in the third person. But mostly, she did not address him directly at all. Now, here they were, speaking as if their relationship was something real. Benjamin allowed his mind to wander back to Nwando's concern about Chuka. Boys will be boys. It wasn't his finest moment of fatherly wisdom, but then he didn't know much about comforting women. What else was he supposed to say on the issue of her son, sent home from boarding school for fighting? Do not most boys who are tucked away in some facility need an outlet? Still, he did not want Nwando to think that he condoned violence, that he believed being aggressive was essential to being male. He wondered if there was something he might say, something to redeem himself, but Nwando's voice suddenly pressed through the phone, asking, "I wonder who he gets it from."

Silence.

"Neither my husband nor I are confrontational—where does he get it from?" she continued. Was this a trap? Benjamin thought. He did not want to get into trouble.

"You know teenagers, they pick up all kinds of things from television these days." After a brief pause, he added, "A girl might be involved."

"Or my mother. Maybe he gets it from her." She sighed.

Silence.

"My mother says it's a curse, you know," Nwando added. "She says it's the family curse."

"Do you think it's a curse?"

"Chuka has never been violent, and now, suddenly he gets sent home from school?"

"I'm sorry."

"Why?"

"What?"

"Why—exactly—are you sorry? Did he get this behavior from you?" Nwando hissed.

"You sound upset. Have I made you angry?" Benjamin asked.

"Did you speak to my mother?"

Ah, finally, Benjamin thought.

"I may have," he said. "Did she say anything?"

"She was not excited about it; she didn't know we'd been speaking."

"I see," Benjamin said.

He stood up from the kitchen stool, thought about going to his bedroom for a nap, then shook his head. How did this happen? He, who had never been a man to take naps, found himself exhausted from the conversation.

"You didn't tell her?" He hoped his voice did not sound accusatory, but he was a little disappointed that their interactions had remained clandestine.

"Was it because of her condition?" Nwando asked, ignoring his question. "Is that why you left?"

"I'll talk to you later, Maggie," Benjamin said. He winced as he realized his mistake. "I mean—Nwando. I'll talk to you later, Nwando."

"Sure, go ahead. Run away when the conversation gets hard."

"Let's not get into this now," Benjamin replied, a little riled up.

"Get into what? I have only asked you a question. Why did you leave?"

▼▲▼

After that first kiss, Benjamin went to Margaret the next Monday.

"I told her," he said.

"Told who?" Margaret responded. She patted her hand softly on her Afro, distracted.

"Cynthia. I told her about us—that we kissed."

Margaret said nothing. It was early in the day; they'd finished the production project but returned to the site for some final interviews. The recording crew were setting up, and Margaret had been preparing one of the market women, a local fish seller they'd scheduled to interview.

"Can we talk about this later?" Margaret answered eventually. She looked away from him, then walked toward the production assistant. Benjamin thought it was a game to her—the way she made everything seem trivial with her lazy laughter. She'd avoided him for the rest of that day, and he tried to throw himself into those final moments of the work. During lunch, she'd said she was not hungry, too much to finish here. Yet, she stood at the setup chatting with the women. They all laughed, their talk moving between Igbo and English and Yoruba and pidgin, their language so braided that it became its own separate thing. He hated that a sentence could begin in English but end in Igbo, which meant that their conversation came to him in pieces. He'd picked up a few phrases in pidgin, but now it only made him feel more alienated. When evening came, Margaret insisted on taking the taxi home, alone. It was an emergency, she said.

"Oh, is everything quite all right? Is there anything I can do?" he asked.

They were standing by the side of the road, under the awning of a closed grocery stall.

He reached out to touch her hand, but she stepped back.

"Sorry," Margaret said.

Benjamin put his hands in his pockets. They both stood in that quiet, neither of them moving. He looked at her feet, her toes peeking through her sandals, the luminous red shine of her nail polish; he frowned, recalling how Cynthia wore a similar color. Benjamin realized in that moment that he barely knew this Margaret, yet he'd looked Cynthia in the face and told her it was over. It was madness, the kind his father had warned him about, but it was already too late. His heart had gone where his heart had gone, and not even Cynthia's tears and accusations and threats could sway him to reason.

Benjamin and Margaret would not come together as a couple for another three months. She wanted to take things slow, said that it was all happening too fast. She'd avoided him all that first week after he'd told her about Cynthia. The week after, she had not shown up at the office at all. He left the radio station and accepted an offer to manage media relations for the director—he'd been assigned an office, a secretary. He told himself he liked the director, that he respected his political ambitions, his grassroots focus; he was the kind of galvanizing force modern Nigeria needed to create a sense of national identity. But there was also Margaret just down the hall from him. For weeks after Margaret resumed work, she ignored him, addressed him as "sir." During meetings when she was called to take notes or verify information, she responded curtly, addressing the director alone. Benjamin began to feel that he was running out of options, so he did the only thing he knew would get her attention. He went to the hallway by her office and lit his cigarette. She ignored him at first, her head in the newspapers she was reading. The older woman who also worked in that space excused herself to lunch. Shortly after, Margaret folded the newspaper, stood up, adjusted her belt, and moved toward the door. Then she stopped, looked at Benjamin. He looked at her, inhaled, then exhaled, letting out the smoke. In that moment, they both began to laugh. She walked up to him, took the cigarette from his hand, and snuffed it out. He was leaning on the wall, next to the window, the city behind them—an old church, buses picking up passengers, schoolchildren running home.

"It's nice and sunny out today," Benjamin said, enjoying her closeness.

"Really? You want to talk about the sun?" she asked, teasing.

Her eyes fell on a book he had rolled in his trouser pocket.

"I didn't know you read Nietzsche," she said, bumping her shoulder against his.

"There are many things you don't know about me," he replied. He searched her face, then peered out the window at the city.

"Same here," she replied.

"Then let's do it," Benjamin said. "Let's get to know each other," he declared with urgency. "I want to know everything about you."

"I'm going to the canteen by the corner. Do you want to come?" she said.

So they had walked outside into the afternoon heat. The weather was so hot that Margaret squeezed her face.

"Here, take my handkerchief," Benjamin offered.

"How many girls do you give your handkerchief to?" Margaret asked.

He wasn't sure what to say, how to respond to this version of her. Was she jealous?

"Relax, I'm teasing, thank you." She moved to collect it but did not wipe her face.

"You have been avoiding me," Benjamin said. He stopped, searched her face, his heart now racing.

"It is true, onye ocha," she admitted.

"Why?"

This time it was Margaret who reached out and held his hand.

"You just came out of a relationship; there's no rush. I want us to be sensible," she said.

Of course, she chose this moment, after she had kissed him, after she had suggested he end things with Cynthia, to be sensible. But because he could not think of any other argument to make, he asked, "How long?"

"As long as it takes."

▼▲▼

"Are you still there?" Nwando asked, interrupting his thoughts.

"Yes, forgive me, I got distracted."

"Will you not answer my question?" Nwando said.

"What question?"

"Why? Why did you leave my mother? Why did you abandon us?"

Benjamin raised his hand to smooth his thinning hair.

"Why does anybody leave?" he answered wistfully. "We were young; it didn't work out. I wish things had been different."

11

The Vagabond

Umumilo, 1905

Okolo had spent three days in Mr. Walter's custody. Having drunk the water they gave him while refusing their food, Okolo now began to reconsider his actions. This Mr. Walter, as he was called, was not one of his wives, and therefore he had no way to understand this refusal of food as a statement of anger. When Okolo turned away from the bowls that were presented to him, no one made mention of it; there were no appeals for his nourishment, no concerned questioning. The man who had the calabash had simply grunted, then carried the food away. After two more refusals, they had simply not offered him any more. He could feel his resolve weaken, hear his stomach growl. He understood that his fortunes might decline further if he did not do something. He had to make a decision quickly. But he wondered: Why this request?

Mr. Walter had started off demanding that Okolo sell out his brothers—point fingers, give names; the man wanted someone to pay for the death of the young lad. When Bassey conveyed the request, Okolo refused. He would not give out the names of men who acted in his honor. It seemed Mr. Walter must have reasoned as much, for he'd come to change his request. He no longer wanted to punish the villagers. What he wanted now was to know more about the vagabond. Perhaps it was a simple enough trade, one story in exchange for Okolo's release. Indeed, Okolo was old enough to have heard the stories of the vagabond's birth; he knew the stories about both of his parents—he also knew the mysteries that tailed the young lad's existence. But knowing these stories was one thing; sharing them with a stranger for profit was another. Olisa the vagabond was a son of the land, but he carried his curse from childhood. When a child is sick, you do not send it into the wild to be eaten by lions. So, despite the vagabond's past, the people of Umumilo turned their eyes away as he wandered the barns of his kinsmen, picking up yams and stealing chickens. He was one of their own and therefore must be allowed to feed.

Finally, Okolo made the decision. If the white man wanted to know about the boy, and if the story would absolve Okolo of the incident with Derek, then he would tell them. He would tell them everything and put the matter to bed once and for all. And he would start at the very beginning.

▼▲▼

1870

Before the great Okolo was seized by the roadside, before the death of the young missionary, before the virgins became pregnant, there was a story. The vagabond's story—cemented in blood and tears and Gods. His was a story of all that is terrible, all that can be stretched and squeezed, distorted beyond recognition, but like many others, it was also a story about love. It began in 1870. At that time, the Uchu River was venerated among the people of Umumilo and its surrounding regions. It was from there—the endeared Uchu River—that the villagers fetched water for cooking and washing. But it was also from there that they consulted their ancestors and carried out cleansings. It was a site of sacrifice, of prayer, of rest and renewal. Yet, as endeared as the Uchu River was to its people, it came second to the first rainwater of the farming season.

In this momentous seasonal occasion, when the rains of a new season came, it was the people's custom to desist from visiting the Uchu River and instead to bring out their clay pots and fill them up with rainwater. It was also their custom, if the rain started while their neighbors were far off on the long trek to the market, or buried in cassava seedlings at the farm, to go to their neighbors' sheds, find their pots, and leave them out to be filled by this rain. No one dared move the pots from their place; not mischievous children who picked up belongings from people's backyards, not heavy winds moving angrily through the village, and not the goats that roamed along the sheds in search of water and food.

The people of Umumilo were taught to hold one another's problems the same way the pots collected the first rainwater—each man seeking to help his neighbor. When a villager's corn harvest caught fire, the people of Umumilo came together and fed his children. When another was attacked by an animal and lost his right leg and sight, the people of Umumilo became his legs and eyes. When a young mother died in the throes of childbirth, there was always another young mother whose breasts the child could suckle. The matter was simple: If it rains, you do not leave your neighbor's pots unattended. When trouble comes, you do not throw your face the other way. However, as one must acknowledge, it was not every problem whose burden the people of Umumilo willingly shared, especially when the people believed that such a problem was the result of a judgment decreed by the Gods. In cases like these, the people of Umumilo knew to stay away and allow the Gods their wish. This was precisely what happened when Oriaku lost her mind.

▼▲▼

Oriaku was the only daughter of Ifedili, the revered town warrior. Ifedili had encountered the woman who would become Oriaku's mother one night after a wrestling conquest. They spent that first night together and Ifedili returned to the woman every fortnight. Their entertainments were kept quiet—the woman being an outcast forced to survive by selling herself to wrestlers, and Ifedili being the beloved town warrior who was already betrothed to a virgin in Amanasa. By the time the woman took with child, Ifedili had exhausted his curiosity of her body. As was his practice whenever he had to break off an affair, he offered the dried skin of a baby goat to the woman, thanked her, and prepared to part ways. But on the night that he would leave, he also learned that he was to be a father. Ifedili counted on his fingers how many times he had known the woman. He counted how many times he had pulled himself out before he reached completion. And he recounted the words of the woman, that first night, telling him that she had drunk the concoction and prepared herself to be known. It was therefore impossible to have made this child that she spoke of. They quarreled. He hit his chest and reminded her of who he was. The power that his name carried. The doors it could open and close. But despite his outrage, she remained pregnant and insisted he was the father.

When the baby arrived, there was no denying where she came from. One could almost say that her eyes were carved directly from Ifedili's face. When she cried, her mouth upturned slightly to the left, the exact same way Ifedili's moved in the grip of a wrestle. Her mother called her Oriaku, child of wealth, though they were both shacked away at the edge of the village, waiting on the generosity of the people.

When Oriaku was just six months old, the woman died. So the woman's sister, despising Ifedili's big name and reputation, wrapped the child in a raffia mat and dropped her in front of Ifedili's shed. It is said that a man cannot deny his blood any more than he can deny the skin that covers his bones. There is no running away from who you are. So when Ifedili found Oriaku in front of his shed, crying and crusted with sand, he knew at once that it was his blood that flowed through her. By the time her nakedness exposed the moon-shaped mark they both shared on their left thigh, he had already sent for the village midwife to nurse the child.

This was how Oriaku was raised—in the eye of her father. When he returned from battle, she was the first he asked for. When she complained of a headache, he sent her off to her shed with cooled goat milk and a command to rest the remaining day. As her beauty began to blossom, and the warriors in the near villages began to take notice, Ifedili sent out word that he would have the head of whoever came near his girl. And they were many, the men who wanted to drink from her, who were astonished by her beauty and frustrated by her elusiveness. It is true that her skin was as soft as the skin of a newborn and her teeth white and shapely, like the cowries that lined the banks of the Uchu River. But it was more than just her beauty that drew men to her. It was more than the fact that she came from a long line of Agwu priestesses—Ifedili's grandmother having served the oracle in her lifetime. It was that Oriaku herself was blessed with the ability to stand before the Gods. She was a healer, gifted by her chi with the foresight of herbs and spices that cured all kinds of fever. And this was paired with a kindness of heart that people found endearing—the way she held a dying child in her hands or looked at a bleeding new mother and offered her consolation. She spent her days on the farms, plucking out green herbs, burning under the sun. Then she spent her evenings visiting the older men whose bones had begun to rot with age, men who had become fragile with time but still wanted to know their wives. She visited the young women who nursed babies with fevers, and the younger ones, virgins, who wanted to learn the ways to secure a man's heart.

When the time came for marriage, Oriaku accepted the hand of Uche, the local welder, and they married quietly in the presence of Agwu and their families. They had met on a hot market day, when one of the village dancers fell in the middle of her performance. Uche swooped in from the crowd and lifted the girl off the ground as though she weighed no more than a bundle of leaves. The dancer was his sister, and it was Oriaku whose healing hands nursed her bones back to health. For three evenings, Oriaku and Uche sat together under the half-moon. Uche insisted he came to keep guard, to ensure his sister had everything she needed. Oriaku said she stayed to administer more herbs. Neither of them was eager to leave. By the fourth evening, the young dancer was well enough to get her own drinking water, and it became clear that she did not need any more guarding or fresh herbs. That same evening, Uche gathered up his nerves and asked Oriaku to marry him.

"I am not the wealthiest in Umumilo, but I work well with my hands," he said to her. "My back is strong. My father and his father before him did not let our mothers go hungry. I can take care of you. Let us build a life together."

Uche was sure Oriaku would turn him down. Yet, he continued speaking, determined he would cast the stone to at least see where it landed.

"With your gifts and my strength, our sons will be known in all Umumilo. If you stand by me, I will not leave your side; I will make you the pride and envy of our people. I will spend my days blessing you. Your name will be sung on the lips of young virgins. I swear this to you. I will treat you with the sam—"

"Enough," Oriaku said, cutting him off. "I will tell my father you wish to speak to him." Then she picked up her basket and walked out of the compound.

After their brief courtship, after Uche had spoken with Oriaku's father and he had given his blessing, after they married, Oriaku left home for the farm one morning and did not return. Uche sought her in the markets, touring through the homes she visited. When he did not find her, he stood in front of their shed, lit only by a small wick of fire, waiting for her. By the time the cock crowed at dawn, Uche had not slept, and he had not sat down. The fire had gone out. The goats had resumed their roaming. Young wives were already up, making their way to the stream. It took a full market week of scouring the village, combing through its sand-caked corners, sending their fittest men to the forest, and finding nothing, before Uche began to make plans for burial.

"Nna, jide obi gi aka—take your heart in your hands; be a man," one of the villagers said to him.

"I have always known that she was too good for this world. The Gods must have claimed her for their own," another villager said.

Eventually, Uche picked himself up from his grief, summoned his kinsmen, and went to bury the ghost of his wife.

▼▲▼

Five years passed and Uche had taken another young virgin as his wife; they had two daughters. His welding business had spread to Umuchu and Umueri, and his name was spoken in city council meetings. Indeed, his people had forgotten the long year of his grief—those months after the burial when he refused to eat. They had forgotten how he abandoned his farm, leaving the leaves to dry and rot; how he swore that there was no woman besides Oriaku for him. That year squeezed out a lifetime of pain, and, as in the way of fetching rainwater, the village people took rotations to care for him. They cleared the patch of rotten leaves from his farm and planted new seedlings. They cooked for him, filled out the holes in the roof of his shed. Even the widows took turns to keep him warm at night, to remind him that although Oriaku was gone, his blood could still be warmed by a woman's touch. When the year had passed and his grief was exhausted, he picked up the fragments of his life and began to build again.

On the evening of the yam festival, five years after her disappearance, Oriaku returned to him. Uche was hosting the chiefs and young welders that night. His shy, young wife had served goat-meat pepper soup speckled with lumps of dried fish. She had pounded the yams, rolled them in molds, and served them hot just like the chiefs liked. The men were drinking and laughing. Their stomachs were full. Even the termites and crickets were peaceful. Then Oriaku walked back into the village, into the compound. A sudden silence fell across the room, arresting the sound of laughter. In the eyes of the villagers, a dead thing had come back to life.

"Obim," she said, addressing Uche by the endearment she fondly called him. It was her, Oriaku, but it was also not her. Her skin had become rumpled, dry, as though with great age, and her eyes had taken on a reddish hue, as if to suggest she had seen the Gods.

"Obim obim obim," she said again, repeatedly, then swirled in front of the men, mimicking the bold dance of virgins.

Uche was sure that his heart had stopped. Yet, what made the evening even more strange, stranger than Oriaku's sudden return, than the putrid smell that followed her into the room, was the young boy-child who stood quietly behind her. He held her wrapper with his left hand and nestled his right thumb firmly in his mouth. As Oriaku spun round and round, loudly singing "obim obim," the boy's face became clearer. The chiefs and the young welders looked at the boy and marveled. It was as though they were looking directly at Uche. That first evening, Oriaku held the boy and walked straight to her old quarters, as though she were merely returning from a short trip. When she found the place occupied by another woman, the hallway occupied by two young children, she sat by the entrance with the boy still firmly in her grip. They slept outside until the cock crowed at dawn.

▼▲▼

"You know what this means, don't you?"

The kinsmen had called for a meeting because they had not been able to pry any sensible answers from Oriaku. She would not say where she had been, how she had lived, or what had happened to her on that fateful morning five years ago. She did not say who the boy-child was, even though he had Uche written all over him. The boy looked to be about four years of age, which suggested Oriaku had already taken in at the time she went missing.

"You know what this means," the butcher repeated.

Uche sat quietly, his head bowed down.

"I am sure you will tell us," another chief chimed in.

"Look here, my man. This question is directed at Uche. He must speak up for himself," said the butcher, then turned his face toward Uche.

"If I knew what any of this means, I would not have called for this meeting," Uche muttered. "If you have something to say, some word of wisdom, this is the time. Speak now."

The clouds had begun to gather, signaling the arrival of a heavy downpour; but the men did not move to retreat into the shed.

"You must send her back to where she came from. Since she has refused to tell us what happened, let her return there. We cannot just erase five years as if they never happened. She owes us some answers," the butcher declared.

"No, no," the men chorused. "You do not tell a man to turn his back on his wife. It is not the way of our people. If her father, Ifedili, was still with us, you would not even dream up such a response. Where exactly would we send her to?"

"The same place she has been these last few years."

"I cannot do that," Uche said, finding his voice again. "I cannot turn my back on her, not after I gave her my word. My home people, she is my wife. We stood before Agwu and made promises. We are bound."

"Brother, do not say such things," the butcher chided him. "We are only bound to the living, to what we see and hear. It's been too many years. We need answers, and if we do not get them, then we must determine to say our goodbyes."

"What about the boy?" someone uttered.

"Of course the boy is our son," the butcher volunteered, sitting up straight. He leaned forward toward the people, his eyes brightened with the importance he attached to the topic. "Of course we take the boy. We raise him in the ways of our people. He is still a child; he carries our blood; he is one of us."

"I gave her my word," Uche said. "You ask me to take her son—our son—and send her away. You ask me to send my wife away? Oriaku is still my wife. She is still my wife."

▼▲▼

The boy was thin and tall for his age. He was also still nursing at the time of their return, though that in itself did not surprise the villagers much. It was other things that disturbed them—the fact that the boy was not eating solid foods yet; that he never left his mother's side, not even in response to gestures from the other children. And he did not speak. The villagers set about to put an end to what they now considered an anomaly; they often tried to lure the boy away from his mother with lumps of fish; they jested after him. Yet, the boy did not say a word. They tried to correct this silence. According to their customs, there were prayers and cleansings required for infants in the village, prayers that the boy certainly must have missed. Perhaps it was on account of this that the Gods forgot to give him his speech. But he was still a child—they reasoned—and his problems could easily be rectified. However, each time they attempted to pry him out of Oriaku's arms, she screamed them off. It was only when Oriaku sent a stone flying at one of the wives that the women of Umumilo stopped with their schemes.

Oriaku's husband, Uche, tried to know his son, to learn about this person who came from his loins. He asked Oriaku what she called him, but she only laughed and refused to answer. Uche decided he would name the boy after his own father. But every time he beckoned to his son, gestured to him, there was no response. The boy sat on the ground beside Oriaku and leaned his head on her arm, day after day, until finally a room was cleared for them. They ate. Slept. Oriaku occasionally picked up a broom and cleaned the compound. She greeted Uche every morning when she saw him. But her eyes were still glazed and distant. Some days she would cook and clean, without explanation. And other times, she would fight and throw stones at anyone who came near her. This was the dance of her life.

One night, she returned to herself long enough to seek out Uche. He'd been lying in his bedchamber when the door creaked open and Oriaku entered. The moon shrouded the room with a haunted presence, so that from where Uche lay, Oriaku's face appeared in his vision as though it were floating in the air. She pulled down her wrapper and revealed her breasts. Her skin there had also aged, and there was still that faint putrid smell that followed her everywhere. It was clear what she had come for—a night with Uche, her husband. He wanted to send her back, ask her to clean herself. He wanted, too, to ask her if she had given herself to other men in the time she was away, if the boy whose face was marked with his was truly his son. Instead, he willed his blood to stir, then pulled her down to himself.

▼▲▼

After that night with Uche, every evening Oriaku would go again to his bedchamber, and he'd take her in his arms even though he knew that the other villagers wanted her gone. It was true that like the boy, she sometimes did not have her words, or could not present them in their correct order. But there were days when her head was bright and clear. She sometimes overheard the gossip from the women who passed by; she knew what their husbands thought of her, of her son, their return. Yet, even within the cracks of her mind, she knew that she did not need to tackle the villagers. What mattered was keeping Uche's gaze on what they shared, what no woman could take from her. And so Oriaku continued to slip through the darkness to Uche's room, satisfied that he had not turned her away yet. That perhaps he would never be able to. The only problem was that after their time together, Uche would begin with his questions. Where had she been? What happened? Who was the boy's father? How could she tell him that she did not know everything about those years of her absence? How could she tell him about the spirits that came out to dance every night, how they flogged her and left her screaming and scratching her back, how they sometimes appeared in the daytime too, taking on the face of villagers. Each time she caught a glimpse of them in the market or by the roadside, she threw everything she had at them, clutched her boy's hand, and ran. She would not tell her husband that she and the boy had lived on a patch of farmland, at the edge of a growing city, with people who spoke a different language. And she would not say how she stole into a small wooden church at night, searching for discarded food when the strange old man who lived there had gone to sleep. How the man in question left bread for her, sometimes eggs, sometimes cooked food. How it was this same man and some others who had come to her aid when she was to give birth. She wanted to explain how she came to finally understand that these people were her enemies, that they wanted to kill her, kill her son, that it was up to her to protect the boy from what was to come. And so she had carried her baby and run off into the night. Sometimes she remembered that she was on a journey to return somewhere, but she could not bring herself to remember where. Sometimes she found herself returning to the church, to the old man who left her bread and water. But then she would sense the danger in his gaze and off she would go again. How could she explain to Uche that she had simply been running, and forgetting where she was running to?

She continued to go to Uche, and he continued to ask his questions, and the villagers continued to seethe at her presence. They determined that she was no longer part of them, that she was no longer their daughter; she was instead Oriaku, a strange body inhabited by evil spirits. She must have done something unpardonable to be struck this way by the anger of the Gods. And so, unable to condone her presence any longer, the villagers marched into Uche's compound full of anger.

"Enough of this nonsense. It is time for her to go," one of the women screamed.

"Ee, our brother, you are not thinking straight, the woman has bewitched you," the butcher echoed from behind.

The villagers reported that they had just uncovered a recent sin of Oriaku. They said that she had beat a twelve-year-old girl who was only trying to help. They said that the girl came in the compound to fill up Oriaku's jars with water and to escort the boy-child to the stream, where he could wash himself. But what they did not say was that the girl carried in her the angry spirits that tormented Oriaku. Of course, the girl did not know that she carried such spirits; this was only as Oriaku saw it. When the young girl had entered their yard that morning, Oriaku saw the spirits as they sat on her face, perched on her shoulders; they laughed and screamed with sadness and fire, their eyes swelling. The villagers also did not report that Oriaku had screamed when she saw the girl approaching. "Hapu anyi aka, leave us alone," she had said. "Let us be." They did not say that Oriaku had begun her dance again, swirling round the compound, slapping her back, and jumping, as though in pain. It was not until the boy screamed out with tears that Oriaku calmed herself down and walked up to the girl. She took the girl by her neck and flung her against the wall. Then she bent over the girl and began to pound.

"I warned you people to leave us alone," Oriaku screamed.

She would have killed the girl, the villagers reported, had they not run to her begging and crying. They spoke of the whole incident deeply aggrieved, determined to expel Oriaku from their midst. This was not their daughter; it was not the same girl who healed their sick. It was time for this imposter to leave, they demanded. Later that night, when Oriaku walked into Uche's bedchamber and pulled down her wrapper, he still took her in his arms. But this time, there were no questions afterward. He no longer wanted to know who had harmed her or where she had been. Once he finished, he turned his face from her, closed his eyes, and willed her out of his presence.

▼▲▼

The woman Uche married after Oriaku held her stomach as she walked back from the market. She'd begun to swell with child, the third she would share with Uche. It had been only a fortnight ago that her morning fevers had stopped. But she knew that this pregnancy, the vomiting, and the fever were not the reason she had not lain with her husband in the last two months. He no longer came to her bedchamber in the evenings after the girls had gone to sleep. Indeed, the younger wife knew that Uche now spent his evenings with Oriaku, but she did not consider this a sufficient reason for his disinterest in her. After all, she was younger, and she was strong. Her skin was soft. Her breasts were full and standing. Even after two children, the men of Umumilo still looked at her as she passed by. It was therefore not possible that Uche would disfavor her for the haggard-looking Oriaku, the once-revered woman whom it appeared that the Gods had cursed severely. She had heard whispers of the council meetings. Yes, Uche was an honorable man, he did not want to put away his first wife, but even honor was bound to run its course. Soon enough, he would understand that Oriaku had nothing more to offer. More so, he could not deny his people's request for too long. It was only a matter of time. Eventually even his pity for Oriaku would wear out.

Lost in her contemplations, the younger wife did not expect to see Oriaku sitting outside their shed, her body sprawled on the floor, blood seeping out from under the weight of her skin on the ground. She did not expect that her woman parts would pull with pressure at this brutal sight, or that the urine would flow out, soaking her legs. The child that Oriaku shared with Uche stood by a corner, watching his mother. His face was without expression, as if he had merely come out to collect the afternoon air. The younger wife forced her eyes from the boy and returned her gaze to Oriaku's lifeless form. She was certain that any moment now, she would lose her grip on the ground and faint, but she could not leave. She held her stomach, moved a few steps back, and began to scream.

Afterward, when the story began to circulate, people would say that Oriaku took her own life. That she snuck the dagger from Uche's hut and sliced her own throat. They said it would have happened quickly, without much pain, that finally Oriaku could rest, that there was no life here for a ghost—someone who had already been buried had to take her place among the dead. Others said there would be no burial because a man cannot bury the same woman twice. Then they asked Uche—for the second time—to be strong; to consider his house, full of young children. Three children now and another child on the way. They reminded him that he had lost Oriaku before and he could carry another loss. And when they were done, they charted him toward the course of a new future. A future for the boy Oriaku left behind.

"What will you call him?" they asked.

Uche thought about his own father in that moment, who had died from an unknown ailment. "Olisa," Uche replied. "The boy will be called Olisa."

The villagers grunted in approval, the afternoon heat fierce on their heads.

"We will take care of you, Olisa," one villager said. But the boy remained quiet, his eyes falling to a space beyond the men. The boy would finish the rest of his life with this same unreadable mask, never able to wear what he was thinking on his face. It would become a point of anger after he defiled women in the village; his accusers would point at his expressionless face and declare that he had no remorse, that his face was in fact the face of the devil.

12

The Lovers

Lagos, 1960s

Margaret liked to lay out her shoes a certain way—all the rights lined in one corner of the room, and the lefts at the other end. She did not have a lot of shoes—about four pairs if you removed the sandals she wore for domestic errands. Still, this arrangement was startling to Benjamin's eye. She'd explained that she spent her childhood confusing her footwear, left shoes going on her right foot, and vice versa, but she'd found a system that worked for her, that helped her to keep things simple. Benjamin laughed, mad with love.

"I find it oddly comforting, you know," he'd said after a while.

"How so?"

"Just knowing that you're not perfect, that you don't know everything."

He'd spent those early weeks of their relationship watching her small habits, determined to learn all there was. It was a simple, primal desire—the eye's longing to become familiar with that which it found affecting. He learned about her love for roasted corn and pears, the way she secretly wished she could shave off her hair, her aversion to fried meats, her aversion to her feet and, much later, to people's feet in general. He'd also learned some other quirks. She did not go much to church, but she prayed. Sometimes the prayers were a mixture of her rosary and traditional chants she picked up from Ma Adaora. She said it comforted her. A ritual that kept her calm, grounded. He'd taken in all the details, startled only by the quirk around her footwear. He'd been rather surprised when Margaret said she did not think that toes should be seen outside.

"But you wear sandals," he'd said.

"Sometimes it's fine, I suppose."

She'd lifted her foot to him one evening in her apartment, laughing. "Don't they look strange, toes?"

"What do you mean?" Benjamin said, brushing her foot away.

"It looks like someone tried to cut the limb in five parts but did not see it through like with our fingers," she said, wiggling her toes.

Her apartment was a modest single-bedroom accommodation that she used to share with her cousin, but the cousin had returned to London, where they had both attended secretary school.

"Look, can't you see it?" She raised her legs again, this time bringing both feet to Benjamin, her skirt held up slightly to reveal her knees. He'd wanted to reach out, touch her legs, but the relationship was still young. Yes, they were getting closer, but they had still not decided what they were, what they could be. It was in this heady phase of their fledgling relationship that Benjamin came to learn one more thing about Margaret. She wanted to wait for them to be intimate.

"We are soulmates," he'd said dreamily, surprising himself. "Our lovemaking will be anything but casual."

"Like it was for you and Cynthia?" she added.

"Are you jealous?" Benjamin chuckled. He touched her face.

"Of course not. I just want to wait."

Benjamin was stunned and sat silently.

"It's not for any religious reasons, though," Margaret clarified.

He remained silent. He knew that she was not fanatical with her Catholicism.

"Is this about your culture—what people will say?" He did not know where the question was going, and he felt foolish to ask.

"You know that sex is not a European invention, correct? People from other cultures do it," she'd said dryly.

"So what is it, then? Or do you just refuse to sleep with your boyfriends?" Benjamin asked.

"What's so special about boyfriends?" She had a small smile on her face.

"You're celibate?"

"There are other ways to put it," Margaret continued.

"Like what?" He felt himself start to get irritated.

It was not just that she was now ruling out sex; it was her reason for it, which was not in fact a reason.

"So let me get this right; it's not for religious reasons."

"Something like that, yes," she said, playing into his sarcasm.

"Do you like me?" Benjamin blurted. "I mean, do you find me attractive?"

"That's not the point."

"All right, do you feel the urges? Because if you don't, there might be something else going on."

"Of course I feel the urge." She looked away, adjusting her blouse.

"And you just deny yourself?" After a while he added, "Or is it safety? We can be safe; you don't have to worry about that."

"It's not safety. Why do you need a reason? Can we not both enjoy each other without sex?"

Benjamin eyed her. "You're sure that is all?"

"Look, I'm a sensual woman; I know what it means to desire," she said stiffly. Then she turned and touched him lightly on his sleeves.

"But I also know that it does not always mean what we think; there's no need to rush into things, as if we are animals."

"We are animals!"

Benjamin didn't mean for his voice to come out loud, didn't mean for the irritation to glaze his eyes, for his hands to clench. It seemed, in that moment, that he was a different man, sitting in front of a different woman, in a world with unfamiliar walls, whose rules he no longer knew.

"You're screaming at me—in my own house?" Margaret asked. When Benjamin said nothing, she added, "Very well. Get out."

"What?"

"Leave my house right away. Get out!" Her voice was shaking.

"Oh, c'mon, no need to be upset. We've just had a small quarrel. Will you forgive me?"

Margaret picked up a shoe from the corner of the room and flung it at him. "Leave," she said again. So he left.

It was the only time she'd really lost her temper with him. She always had a certain air of composure about her—her hair in place, her clothes ironed. Her anger was quiet, fleeting. She was stubborn, saw the world in very fixed terms, was not given to compromise. Many times Benjamin believed it was the usual mood swings, women's trouble. He even chided her for it, told her to keep her monthly issues under control. He teased her, poked the sides of her waist, saying that she was too sensitive, too fragile. But in the end, it did not seem to matter—their disagreements, their different perceptions of the world. They were in love. Both of them caught in the storm of their attraction. So Benjamin had agreed—no sex. And he agreed to no further questions about her family, her parents' sudden tragic death—a truck transporting tomatoes from the north had crushed a taxi they were in. Everyone died on the spot. She was just sixteen, an only child. He willed himself to understand her guardrails. No public displays of affection either. They would see each other every other weekend, Margaret insisting that it was good that they have time for themselves. They shared their dreams, hers of becoming a lawyer, lobbying for a public service position, entering spaces that women rarely did. His of writing a novel, going into publishing. They talked about Nigerian writers, ignited by Chinua Achebe—a recent acquaintance Benjamin had made. They talked, too, about Nigerian politics, the frustrations of Ndi Igbo; she'd said that Nigeria's independence was premature, that the people still had no national identity. Nigeria was created by the British, which means it was an illusion; the people needed time to get used to the idea of their tribal identity coming only after their national one. Benjamin disagreed. Independence was necessary; it was sweeping across the continent. And so their relationship had been food and talk. Occasionally, their bodies would stray, their hands reaching to the other's chest, face, hair. Margaret was his life, his heart, but she had no patience for people who did not sway to her plans. There were a few times Benjamin thought about how easy things had been with Cynthia; their conversations were soft, often revolving around ordinary details of shared life. Margaret, on the other hand, demanded a certain solidity. She wanted opinions, arguments. Her passion for structure and order had sometimes been alienating, so she led a modest social life and grappled with the intense loneliness of those often misunderstood.

▼▲▼

By the sixth month of their courtship, Benjamin made a service-operated phone call to his mother in London. He announced he was to be married.

"You can't be serious!" Mrs. Fletcher said, then began to cry.

"Is she a Black?" his mother then asked, to which Benjamin replied by asking how it mattered, since he, too, was a Black.

"Is she Catholic?"

"Mother, she's Christian. Surely that means something," Benjamin had responded. "I called because I want you to meet her. I want you to come down to Nigeria."

Benjamin's mother said she'd think about it. That it was not just a casual affair, to travel all the way there. There were plans to be made. Factors to be considered. Besides, why could they not wed in London? When was he coming back?

At the time of this exchange, Benjamin had not yet asked Margaret to marry him; he wanted to get his mother's consent first. For months, his mother sent him postcard after postcard, asked about mosquitoes, about the food, about how many people in Lagos could speak English, and how well Benjamin could carry on a life in such quarters. And he had sent back general replies—empty observations with no real update on his personal life. Margaret's existence and his intention to marry her came as a surprise to her, and he had, to be fair, anticipated her hesitation, understood her worry. But he wanted her to know that he had made up his mind. After that call, he wrote to his mother: "By the time you read this I will have asked her to marry me." "Father would have approved," he added at the end of his note, thinking about the grandfather he never knew. His mother, naturally, would become much more agreeable once they were engaged, he thought. And so, that same day, he went to see Margaret.

When Margaret opened her door, she was wearing an A-line skirt, knee-length, black but much faded from its original shine. Her hair was held in a net, spilling out around the edges.

"I want to marry you," Benjamin blurted. "I know; it's been less than a year, but I think we're ready. I know I'm ready, Maggie."

Margaret said nothing. She walked to her bedroom and sat on the bed, running her hand over the sheets, looking pensive. "I knew you were going to ask me this today," she said.

"You knew?"

"I had a dream," Margaret said; then she smiled.

Benjamin stood there, not sure what had made him more uncomfortable—the odd reference to the dream or the fact that she had not given him a response. He sat on the bed beside her, tired of standing.

"You've not given me a reply," he said. She looked at him, then inched closer and hugged him. Moments later, as she set to make him a quick lunch of spaghetti and tomato stew, Benjamin asked, "So, you had a dream?"

"Yes."

"I didn't know you had dreams about me," he said, pinching her. She giggled.

"I dream about many things you do not know."

At the time he asked her to marry him, he had not worked out the finer details of their union. He'd been so consumed by the notion of spending his life with her, of thinking whether she would say yes or no, whether they would return to London at some point, whether his distressed mother would finally give up on him, that it had not really occurred to him where the marriage would take place. He'd suggested they simply go to the registry and worry about a ceremony afterward. But she'd begun to talk about a church wedding.

"It's all ceremonial, anyway," he said.

"No, we have to do it in the church," Margaret announced.

"We have to do it in church?" he repeated. He thought again about the no-sex thing.

"Don't say it like that," she chided.

"How am I saying it?" He laughed, unable to stop himself. "Very well then, in a church," he said finally.

They planned to visit Umumilo together, where they'd see Ma Adaora, and where Benjamin would get the opportunity he'd been seeking all along, a chance reckoning with his own ancestral past. He'd come to learn that everyone called Ma Adaora Mama, except Margaret, who sometimes called her Ma Adore. "It's because I adore her," Margaret said, laughing. Benjamin thought it was a lovely name, and he told Margaret so.

"I am named after her, you know," she'd replied. "But my mother preferred my English name." He had always preferred the native names; he loved the meanings that often followed such names, a name that rang as both a prayer and a promise, names that were not just labels, but vows—Adaora meant the people's daughter, belonging to many, cherished by many. Benjamin tested the name in his mouth for weeks. He moved between calling Margaret Ada, Ada'm, and precious Adaora, at which she would eye him wryly and say, "Please, call me by my Christian name."

▼▲▼

They arrived in Umumilo late at night, having taken the bus from Lagos to Onitsha, then a shuttle to Ekwulobia, before hailing a small taxi that went into the village. No one knew they were coming, which made the journey more thrilling for Margaret. Still, when their taxi, as worn out as its occupants, pulled into the compound, they found Ma Adaora seated on a wooden chair in front of the bungalow her late husband, Mazi Okolo, had built for her. Benjamin was quick to take in the faint sketch of her presence under the moonlight. He thought it was interesting that she kept her face straight, without craning her neck to see who was coming into the compound. She was considered an elder in her clan, having outlived her husband by more than nineteen years. Benjamin remembered the descriptions of Adaora from his great-uncle's journal—she was one of the women who had gotten pregnant, rumored to have been raped, though his uncle wrote the child could also have been the result of an affair. When he was a teenager, the journal had a speculative component: pregnant virgins, sexual encounters without consciousness. And now, here he was, in Umumilo, after two full years in Lagos, standing with Ma Adaora, telling himself that he had done the impossible; he had walked backward in time and now could confront the past.

This was Margaret's family, but also one that intermingled with his—the world so small in the way that it circled out and back onto itself. It occurred to Benjamin to ask Ma Adaora if she knew his own grandmother, Priscilla. Perhaps they were friends; they were certainly of the same age-group. Perhaps Ma Adaora would tell him what happened, how his grandmother's story ended. There was so much he wanted to learn, but it would all come out in time, he told himself. He had time.

Ma Adaora called out into the night, her voice shrill. "Maggie anyi, is that you?"

"Mama, it is me, your Margaret," Margaret responded. She stooped toward the old woman and embraced her.

"Emeka," the matriarch called, her voice suddenly strong, surprising Benjamin. One of the houseboys, who seemed to have been asleep, staggered outside. Ma Adaora had not said anything to the boy, simply assumed he'd know why he'd been summoned. The boy looked at his matriarch, then at Margaret. Then he moved to collect her bags. Both Benjamin and Margaret took that as their cue to retire, feeling the severity of their tiredness. They made to move into the house when Ma Adaora raised her hand to stop them.

"Onye bu nke a?" she asked, eyeing Benjamin. "Who is this you have brought to my home?" she repeated louder.

"Mama—you asked for my suitor and now I have brought you one," Margaret replied, smiling.

"Onye ocha?" Ma Adaora asked, her displeasure clear. "Of all the men in Lagos, you chose to bring back a white man?"

"Mama, he is one of us, I will tell you all about it tomorrow," Margaret said in dialect.

Benjamin stood there, holding his suitcase. Emeka, the houseboy, had collected Margaret's luggage but had not raised a finger to take his. Benjamin had imagined that there would be concerns about Margaret traveling in the presence of an unmarried man. But the disapproval he sensed in Ma Adaora's tone worried him. Perhaps they were all just tired, he convinced himself.

The next day Benjamin woke up at about noon. It was the second houseboy, one they called Obiora, who'd stirred him awake. Benjamin had opened his eyes after nearly twelve hours of sleep and found the boy's face closely peering over his. The houseboy stepped back, looking startled as Benjamin stared at him. In the coming days, Benjamin would learn that the second houseboy was a newer member of the household. He was not from Umumilo; therefore, he did not hold the usual sentiment toward foreigners that the village held. This was the reason Emeka had been cold; the people of this community did not take well to strangers.

"Your food is ready," the houseboy said, then slammed the door shut.

Benjamin got up hurriedly, stretching out his hands. He decided he'd find Margaret first; he could always clean up after he knew how she was. He stepped out of the room, into a hallway, then into what appeared to be a living room. There was a wide black-and-white photograph of a well-built man. Benjamin immediately understood that the man in question was Okolo, Ma Adaora's husband. Margaret's adoptive grandfather. He thought about his great-uncle's journal. According to the entry, it was in this man's honor that the people of this village had killed his own grandfather. His chest tightened.

He sensed that he was not alone, so he turned to find Ma Adaora watching him. Margaret stood a few inches behind her.

"Good afternoon, madam," he'd said to Ma Adaora, bowing slightly. He was embarrassed, feeling somehow that his thoughts about Okolo were transparent. But he reminded himself that he'd done no harm; besides, people generally did not read minds. Ma Adaora kept her eyes on him, but she did not respond to his greeting. After a few moments, she nodded to both Benjamin and Margaret and walked outside.

"We need to talk," Margaret said. She gestured toward the dining table. Then, in her usual Margaret matter-of-fact way, she told him that before they could marry, before the kinsmen would even entertain his request for a formal introduction, there was something they had to do.

"We have to see the village priest."

"Very well—this is not a problem, Maggie; it's a part of the process?"

"Not really," Margaret continued. "It seems that our pasts are more connected than we knew—Mama is worried."

"Wait, no, no, I know we are certainly not related," Benjamin said.

"Well, in a way we are cousins." She could not resist teasing him.

"Not by blood," Benjamin said, his voice charged.

"Of course not," Margaret said, then laughed. "Stop playing," she continued. She pushed him lightly on his shoulder. "All right, let me explain. Your grandmother did some things that were unpardonable."

"Yes, yes—she had an affair," Benjamin said impatiently.

"Not that. This was after. She deceived the village about her relationship with my grandfather—my biological grandfather."

"I don't follow," Benjamin replied.

"Some villagers say that your grandmother connived with my grandfather and helped him escape," Margaret explained, searching Benjamin's eyes. When his silence suggested that he still did not understand, she continued. "You know my biological grandfather committed a grave crime—"

"Yes. Allegedly. And my grandmother had something to do with this?"

"No. I mean, yes. You see, she hid him. She helped him avoid his verdict."

"What does this have to do with us?"

"Mama says she was sent away; that's all she knows."

"Yes, I presumed so; she disappears from the journal as well," Benjamin said.

"There's more. Mama says there's a curse on her—your grandmother." Margaret paused, searching his face. "She said that the elders of our village were so enraged by her actions that they vowed that her lineage should never continue in our village."

"I never heard this part of the story," Benjamin said, his tone accusatory.

"It's true."

"Well, my uncle never mentioned it; it's not in his journal."

"You already know the journal is incomplete."

"This makes no sense."

"You're angry?"

"I'm not angry."

"You are clearly upset," Margaret said.

"What about the vagabond?" Benjamin asked. He did not mean to sound irritated.

"The vagabond—Olisa—is the least of our concerns."

"Was he also cursed or was that judgment left for my grandmother alone?"

"There was no need to curse him." Margaret bit her lip. "But that's because he was already cursed. His own mother was cursed and so the only punishment meant for him was death."

"And your people believe these stories?" Benjamin shook his head.

"Stop this, Benni." Margaret was now stern. "Look, it's not very clear to me either. The man was already cursed, and they say that your grandmother, Priscilla, knew better than to help a person whom the Gods wanted dead."

"All right. This curse, what has it to do with us?"

"Let's just go and see the dibia," Margaret said. "I'm sure it's nothing."

"Today?" Benjamin asked. He put his hand in his pocket.

"Ma Adaora has sent for a relative. He will tell us when the dibia is ready. It won't be long." After a moment, she added, "You're still angry?"

He looked at her face, still shiny from her pomade. He thought about Priscilla. He frowned.

"You're still angry?" Margaret asked again. She inched closer to him, touched his chest, but he held her hand away.

"It makes no sense," he muttered.

▽△▽

They spent the next two days moving about the village, Margaret serving as his guide. He drank fresh palm wine tapped locally by a villager; they went to the farm that belonged to Okolo, and then they walked to the parish where his great-uncle had served. Margaret told Benjamin that his grandfather was likely buried in the church, but there was no mark, no stone. The young man had followed his heart and look what happened.

Three days after they arrived, Benjamin and Margaret went to see the dibia at the shrine. Ma Adaora stood with them in the meeting—she had her cane for support though she stood upright and did not seem to need it.

"So you mean nothing can be done?" Ma Adaora asked.

"It appears it is not to be so," the dibia answered. He was a middle-aged man who'd lost one eye.

"They cannot be married without grave consequences. The crime is too much—the blood of the defiled women, the younger one in particular, is still screaming. The vagabond should have paid for his sins. The woman should never have helped him. It is too late now."

Margaret gasped.

"You know why our people are angry with his ancestor? By hiding the boy, she not only stole from the Gods; she stole from the innocent," the dibia finished.

"Tell me, what is it? Tell me what is happening," Benjamin said.

"But this curse, what has it got to do with my granddaughter? It is Priscilla who erred." Ma Adaora leaned in toward the dibia.

"Her grandfather's sin hangs above her too. You know our customs. You know a sin cannot sit in a vacuum. It must be atoned for. It must be cleansed."

"What about me, my involvement—I was one of the women involved. Do I get a say in the verdict?"

"Mba." The dibia shook his head at Ma Adaora. "It is not your punishment to bear or absolve."

Margaret stared at the dibia. "What happens if we marry?"

"I will speak no further about this," the dibia said.

"Tell me what is happening," Benjamin said again.

"Mama was correct; he says we cannot marry," Margaret replied hurriedly.

"And what is his reason?"

"Can we talk about this later?" Margaret whispered.

"But we might not have a later, am I correct?" He felt his palms start to sweat.

"There's nothing that can be done?" Margaret asked the dibia in broken English, for Benjamin's benefit.

"Our people will hear none of it," the dibia responded in dialect.

From behind them, Ma Adaora said something to Margaret, to which Margaret hissed a response.

"I'm still not sure what is happening," Benjamin said to Margaret once they returned to the compound.

"You won't understand."

"Then explain it to me."

"Very well. After your grandmother did what she did, the village sent her into exile."

"Into exile?"

"Yes, Benjamin. Exile."

"All right, then what?"

"You still don't get it. When a person is sentenced to death by the Gods, only the Gods can overthrow that verdict. They say Priscilla interfered with the decision of the Gods."

"All this talk about Gods—you confuse me." After a while he added, "So our marriage is cursed?"

"I don't know—no one can be sure."

"Where does that leave us?"

Margaret started to cry. "We can't just go against the laws," she said to herself.

"So you accept it?"

"You make me sound flippant."

"Do you believe these reports? For God's sake, Maggie, you pray the rosary."

"It doesn't matter. My people believe. My kinsmen—they believe on my behalf."

"Where do we stand? I need to make plans." He was angry.

"I don't know. I'm not sure," Margaret said.

"Very well, I will leave for Lagos in the morning."

▽△▽

They returned to Lagos, to Margaret's bungalow, on a Sunday evening. Once out of the taxi and in the compound, Margaret walked in front, and Benjamin followed with their traveling boxes, the night air stained with the smell of peppered stews and plantains. He was tired, as they both were, and there was much about the trip that still felt largely unresolved. But he wanted to see that she was safely in her apartment before the taxi took him to his. They had been away for six days, but it felt longer. The journey had demanded new things of them, so that they had to decide who they were, what they would become. How did a journey toward answers culminate in more questions? His mother would be thrilled by the turn of events. Perhaps he'd go back to London after all. Margaret, on the other hand, seemed unperturbed. During the first half of their trip, she'd made endless comments about the villagers, explaining in detail how palm wine was tapped, pointing to the primary school her mother attended. He listened. Smiled. Held her hand. Touched her face, as though he needed to preserve her words in some kind of material form. But still, he felt like his head tremored slightly. Surely, the world of their love was unmoored, and soon they would settle back to earth—to a reality of hard questions.

And so here they were, back in Lagos, in the same space where he'd asked her to marry him. Margaret's apartment felt askew—the yellow painted walls, her carefully aligned pairs of footwear, the thick flower-patterned curtains. The power had gone out, which meant that the rooms were dark. Margaret drew back the curtains, allowing the streetlights to filter in while she moved between the kitchen and the bathroom, opening shelves, taps, searching for candles, for a lamp. She brushed against him in the dark—"Ah sorry, where are those matches?" she said—but she did not move away. She touched his waist, his chest, daring him to respond. And he did, his questions momentarily forgotten. They moved through the shadows toward the bedroom. Margaret hissed when she kicked her foot against a shoe, and they both laughed, completely in sync as they always were. They sat on the bed, and Benjamin was on her again, kissing her face, her neck. He reached down to her skirt, the large plastic buttons; he could feel the silk of her underskirt.

"And they said we should not marry, can you imagine?" Margaret said. He searched her face, as if pulled back to reality.

"You're laughing?" Margaret said.

"I am laughing."

They kissed and touched, the world settling back in place for Benjamin. The taxi driver honked from outside the gate, startling them both.

"I'll see you tomorrow." Benjamin promised as he whistled out the door.

"And many more times after tomorrow," Margaret said.

Benjamin stopped and stared at her intently. The driver honked again. Margaret laughed.

13

Margaret

Lagos, 2005

It had been a couple months since Margaret left Nwando's home and returned to Arina Estate. Life had not changed much, except in two crucial ways. First, there was the incident with Chuka, and then, there was the agreement with Nwando. An agreement. Is that what it was? Margaret thought to herself—did an agreement not involve two parties who could negotiate equally? Still, this was the way Nwando liked to refer to it. Just that morning, during their brief exchange on the phone, Nwando had paused and said, "I love you, Mama, don't forget our agreement."

The so-called agreement came about after a small but well-intentioned incident that happened a few days after Margaret learned about Chuka's fight. As Nwando explained, he'd come home following his suspension from school. Margaret had been waiting in her room, edgy, since Nosa went out to pick him up. The moment she heard the car horn, the doors open, she put on her slippers and went outside to greet them. Chuka was a bit restrained this time, perhaps from the tongue-lashing Nosa had given him on the way home. Chuka did not run to Margaret like usual, and he did not lean down to kiss his mother.

"Good afternoon, Mama," he'd said to Margaret. "Hello, Mum," he muttered briefly to Nwando.

"Don't hello me, you're not supposed to be here."

"I have told him," Nosa added from the dining area before going upstairs, "if this happens again, he can forget about university abroad."

At that statement Nwando looked at Chuka. "Well, won't you say something?"

"I'm sorry I've disappointed you," Chuka said, his gaze turned down toward his shoes.

"And?" Nwando added.

"And it won't happen again," he finished.

Nwando beamed. "That's my boy, oya come, come give Mummy a hug."

"But we don't know that," Margaret suddenly said. "He can't say for sure whether it will happen again."

"Ma?" Chuka said, his face to Margaret.

"Don't mind Grandma, she's tired today," Nwando added.

"Do I look tired?" Margaret said, turning to Chuka, who had already reached out to hold her hand.

"Remember what we discussed, Chuka?" Margaret said to him. He looked at Margaret, then his mother, but he did not respond. Margaret pressed again. "My darling, you remember, abi? Tell me you remember." Chuka said to Margaret very gently, "Yes, Mama, but I'm not seeing anything, don't worry," then squeezed her hand.

"Remember what? Mama, I hope you've not been putting ideas in Chuka's head," Nwando said, then turned to her boy. "What is she talking about? What are you supposed to remember?"

"Nothing."

"Chuka, don't play with me, you're in enough trouble already. Look at me; I'm talking to you, mister grown-up."

Chuka threw a quick glance at Margaret, his face apologetic. "Grandma has been telling me about our history, that's all. I asked her to tell me."

"Okay. And? Chuka—I said—and?"

"It's just some stories, Mum; she told me about Okolo and Olisa."

"It's not just stories," Margaret said. She stood up, moved to the door, and checked that it was locked.

"When last did you see him?" Margaret said, forgetting Chuka's earlier promise.

"See who?" Nwando asked. "Chuka, go upstairs and freshen up," Nwando said, then she went up to her bedroom, muttering under her breath.

The next morning, Margaret woke to a knock on her door. "Mama, could you step outside when you have a moment, please? There's something I want to show you," Nwando said from the other side of the door.

Margaret had come into the living room, eager to take up the conversation from where they left off the night before. Perhaps the creatures had appeared to Chuka by now. Perhaps Nwando was finally ready to reason. But when she stepped out, she found two middle-aged men dressed in polo shirts and clean-cut cotton trousers. As soon as she saw them, she knew—doctors. She would later learn they were from the psychiatric hospital in Yaba. It was a house call; they hoped that Margaret was doing well these days, especially after her last incident. Was everything okay? Was she sleeping well, eating well? Had there been any sudden disruptions in her schedule? Margaret sat, answered every question, laughed when she sensed she was supposed to laugh.

"And what about your medicines?"

"My medicines?"

"Yes, your daughter says you've not been taking them."

"That's not true. I've been taking everything, every single one of them."

"Mama!"

"Tell them, Nwando, I'm taking my medicine," Margaret said, then added, "Biko."

"Mama, you've been very stressed lately."

"Just a little tired, but I'm taking the medicines."

"You've been having all these ideas—we don't want you to have a relapse."

"No, no, look at me, there's no relapse."

"What about Yetunde?"

"It's okay," one of the doctors added. "It could have been the phone call you mentioned that aggravated her. Let's observe her for another two weeks."

"Observe me. Where?"

"Here, Mama," Nwando said. "If you promise to take your medicines, all of them o, not just some, and your supplements, too, if you promise to take everything, then we'll not see our friends here again."

"Yes, yes. I'll take all of them."

"All right, this is our agreement o, we have witnesses."

"Yes."

The agreement could have stayed in place the way it was intended, all things considered. That first night, Margaret opened her palms by the kitchen sink as Nwando placed a cocktail of pills in them. No questions—this was the plan, a dutiful submission to her daughter's wish. She took the tablets in twos and threes, drinking down the water in the tumbler, and they both continued this way, morning and night, until the two weeks' probation came and went. During those two weeks of supervised medication, Margaret became slower to leave the bed in the mornings; sometimes she forgot to eat, or forgot that she was eating. She referred to Chuka as Peter, repeatedly, and when Chuka corrected her, she apologized but called him Peter again. Things would have remained this way if it was not for that opportune intervention of fate.

On the Saturday before Chuka was to return to school, Nwando was setting the table for dinner, while Margaret lay on the sofa, where she was snoring lightly, her eyeglasses askew on her face. Chuka came in through the back entrance that connected from the kitchen, and he started when he saw his mother in the kitchen.

"Where are you coming from? I thought you were in your bedroom."

"I went out," he mumbled, turning to climb the stairs up to his room.

"Young man, come back here; I'm still talking to you," Nwando said.

"What is it now? I'm tired," he mumbled.

"Ehen, and what has made you tired? Where are you coming from?"

Margaret stirred in her sleep, her hand slapping against the air, then she was quiet. Both Chuka and Nwando turned briefly to watch her.

"Maybe we should wake her?"

"Don't worry about her, she's probably dreaming."

"Can I go now?" Chuka said.

"Go where? Don't play your games with me, Chuka—your father put you on a curfew; you can't just do what you like."

"Okay, sorry." He turned to the stairs again.

"Young man, get back down here. I'm not done talking."

"But I already said sorry. What do you want me to do?"

Nwando stood there looking at him.

"Can I go now?" he asked again, louder.

"No. I need someone to clean my car. The keys are in my blue purse."

"What about Joseph?"

"What about him?"

"Can't Joseph clean your car?"

"Joseph can take a break today; I want you to clean it."

"You want to control me like you control everyone?"

Nwando laughed, clapping her hands together in disbelief.

"Don't talk to your mother that way, nna," Margaret said, straightening up. Her voice sounded strong for someone who had just woken from sleep.

"But it's true, see how she controls you, controls my daddy," Chuka said. He looked around the living room, walked to the door, walked back. "I'm tired of this stupid house. Everything here is stupid." He made to go upstairs again but Nwando stopped him. "I said I need you to wash my car."

"I don't want to wash any s-s-stupid car," Chuka shouted. He took a quick step toward Nwando, then stopped, grabbed a tumbler from the dining table, and threw it against the wall. Margaret flinched. Nwando screamed, her hands raised to shield her face from the shards. Chuka sulked off to his room.

After a stunned silence, Nwando turned to Margaret. "Mama, are you okay?" She moved to sit beside Margaret, though she was not looking at her.

"I'm all right," Margaret said. She paused, then scooted toward Nwando, placing her hand on her thigh. "I should be asking you—are you all right?"

"What just happened, Mama?" Nwando said, her hands shaking.

"He's just upset. Give him some time to cool off."

"Cool off from what? He has never behaved like this before." Nwando started crying.

Minutes later, Chuka came downstairs to wash the car, though he refused to speak to his mother, his father, or even to Margaret.

So you see, the agreement could have stayed in place. Margaret would have taken every medical prescription, and perhaps there would have been a relatively lengthy time of peace between mother and child, between Margaret and her demons—but the thing with Chuka had happened.

That night, Nwando quietly entered Margaret's room and sat beside her mother.

"This curse that you've been speaking of—"

"What about it?" Margaret said, already drowsy. These days it seemed she was sleeping more than she was awake.

"It's not real."

"If that is what you believe," Margaret said.

"There's a reason for these things. You can't just be explaining everything as a curse when doctors have a solution."

"All right, maybe Chuka should see a doctor, then. You can tell the doctor that he was fighting in school," Margaret said with a yawn.

"I'm serious, Mama, I want to do the right thing."

"And I want to sleep."

"Okay, Mama, I will leave you." She got up from the bed, moved to the door, and waited. Finally, she turned back to Margaret.

"Mama?"

"Yes?"

"Let's assume this is a curse."

"Hm-mm."

"I'm not saying it is. But let us assume. How can we get rid of it?"

Margaret sat up and looked at Nwando. "Come in," she said. "Close the door behind you."

▼▲▼

Margaret had been Margaret Okolo all her life. She did not change her surname at twenty, when a girl at the hostel in London asked her if Okolo was the native translation for monkey, and she did not change it when Benjamin swore to love her until they were both old and spent. As a child growing up in the great Okolo's compound, Margaret was teased for belonging to an elite clan; her kinsmen were regarded as among the earliest in Umumilo to embrace the white man's ways—going to school, giving up their local dialects, occupying the spaces that the foreigners carved out for them. But even when the villagers teased her, Margaret knew that it was all envy, that the laughter of the young villagers could not wound her because it came from a place of their own muted hungers—did they not also revere her grandfather Okolo? Did they not adjust their wrappers and beam at him when he made his way through the market? And how often did they come to the compound to see him, to seek out his favors—favors that only his association with the white men could afford him? Ma Adaora told her all the stories when she was a child. But even now that the great Okolo was dead and Margaret was grown, was it not still these villagers, their children and descendants, who often wrote her asking for money? Some still asked for scholarship opportunities, for connections to jobs in the city. And so their moralizing about the source of her family's wealth had no impact on how Margaret perceived herself. What truly bothered Margaret was not that the people condemned Okolo's means and legacy, but rather the limits of the name he bequeathed her. It was the fact that a name—no matter how noble or esteemed—was still an external thing. Like a label. Names could not sit in the blood. They revealed nothing about the people whose lives they marked, about their secrets, their demons. Margaret was in every sense proud to wear the Okolo name, yet she was not exactly an Okolo. She was an Olisa. Her true grandfather—the one whose blood flowed in her—was known to be a vagabond and rapist. A criminal. A man cursed by the Gods. Sometimes she wondered what it meant to belong to a lineage—to be part of a history, a terror that was not of your making. Yes, she was Margaret Okolo. But she was also something else.

Margaret often tried not to entertain these thoughts about who she was, where she came from, and whose legacy she carried. But things were different now after the incident with Chuka. Her people were coming to Arina Estate. That is, Okolo's people—her kinsmen, if she had the right to call them that. She'd woken up at five a.m., prayed, read her Bible, and then, by habit, recited some local incantations that Ma Adaora had taught her as a little girl. They were mostly phrases repeated in a rhythm, intended to calm the mind or chase away wandering evil spirits. Margaret considered herself a Christian in every sense, but she was also, like her matriarch, Oriaku, born into a line of priestesses. She had seen what the psalms could do to her anxious heart. But she also knew the sturdy touch of her ancestral rituals. She reasoned that she belonged to both worlds the same way that she belonged to both Okolo and Olisa. What did it mean to choose one side, to become one thing?

In her younger years, she wanted to have a faith that was clean and tidy—singular. Margaret had moved from church to church, scouring preachers for powers. She wanted healing. Deliverance. And she had spent a lifetime praying for this healing. But healing from what? When she visited the preachers, she tried to explain to them that she was being watched. That she had sinned by marrying without her kinsmen's approval. That her ancestor had done a terrible thing and their Gods insisted on passing on his curse to her. But the preachers seldom found her stories plausible. They asked her to be good. To give more. To have faith. There are no curses with God. But the faith she had desperately clung to had not brought her the salvation she sought. She understood now that instead of faith, she needed answers. If not for her sake, then for the sake of Chuka. God in heaven would understand.

▽△▽

"Ada anyi, we see you have been well."

It was four p.m., but the sun was already beginning to sleep. The security officers were at their workstation, and the estate itself was cloaked in a kind of heated silence, such that Margaret, no matter how much she wished to, could not pretend she had not heard the statement.

It was Matthias who spoke. It was his voice Margaret was trying to ignore.

"Ada anyi," Matthias said again, looking at Margaret, waiting for an answer. He was a man used to being acknowledged—evidenced by his two chieftaincy titles. He wore, in that moment, his red feathered cap, a symbol of his authority, a reminder that he was a man of impressive social standing even if it was just among local villagers. Although he was only fifty-two, he referred to Margaret as ada anyi—our first daughter, our eldest daughter. It was a name that was also a title, used to accord respect to the older women in the clan. It was also used for unmarried older women who were still in their fathers' homes.

"Yes, Mazi, I am fine, a dim mma," Margaret said.

"That's very good, that is excellently very good," Matthias continued, nodding his approval. There were three kinsmen present, but it was Matthias who led the delegation, and it was he who would return first to Aba, and then by the next morning bus to Umumilo, where he would consult with the family dibia on the treatment plan for Margaret.

Forty years ago, Margaret would have laughed at the idea of such a plan from a local dibia. She would have called security to escort these men out of her home for suggesting such a thing. She would have told them to chew on their sanctimonious spiritualism rooted in fear and ignorance.

"What do you mean they're giving you a treatment plan?" Nwando had asked during their phone conversation.

"A solution—a way to right the wrong from the past."

"Mama, if this is about the conversation we had the last time, let's forget about it. I was just worried, that is all," Nwando assured her.

"Yes, yes, but what about Chuka?"

"What about him?"

"Don't be stubborn; we have nothing to lose if we try this path." She knew how distressed Nwando had been since the Chuka outburst, so distressed that she had stopped supervising Margaret taking her medication.

"Have I not been taking my medicine, or are you ready to admit that the medicines don't work?" After a moment she added, "You know that the last man in our family who was violent raped innocent women. What is this business of Chuka and anger?"

"Jesus Christ, Mama, what do you mean? I've told you that this curse is all in your head."

Good, let her be outraged, Margaret thought.

"Mama, Chuka is fine. He's just trying to be grown up. We have spoken; he is very sorry."

"Okay, forget Chuka, what if something else happens?" Margaret asked, her voice a whisper.

"Something else like what?"

"You know what I mean," Margaret hissed.

"I hope this is not about what happened with Yetunde."

"Y-you just don't listen, all these stories I have told you all these years, why don't you ask your father, since you won't listen to me. He understands what I mean."

"Mama, you know I don't believe in these things. Keep taking your medicines—you will get better."

"For God's sake, this is not about me. I'm doing this for Chuka and Chuka's future children—we've talked about this."

"We may have to reconsider."

"Are you willing to live with the consequences? As a mother, can you say you've done everything for your son?"

"Mama—I don't like it when you talk like this."

"Good. We'll do the cleansing and get it over with," she said and dropped the phone.

▼▲▼

"We are your people—your chosen blood. If anybody can make this right, it is us," Matthias continued.

"I have some wine; can I get you some wine?" Margaret asked. "Bayo," she said, calling for her new housekeeper. "Where is that Bayo when you need him?" Margaret continued to no one in particular. "Ah, there you are. Can you help with some glass cups? Three, no, four. I think I'll join them."

"Are you sure you should be drinking?" the other kinsman asked. Then he cackled, as though he had told a secret joke that only he could understand.

"With your condition, you know, I wouldn't want to roughen things up." He laughed again, looking around the room.

"I can have a glass occasionally," Margaret replied. She started to wonder what these men were doing in her home.

"Perhaps you should wait for us to leave; then you can drink all you want." It was the third man who made the final statement; then he looked at the second, and they both began to laugh.

"Gentlemen, gentlemen, today is not the day for jokes. Let us not forget why we are here," Matthias chipped in, quick to remind the other men who was truly in charge.

"No, no, they are right; I'll have water instead," Margaret said. She adjusted herself on the sofa, smoothing out her boubou.

They had already broken kola. Matthias had led the traditional kola prayers; they had reminded Margaret that they had come on her behalf, specifically at her request. Then they had asked if their presence was still welcome, if she was sure this was something she wanted. "Yes," she said, clearing her throat. "Yes," she said again, this time louder, her stomach unsettled but her verdict final.

As Margaret sat in the living room, taking in the hum of the passing evening, she knew she was making the right decision—should this thing she received from home not be solved by returning home? She looked at Matthias, then at the other two kinsmen, and she concluded what the great injustice of life was. It was not death or poverty or the ineptitude of self-possessed politicians. It was family. To be birthed into a home you did not choose, to a people whose fate becomes so intricately linked to yours.

"Hmm, the pepper soup, it is very good," Matthias said, stopping to chug a glass of cold beer into his mouth.

"Very good," the other two echoed.

Margaret had already arranged for the taxi driver who would pick them up, then drop them off at the hotel where they were staying. She had paid for their rooms. She had also sent the check that paid for their transportation to her home. And now the cash that would cater to their return. One of the men, between swallows, had hinted already that his eldest son was fresh out of the polytechnic, in need of a job;

he was sure there was something Margaret could do, and of course there was another son, who was an artist in the making, hoping to go to Europe to find opportunities.

"These young men, they have their heads in the clouds," Matthias had said almost immediately after the second man narrated his son's ordeal.

"But he is your son, correct? I will give him your number. He will call you soon—anyhow you can assist, ada anyi, nothing at all is small," the man finished, ignoring Matthias.

Margaret listened and nodded and smiled. This was also what family meant, stones strapped to your back, a log of wood you had to drag behind you. Family emerged when resources had to be shared, poverty passed about like a basket, in which everyone had to dip their hands, participate in their share of mutual want. But family was also the place where shame could be deposited. It did not matter which uncle you had not seen since you were six years old, or which aunt did not speak to your father from the moment you were born; when your shame was passed around in the basket, everyone partook of it. It was in this family, two years before, when a second cousin was deported from Malaysia for carrying drugs, that the people had rallied prayers, scraped loose their last threads of connections, fought for him to be returned home a disgrace rather than face execution in another man's land. She refused to be put off by the way they peddled their needs; after all, she peddled hers too. It was better that Margaret resort to sharing her sickness with these strange people than to have it flaunted publicly in Arina Estate. When everywhere else becomes uncomfortable, you know it is time to go home.

14

The Lovers

Lagos, 1960s

There was something about that trip to Umumilo—that verdict—that emboldened Margaret and Benjamin. Their love had taken the shape of sacrilege—forbidden, and therefore much more desirable. The lovers spent many evenings together in Margaret's flat, on the veranda, which opened onto the back street of her neighborhood. They watched local vendors sell food by the roadside, the lazy banter of customers, the sun setting behind electrical transmission wires. They listened to the radio, read the newspapers. Sometimes they danced, and always, they ate—their food coming from restaurants, but also from street vendors—fried eggs, roasted corn, African pears. Sometimes they fed each other, compared their choice of condiments, Benjamin preferring his roasted corn with coconuts, while Margaret favored the pears.

One evening, as was his habit, Benjamin moved to the veranda for a smoke while Margaret fussed about in her small, cramped kitchen, where she was making fried tomato stew with turkey and boiled yams. She laid the meal on a tray and used her foot to kick the door to the veranda open, the smell of smoked peppers following her outside. To the unsuspecting eye, they were just another couple, home in the evening after work—an ordinary domestic scene. Margaret wore a flowered green dress with a low-cut V-neck that Benjamin had frequently complimented; she even had red lipstick on, just as he liked.

"You better enjoy this while I am still willing to cook for you," she teased as Benjamin sniffed. He tried to laugh but instead started to cough.

"Are you all right?" Margaret asked.

"Yes, water, please," Benjamin said, still coughing.

He drank, raised his hand to wipe the sweat off his face.

"It's very good," Benjamin said with a weak smile.

Moments passed.

Benjamin asked Margaret if she was hot, then he began to unbutton his shirt, still coughing. He said he needed to take a piss—he stood, paused another moment; he felt the floor shift. He paused again and felt himself stagger. Then he fell to the ground.

The neighbors rushed in when they heard Margaret's scream. They lifted Benjamin, who was barely conscious, into a taxi that took him to a local clinic; from there he was sent to the general hospital to see a specialist, where despite the queue and the long wait for appointments, he was given his own private ward. By the second day of his hospitalization, Benjamin still had a fever, although the doctor assured Margaret that the worst had passed. It was malaria and a little typhoid, they said. He'd grown lean and pale overnight; the skin on his lips and head was cracked from dryness. Margaret sat on a stool beside him, holding his hand, her face without expression. She took notes when the nurses did their rounds, asked questions about medicines, injections. Benjamin tried to say something humorous, make her laugh, but his voice was so hoarse that every attempt at speech felt like a plea; he tried to squeeze her hand, but he was too weak, and it seemed Margaret did not notice any of his efforts. It occurred to him that he had gone two days without brushing his teeth, taking a bath.

By the third day, he said to her, "You don't have to stay, you know." She smiled and patted his hand. One of the nurses had come in, touched her shoulder, and said, "Madam, don't worry, your husband will be fine."

"He's not my husband," Margaret said, without glancing up. The nurse looked at Margaret, then at Benjamin. She shrugged and walked away. It was the longest they'd stayed quiet by each other, but with every minute that passed, Benjamin felt a wide gulf open between them. Perhaps Margaret did not want to see him like this; he could barely stand to see himself like this. Earlier in the day, when Margaret had gone home to change, he'd called for the nurse, saying that he needed a quick shower. But he was still weak. He'd brushed his teeth, spat into a bowl the nurse held out for him; his chest and underarms were wiped with a damp towel. If Margaret returned and still did not speak, he would insist that she leave, that he would come see her when he was recovered, that she go back to work. But she returned, and they both resumed their silence.

Then evening came. Margaret was asleep on a mat she brought from home. The hallway was dark. Certainly, the nurses on the night shift would not hear if he called, Benjamin thought. He felt his bowels move, so he turned to his side and strained himself, trying to reach the bell. Margaret stirred.

"What is it?" she whispered.

"I need the nurse," he said, pointing to the bell.

"What do you need? Let me help," Margaret said. She made her way to him, sat by the side of the bed.

"All right, please help me up. I need to take a piss," he said.

"Should I bring your bucket?" Margaret asked.

"No," he said, "I want to go to the loo."

Margaret raised his hand across her shoulder as he lowered his feet to the ground. She was strong, seemed to carry his weight well, even though he was a full head taller than her. She opened the door to the restroom, turned on the light. Benjamin staggered a little and they both stumbled.

"I need to sit," he said.

She lowered him to the toilet bowl, pulling down his undershorts. She adjusted his legs to create some support so he could sit by himself, then she squatted in front of him, waiting.

"I can manage from here."

"Are you sure?"

"Of course I am sure," he snapped.

"All right," Margaret said. "I'll leave the door open, just in case."

Benjamin saw the toilet paper; he saw the kettle with water for washing himself. He bent forward, tried to reach the toilet paper, still out of his grasp. Nausea rose from his chest to his neck; he hissed, then he tried to get up. He forgot about the toilet paper. The kettle. The bucket with water to flush the toilet. The world was a daze. He pulled his shorts up, smoothed his undershirt, then he fell on the bathroom floor.

"Get the nurse," he said to Margaret as she rushed in, but she did not. Instead she brought a rag, cleaned the shit from his kneecaps, from his chin, outside the toilet bowl. She carried him back to the bed, all the while showing no emotion. Benjamin stared at the ceiling; he could not bring himself to look at her. After another long silence, he felt her hand on his wrist, and he turned.

"The curse," Margaret said in a whisper.

"What curse?" He recognized the concern in her voice.

"What if the dibia was right?" she asked.

"The dibia?"

"Listen," she whispered, "what if this is what he warned us about, why we must not marry."

"What do you mean?"

"You have not been seriously sick since you've been here. Why now?"

Benjamin laughed softly. "But we are not married. We have not broken their rules."

"Perhaps we shouldn't," Margaret said quietly to herself.

"What are you saying?"

"Never mind. I was just thinking." She patted him on his chest and returned to her corner of the room.

That same night, Benjamin's fever broke.

▼▲▼

Shortly before their wedding, Benjamin's mother wrote to Margaret, the first correspondence between them. She had just newly recovered from a fever herself, her letter said, but her migraines were endless and her health still fragile; she could not come down to Lagos, but she was eager to meet her daughter-in-law when they both arrived in London the following summer. Margaret sat under the fluorescent bulb in the kitchen, in the newly built two-bedroom apartment that Benjamin had rented, the home she was to share with him. She had a kettle of water boiling on the stove. She squinted, read, adjusted the paper under the light, laughed.

"Let me see," Benjamin said from behind her, but she waved him off. "Read your own letter; this one is addressed to me."

"I hope she's not said anything embarrassing." Benjamin sighed, turning off the stove.

"She's sweet," Margaret answered, wiping her forehead.

"As sweet as I am?" Benjamin pulled Margaret toward him. Her hand brushed against the kettle's handle.

"Mister man, do you want to burn me before our wedding?"

"I wouldn't dare."

Benjamin tried to kiss her cheek, but she stretched her neck, shifting out of reach. They were both laughing, holding each other. Benjamin moved to kiss Margaret's other cheek, but she turned her face again, wiggling in his arms but careful not to leave. It was on this evening, after reading his mother's letter and placing it on a table, while avoiding Benjamin's kisses but staying in his embrace, that Margaret first had the thought, sudden and jolting: someone was watching them. The thought passed as quickly as it came.

They scheduled a day in court to be married—without Ma Adaora's notice or the family's blessing. This was neither the Catholic church wedding she had preferred, nor the prerequisite traditional ceremony. Benjamin had not paid her bride price, as was the custom, and in the absence of that rite of passage, she felt like a child who had gone to the neighbor for food because the mother was taking too long. Her people would not recognize this marriage, regardless of what document she presented. Without the bride price, Benjamin would be considered an intruder who had carted away stolen goods. But what was the alternative? They had this conversation about moving forward with their plans after Benjamin's hospitalization, when he'd assured her and she'd agreed that malaria, which attacked thousands of people daily in Lagos, was surely no sign of the Gods' disapproval. Besides, no one in the village knew that they were carrying on with their relationship.

"We love each other. We should be together. It's as simple as that," Benjamin said, while Margaret nodded. In choosing to marry Benjamin this way, Margaret understood that her *yes* to him meant the potential dismissal of her own people. So she reasoned that it was perhaps the idea of betraying Ma Adaora that gave her the sense that people were watching her. Or perhaps it was just fear. In any case, it was silly to bring her concerns to Benjamin, she thought to herself, to say to him that she was afraid, that something about her time with him in the hospital had crept under her skin and she had not been able to shake it off. There was nothing to suggest that their shiny marriage certificate would persuade her people, or Ma Adaora, who had warned her clearly that she was playing with fire.

To Benjamin, the events of the village had receded in his mind. All that remained was the fact that she had agreed to marry quietly, to go to London to meet his mother. They were even contemplating where they would settle. So yes, he'd forgotten the dibia's words, Ma Adaora's firm disapproval. He had even made his peace with his grandmother's disappearance from the village, both in his great-uncle's notes and in the wider narrative of his own history. Priscilla. That poor woman. It did not matter now since there was no point in digging up a grave that did not exist. He would focus on the present. There was no other woman for him but Margaret, and he knew this to be undeniably true. And so they agreed together that, yes, they would wed, and the kinsmen would see reason; they would learn that Benjamin and Margaret could not be stopped. This was fate.

They married on a Thursday afternoon in February, in a courthouse, with the heat pressing through the back of Margaret's off-white linen dress. Neither of their families was present. They told themselves that they would wait till December to inform Ma Adaora, perhaps have a proper wine-carrying ceremony in the village. But Margaret had a friend whom she considered dear from her secondary school days, and Benjamin had his friends from the radio station. They both brought the full weight of their colleagues from the director's office, so that the evening reception was a small but pompous affair. They returned to the flat after their wedding, tired, eager, nervous.

"Shall I make you some tea?" Benjamin asked.

"No," Margaret said, taking out her hairpins.

"How about a sandwich?"

"No," she said again. She moved to the bathroom, and Benjamin was glad for the extra time to allow the fan to cool the room. He went to the kitchen sink, washed his face, his hands. He started to unbutton his shirt; then he stopped. Finally, Margaret emerged from the shower in silk nightwear, her face wiped clean, her Afro tied in a bun. He was not sure what to do or say, so he moved toward their bedroom, stood at the entrance, and gestured. "Welcome home, my love." Margaret smiled and followed him.

▼▲▼

The dreams began in earnest the same week as their wedding.

They were seated at their dining table, a small two-seater space where they ate a late breakfast, toasted bread with butter, and a bottle of Coke for Benjamin.

"You're quiet this morning. Sleep all right?"

"I slept fine," Margaret said. She sipped her tea. "Well, now that you mention it—I had a dream. Last night. I've been having these dreams." She frowned.

Benjamin gulped his Coke from the bottle, ignoring the straw Margaret had placed on his eating tray.

"I think they might be watching us," Margaret continued. She was no longer eating; she was looking at Benjamin in earnest.

"Who?"

"Our people, the village," she said.

"You saw this in your dream?" Benjamin asked. He reached across the table and held her hand.

"No, not there. I can't explain it," Margaret said. She pulled her hand away from Benjamin. "I can sense it."

"You can sense the village?" Benjamin laughed.

"Go on. Mock me. Laugh at my expense," Margaret said. She scooted the chair back and made to leave.

"Forgive me." Benjamin reached across the table again, held her hand. "Please. Tell me about the dream. I want to know."

"I can't remember the dream. I mean—I can't remember it exactly," Margaret said, "but I don't think it was good. Something feels wrong."

"And it has to do with the village?"

"Yes."

"How do you know?" Benjamin asked, perplexed.

"I just know. I can't explain it," Margaret answered. Then she began to cry.

▼▲▼

Weeks into their marriage, Benjamin began to wake from sleep in the middle of the night to find Margaret's side empty. At first he told himself that these odd incidents were merely her quirks revealing themselves, that he had arrived into that dawning realization that descends on young couples when they learn that despite their love, they have in fact married a stranger. So the first time Margaret was missing from their bed, Benjamin was sure that it was a bathroom call. She was the sort of woman who made midnight bathroom trips. He'd turned to the other side of the bed and gone back to sleep.

The third time it happened, he picked up a lantern and went to the bathroom. When he did not see her there, he called out. Then he found her sitting in their living room, her hand under her chin, as though she was deep in thought. Still, he shook it off. So what if he married a worry-prone woman? His own mother could barely cross the streets in London without fearing some grave danger befalling her, so it was perfectly normal that Margaret, who feared some lurking danger from the village, would also start to lose sleep.

Otherwise they were still happy as a couple, still mad with love. They held hands while they walked across the street, while they listened to the radio in the evenings, their hands and legs often straying to find each other in the living room, under the dining table, in the taxi. But there were moments when Benjamin sensed a distance, times when Margaret seemed far away. Once, while taking a stroll in the evening, they ran into one of Benjamin's former colleagues at the radio station.

"Mr. Fletcher! Benjo!" the colleague shouted from across the road, waving. He'd just gotten out of a taxi when he saw them, and he now jogged across the main road toward Benjamin.

"There's Kunle, my good friend," Benjamin said happily, nudging Margaret. When she looked across the road, she started, squeezing his hand.

"Are you all right?" Benjamin asked.

"C'mon, let's go," she said.

"One moment, it's Kunle," Benjamin said again happily.

"Do we have to stop?"

But it was too late. Kunle was already there.

"My man. Long time, what a coincidence to run into you," he said. He was all smiles. "And your madam too." He made to embrace Margaret, but she stepped behind Benjamin and nodded curtly.

"A coincidence indeed, and a happy one too," Benjamin said. He laughed and embraced him. The men chatted for a few minutes, then Margaret and Benjamin continued their walk. Benjamin felt odd about Margaret's awkward retreat, but he assumed it was something cultural. She was being conservative. Newly married, why should she embrace his colleague? She hesitated because she respected him. He thought about Kunle again—and smiled.

"Do you consider that man a good friend?" Margaret asked after they'd walked a few blocks. She'd taken Benjamin's hand again.

"What man, you mean Kunle?"

She nodded.

"He's a good man—yes."

"There's something about him. He frightens me."

"What are you talking about? He's our good friend; he was at our wedding."

"He was? I don't recall."

That evening, after dinner, as Benjamin was cleaning the kitchen sink, he said to Margaret, "Maybe we should go to London."

"I thought we agreed next summer."

"Next summer. Now. It's all the same."

"Why now?"

"No reason." He shrugged. "You may like the change of environment," he continued. After a pause, he said, "It may help with the dreams."

There was no response, so they settled onto the sofa to listen to the news. When the television became static, Margaret turned to Benjamin.

"You are worried about me?" she asked.

"Should I not be?" Benjamin said.

"Because of your friend? Because of what I said about him?"

"No." After a while he added, "How can you not remember he was at our wedding?"

"It's not a crime to forget."

Benjamin recognized a quarrel when it was coming, so he said nothing. He reached for his cigarette on the side stool and walked off to the veranda. When he returned, Margaret was still seated, staring at the static television.

She turned to him and said, "Perhaps you're right. I've not been feeling well."

"Is that so?"

"I'll go to the hospital. I will even tell the doctor about my memory loss," she said, poking him in his sides. He smiled.

"Do you want me to come with you?" he asked.

"No need, my darling."

When the time for the doctor's visit came, Margaret explained to the doctor, who nodded and smiled. He asked Margaret when she last saw her menses. She said she did not remember, surprising herself with the answer. And so the doctor had sent her to the lab to run some tests. This was how they learned she was pregnant.

"I must write to my mother immediately, and we will go to London this Christmas," Benjamin announced that evening, elated.

"How do you feel?" he asked, raising the back of his hand to Margaret's forehead.

She moved away and laughed. "Onye ocha, take it easy, please," she teased.

"All right, all right," Benjamin said, bowing lightly—a gesture he knew amused Margaret.

"At least now we know it's not the village curse," he said, winking at Margaret.

"Abi?" Margaret said in pidgin.

"I'm just glad we can do away with all that backward philosophy," Benjamin said as he smirked.

"Well, it might not make sense to you; that doesn't mean it is backward," Margaret responded.

"I'm sorry, I didn't mean it that way."

"I wish you would take it seriously."

"If we took it seriously, we would not have married," Benjamin said. "And we would not be expecting this wonderful child," he added, walking to Margaret.

He rubbed her tummy, then tickled her sides. Margaret squealed. She walked to the fridge, then to the bathroom. By the time she came out, she was still smiling.

15

The Kinsmen

Umumilo, 1905

There are three ways to know a man, Okolo thought. One is by the sex of his first child. If he bears a son, it is because he is a man who shoots his arrows once, who hits his target with a single determined look; the kind of man who sets out to the forest and returns with the head of a leopard or the dull tusk of a slain elephant. If, however, he fathers a girl first, well, it means he is a man who must try again, whose life is given to second attempts—a man whose efforts are, at best, quivering and unsure. In this regard, Okolo was a man's man. He had five sons, three of whom were old enough to tend to their own patches of farmland.

The second way to know a man, Okolo considered, was to observe the way such a man handles a victory. If, weeks after a battle, a man continues to move around the village, relishing the praise of women and children, it is because his glory days are behind him. True warriors know that every celebration is short-lived, for the next battle is always around the corner ahead, waiting. Okolo had tasted this kind of manhood too. He had known the triumph of picking up a man from the ground and raising him above his head. He was familiar with the roar of onlookers, the whistling of winds against palm leaves, even the squawks of the birds, all witness to his public victory. He'd been a man—a real man. Yet, there was that third haunting index by which Okolo measured these things. A real man can also be known by the way he protects his people. The way he guards them. A real man was a custodian of culture, a keeper of his people's stories, their secrets. It was in this regard that Okolo knew he had failed utterly. The feeling of wretched anxiety was so strong in his body—sitting even on his shoulders and arms, in his thighs, wrapped around him with his loincloth. Back at the secretariat, when Okolo told Mr. Walter the story of Olisa and his mother, Oriaku, Okolo believed he was exacting a kind of justice for the violated women—justice also for his sister Priscilla, who, in addition to being shunned by the village, had become sick in her body since the death of the Irish boy. But every time he watched Mr. Walter scribble in his notes, or grunt in approval, or prod Bassey with more questions, Okolo felt as though he had taken his own father's name and offered it to this stranger.

"Interesting," Mr. Walter said repeatedly, so much so that the word *interesting* cemented itself in Okolo's mind, the first English word he would learn. Every time Okolo finished a part of the narrative and asked when Olisa would be executed, Mr. Walter had merely adjusted his glasses and scribbled further, before signaling to Bassey—"More. Tell him to tell us more."

The morning after Okolo told the stories, the officers said he would soon be sent home, but only after he spoke with Mr. Walter again. He'd thought that he was done, that he had said all that needed to be said; still, he walked confidently and with a little impatience into the room where Mr. Walter sat waiting. It was afternoon, but because the room had neither windows nor a lantern, it appeared dim.

"Please, sit," Mr. Walter said through Bassey.

"Tell your master to speak and to speak quickly," Okolo said to Bassey.

Mr. Walter brought out a small piece of folded cloth from under the table. He looked up at Okolo, smiled, then very carefully opened the cloth to reveal five manillas—a currency of trade.

"Go on," Mr. Walter said to Okolo, gesturing to the package. "It is yours, a friendly token." He was speaking to Okolo directly, while Bassey tried to match his pace with the interpretation.

Okolo glared at the money, then at Bassey and Mr. Walter. Then Okolo laughed.

"What is this for?" he asked.

"A gift—for speaking to us. There is more where that came from," Mr. Walter said. He stood up and walked to Okolo, looking him in the face. "Think of all that you can do for your family, for your people, with all that money," Mr. Walter continued.

Okolo turned to leave, but Mr. Walter caught him by the hand. "Tell him," Mr. Walter said to Bassey without looking at him.

"Th-they are going to arrest Priscilla," Bassey stuttered. "They will send her away."

"What for? She has committed no crime," Okolo said.

"Yes, but you have."

"What crime do you hold over me now? I have told you about the vagabond as you requested."

"You are absolved, but the crime must still be punished."

"Your master will punish my sister for my sake?"

"It doesn't have to be so if you work with us."

"Nonsense."

"Just listen to him," Bassey said. "Hear him out."

That same afternoon, they released Okolo and told him to return in two days with his response to their offer.

Now he was back in his own compound, full of contemplation. He was already a chief. He was already in favor with his people. There wasn't much that needed to change in his own life. But Mr. Walter had made his request rather clear. Okolo had much to give. His influence in the village would make them more accepting of the incoming changes. But what kind of a man would champion the cause of the people who killed his brothers, regardless of what was promised?

Shortly after his return, his kinsmen came out of hiding. They were elated that he was back. They wanted to celebrate.

"What is there to celebrate?" Okolo replied, distracted. "You do not feast when your house has just been raided." His frown was visible, but that did not dissuade them.

"We heard the rumors, nna anyi," one chief said, his voice strained. "We heard of how they lifted you off the ground, how your wrapper went flying in the air, your thighs exposed." The man lowered his head and shuddered.

"Ee, it is true. My errand boy saw it himself on the way to the stream," another villager chimed in. "He said you were brave, that you commanded them to put you down at once, but they did not. He said you were stronger than three of their best men. But they had their guns, those terrible things—did they not?"

Okolo wondered what his kinsmen would say if they heard how the white men treated Olisa; how the vagabond had been eating their bread, drinking their water, their milk. He wondered about the manillas that Mr. Walter offered—the invitation to serve the British administration, to rule over his people as a different kind of chief—a warrant chief. He remembered the threat Mr. Walter made to banish Priscilla. His chest tightened. And what about the child? It occurred to him now that this Mr. Walter man made no mention of the child. Would they banish the child too? It pained Okolo that Thomas and Boko, his good friends, were dead, other villagers were dead, too—for nothing—while Olisa lived. It pained him even more that the verdict of the Gods was now left in the charge of the white men. His kinsmen were still around him in his obi—sitting on the floor, on the bench. They, too, were waiting for answers. He looked at their eager faces and finally responded.

"You have not told us all that happened."

"You know all there is. I was away and now I have returned."

"But why? Why did they send you back?"

"I suppose they got tired of me." He shrugged.

▼▲▼

Walter sat on a wooden bench, reading. It was in the small room where he'd been assigned to lodge. Usually, he would read with a glass of whiskey, but he had run out of spirits. His back was slightly curved from lurching forward to peer at his notes through the dim light of the kerosene lantern. A few weeks had passed since he made the first move to Okolo, and while Okolo had made no commitments yet, he was sure that Okolo would return. He had a sense about these things. From his experience with these negotiations, he understood that it was hard to turn down one's family. But it was even harder to turn down power. He had called for a few more meetings with the man. And yes, it was true that each meeting was followed with a quarrel. The man, Okolo, had a way of asserting himself. But he kept showing up. He had not told his kinsmen about the offer. More so, he collected the manillas. He did not refuse them. Walter had decided in that moment that he would go ahead and write a short profile on Okolo and make the necessary introductions for the officer who would be posted to take his place. This, indeed, was what he set out to do when he retired to his lodge on this particular night. He had picked the lantern for this purpose, along with his writing materials. But he had not long since sat down to write before he admitted the impossibility of the matter.

There was one misplaced but crucial factor. It was the vagabond—he had gone missing. The officers had woken up that morning and found his quarters empty. Walter had covered it up immediately, admitting that indeed, it was he who had released the vagabond. It was a lie, but what was the alternative? To suggest that the secretariat had a mole, that the officers were not as in control as they thought? That was not a story he intended to tell his superiors, so when the matter came up, he told the officers, Bassey, and eventually Okolo that, yes—I let him go. I reviewed all the details; his crime is of no consequence.

As for the consequence of the crime—whether or not the vagabond had done those things, Walter continued to sit on the fence. One of the virgins had died. Tragic. The other one, Priscilla, turned out to be a carefully concealed affair. It was all up to Adaora now to tilt the scale of his reports. It was up to her to finalize what had happened, but she was not forthcoming. She had stopped speaking during their sessions.

On two occasions, Walter walked into the room where the vagabond was, making sure to take his pistol with him. He had made Bassey come in, too, as well as two other officers. It was unnecessary—the boy, as they liked to call him, had shown no sign of violence, or of intelligence. His body had that tired, worn-out shape of someone who had lived a rough life, and though he was nearly a head taller than Walter himself, his face was still the face of a child.

The first time Walter went in, he'd wanted answers. He wanted to finalize his report and close the file.

"Do you know why you are here?" Walter asked the boy. Olisa listened to Bassey interpret the question; then his eyes fell on his feet. There was no answer.

"How did you do it? How did you get the women to stay asleep?" Walter asked.

Walter remembered that Okolo had said the boy was a descendant of priestesses, but that was just another superstition.

"How did you do it?" he asked again, his voice raised.

Olisa crouched even lower. The stench of his blood and sweat filled the room. He turned away from Walter and faced the wall. When moments passed and he still did not say anything, Bassey raised his legs and kicked the boy—twice in the shoulder and once on his head. Walter had sometimes suspected that Bassey was an impassioned man, that there was a kind of energy with which he went about his day-to-day affairs; there was an exacting authority in the way he spoke about his life, his people—the activities of the village. But Walter would not have taken him to be a forceful or violent man. Then again, there was that singular occasion when he raised his hand and struck Adaora. Yet, here he was, kicking the boy on the floor. It took the two other commanding officers to get Bassey out of the room. Later, Bassey would explain that he was only trying to help. That he was doing the work they had called him to do. That if language fails, one must not be afraid to use fists—after all, what the vagabond had done was unpardonable; after all, one of the virgins, the youngest of them, had died. Walter had looked at him, silent, incredulous. Four days after that incident, the vagabond disappeared.

▼▲▼

Bassey typically did not retire to his sleeping quarters until the officers had all left for the night. In the room that was assigned to him, he slept on the floor, atop a mat that he bought from the Nkwo market. The ground was often cold and damp, so that Bassey, on occasion, had to spread his day's cloth beneath a wrapper before he could lie down to sleep. However, regardless of the hardness of the floor or the coldness of the night, once Bassey's head touched the ground, he drifted into dreamless sleep. In this sense, he considered himself blessed. This ability to sleep through any situation had followed him from the time he was a child, so much so that as a young boy of eleven, he had slept through the commotion of a compound fire, awakened only after his people noticed he was still inside. They found him asleep in the midst of the fumes, had kicked him awake before dragging him through the smoke to safety. Yet, this blessing of sleep seemed to have run its course.

It began on the first night Okolo was arrested. That evening, as Bassey returned to his room and walked to the tap to wash his feet, he felt within him a growing unease, though he did not know what it was. He squatted at the tap, waited for the dirt to run out first, for the clean water to emerge. His hands were under the faucet, the water rushed out, but his vision was blurred. He moved closer, placed his face under the tap, and shook his head, letting the water fall to his neck and chest. Then he lost his balance and fell. When he got up, he wondered for a moment where he was; then he closed the tap. He must be tired, he thought, raising his hand to clench his stomach. He then hurried to the bush beside the quarters, where he vomited everything he'd eaten for supper.

The fever started the next night, after he vomited again. Earlier in the day, he had gone about his tasks with a sullen look. He was already a small man, but now his shoulders felt tighter, constrained. His eyes seemed to sting under the sun. And in one instance, while Mr. Walter was speaking with one of the natives, Bassey had pulled out a bench and sat down. Still, he had executed his tasks that day reasonably well; he had even waited for Mr. Walter to finish his drinks with the other officers before he retired. After two nights of fever, and after nearly fainting on his return from work the third day, Bassey decided he would visit the nurse. She said it was malaria and gave him medicine for it. He was told to take it for ten days. There was only one small problem: he had had malaria before—too many times. He was familiar with its signs, and this thing he carried now, it did not feel like malaria. He had taken the first tablet and felt sorely worse in his body. He did not know where the sense came from, only that he had a firm understanding that something was wrong. He felt that he was about to die. It was not fear. It was not even the sickness that made his stomach retch, just a simple knowing—his end was almost here. In the face of this self-imposed verdict, Bassey realized he did not know himself anymore. He did not know who he was, where he stood with the customs of his people. He did not know where he would be buried if he died; if the white man considered burial rights for people like him, if his father's people would take him back. The church would have buried him had he still been stationed with them. But with the consulate, he was not sure. Now he wondered who would claim him when his body could no longer render those services.

He'd discussed these fears with Okolo one evening when they met, his eyes red and sunken, his voice hoarse.

"You must seek a healer at once," Okolo had said.

"I am taking some medicines; it will be all right," he replied, but his voice belied his confidence.

"Nonsense. Take your medicine, but seek more help. You work for the white man; you have two ways of living now—is it not?" Okolo said.

"And you?" Bassey asked. "You do not work for him?"

"I serve myself and my sons. I work for my family."

"So you will do the right thing?"

"What do you mean?"

"For your sister. Priscilla. A shame to see her suffer for nothing."

Okolo grunted.

After that discussion, Bassey decided to seek the mercies of Agwu.

He thought that there was some truth to what Okolo said. He was taking the medicine, but why could he not do more? He found a dibia outside of Umumilo and he went there determined to make the journey by foot, even if he had to crawl there. When the priests told him what he had to do—he sat dazed. He'd been grateful that the dibia had given him a potion for the fevers but was stunned that the Gods knew him. The dibia had painted vivid images of his boyhood days, of the disappearance of his younger brother, of his falling out with his own father, and then of his father's sudden illness and death in the missions. Bassey nodded, swallowing his spit, terrified but also grateful to be known in such a way. And then, because he had told the dibia that he wanted—above all things—to be accepted by his people again, that he even wanted to take a wife, for it was not just death he feared, but dying alone, the dibia told him what the Gods wanted in exchange. It was a simple task. He had something that belonged to them. Someone. Even before the dibia said the words, Bassey knew what he had to do. The Gods wanted their son. They wanted the vagabond out of the white man's clutches. The boy had wronged the women of the land, and the women had to be avenged. His crime must be punished. It was the way of the soil. Bassey's assignment was simple—he was to release the vagabond so that the village could carry out his punishment. Yet such a task would cost him not just his work, but his freedom as well, perhaps even his own life. He was not sure how he would go about such a mission. He did not have the key to the room where the vagabond was kept, though he knew where it was. He decided that he would do it on a Sunday, during the church service. Not that Mr. Walter ever attended, but Mr. Walter had taken to long walks in the village on such mornings, strolling past the Uchu River, where he would stop and stare into the far distance. After Bassey decided when and how he would carry out the assignment, the next thing he had to do was to put on a performance to disguise his intentions. There could be no suspicion; not even the slightest sense of sympathy could be detected. And so, on one occasion when Mr. Walter was questioning the vagabond, Bassey did not think too much about raising his boots to the boy's head, stomping and stomping, until the boy began to bleed from his nose. For a moment, Bassey believed his own rage. Once he had put on the performance, he knew that there was no going back. He had started a course of action that he could not change any more than he could turn back the hands of a clock.

Sunday morning arrived. Mr. Walter went about his walk as expected. Bassey waited for some time, convinced there was no company save for the cook asleep in her quarters and the chickens in the backyard. He opened the door and saw the vagabond standing, almost as if he had been waiting, as if he knew. Or maybe he had merely stood when he heard the door being opened. He was tall, this vagabond. His clothes old and worn, his hands caked in dirt. But his face was clean, the face of a boy lost.

"Come." Bassey gestured. "Take the back door. Tell no one of this."

That night, after the deed had been done, Bassey slept well again, the fever having disappeared. All was restored. Perhaps now he might find a wife, have a son or a daughter, little children he would train in English. Perhaps they would even go to school, get a formal education. Children who would be better than him and his father. He allowed himself to dream and plan. He entertained ideas of potential arranged marriages, of a flamboyant wedding in the village square, of his mother's visit and her approval. He had even come to entertain the idea of a genuine friendship with Okolo, a relationship where he was more than his informant—he was his equal. However, two weeks after he released Olisa, Bassey died in his sleeping quarters.

He'd shown no symptoms. He had—just the day before—attended a wrestling match at the village square. He had his eyes on a young virgin on the scene, though he never got to the point of speaking with her. And he had even declared to Mr. Walter his intention to visit his ailing mother in his home village. The day was well spent, and he retired to his room. Then he slept and did not wake up. It was as simple as that. The parishioners buried him behind the church quietly, without ceremony. By the time the news reached his sisters and his mother, all that was left was the ground in which his remains lay.

16

Benjamin

Atlanta, Lagos, 2005

"She wants you to come home," Nwando said on a call to Benjamin.

He raised his hands to his chest. A few moments passed before he realized he'd not responded.

"What?" he said finally, his voice a murmur.

"She wants you to come home; she asked me to call you. It's about her health."

There was a long pause. Benjamin played around with the question in his head, willing himself to breathe.

"Her health. Is she all right?" he asked at last.

"Yes, yes, she is. It's also about some other things, something about a family cleansing. She said you'd know about it," Nwando clarified.

"Hmm."

"At least tell me you'll think about it," Nwando hissed.

"How is she these days?"

"You mean is she sick again?"

“Not really,” he said, lying.

“Some years are worse than others. What should I tell her you said?” Nwando pressed.

“Tell her about what?”

“About the request—to come home. She’s going to want to know.”

“There’s a lot to consider.”

“Like what? Nobody is going to make you stay if that’s what you’re worried about.”

“Nwando, you know my condition. I can’t just get up and leave. I just had a heart attack.” He was reaching for every defense he could find.

“Please—”

“Can I think about it?”

“I’ve never asked you for anything,” Nwando said. “This is the least you can do.”

“When is the cleansing?”

“September twenty-sixth.”

“That is in less than five weeks.”

“I know. You don’t need to do anything. We’ll plan everything. My husband, Nosa, will book your flight. You will stay at our place. You will meet Chuka—and then we can all get to know each other better. Is it not what you’ve wanted?”

“And there’s the cleansing?” Benjamin said, as if to remind her.

“Of course there’s the cleansing, but it’s only to humor her. You don’t have to do anything.”

“Let me at least think about it,” Benjamin said.

“All right. I’ll call you this weekend to discuss the travel plans.” After a little hesitation, as though thinking of her words, she then added, “This is a good way to make up for the past, you know?” and she hung up the phone.

▼▲▼

"Take a deep breath for me."

"Take another deep breath, Mr.—?" The doctor turned to Benjamin's chart on a monitor. "Fletcher?"

"Call me Ben."

"Okay," the doctor said without raising his face. "Everything looks clear, in tip-top shape."

He was young—this doctor—the youngest-looking Benjamin had met so far.

"How old are you?" Benjamin asked, regretting the words as soon as they came out.

"Old enough to interpret your chest readings," the doctor said with a small smile.

Benjamin looked at the doctor's dark hair; black, straight but not spiky. Maybe slightly Asian? he thought. The doctor was thin, his shoulders a little slouched; his glasses hung lopsided on his face; his nails appeared bitten, like he chewed on them. There was a dark undertone to his white skin, perhaps someone with Greek roots? A Persian heritage? But it was the young doctor's nose that decided things for Benjamin. It was the most prominent feature on his face, large enough to draw attention to itself without distorting the face. Must be Armenian, Benjamin thought. Yes, this is certainly an Armenian nose.

Benjamin sat upright on the exam table, trying to ignore the smell of the place. It was an examination room, painted a dull yellow. The table was covered in a thin blue sheet, the same one that also covered his chest now.

"Tell me what you are eating these days," the young doctor continued.

"The usual—all the clean stuff," Benjamin replied, sounding as American as he could.

"Exercise?"

"A few times a week."

"Rigorous?"

"Not too rigorous; some weights when I can manage."

"You have the heart monitor?"

"I have the heart monitor," Benjamin said in a shrill voice, mildly mimicking the doctor. He straightened his back as soon as he responded, suddenly aware that he might appear surly.

"All right, then, I suppose I'll see you in three months."

"Of course."

The doctor began to type into a screen, deciding he was done with the patient.

"What about travel?" Benjamin asked, finally broaching the question that had been on his mind.

"Travel? Like go on a trip?"

"Yes, most people would define that as travel."

The doctor smiled this time, and Benjamin found himself strangely relieved. The doctor, however, did not respond, just continued typing into the screen.

"Well?"

"I would imagine you can travel; I would just keep the same dietary restrictions—you're going to want to do your exercise, monitor any discrepancies."

"So, it's fine to travel? I mean—to travel abroad?"

"I suppose so—yes."

"I mean to Africa—to Nigeria? Is it safe to fly for that long?"

"If you have concerns about traveling that far, you could postpone the trip," the doctor replied. He stood, unconsciously stretching out his back.

"I don't have concerns—it's my family," Benjamin said. "My family needs me," he added, testing out the words.

If the doctor was surprised at the idea of Benjamin having family in West Africa—in Nigeria—he did not show it. Instead, he moved toward the door, a clear indication that this examination was over.

"Is there anything the nurse can get you?" the doctor asked. "Or anything else you'd like to ask me?"

"You mean besides how old you are? You never answered my question, you know," Benjamin said, pulling his shirt over his head. He did not bother to smile, his mind already running to other places. But the doctor laughed.

"I'm thirty-four next month," he said. Then he added as he opened the door, "Have a good trip, Mr. Fletcher."

With the doctor now out of the room, out of his sight, Benjamin turned his thoughts toward his father, this time with more tenderness than he'd shown the man in his last months alive. The last serious conversation Benjamin had with his father was back in '60, shortly before his father slumped dead at home, his legs askew, his mouth open, his eyes only half-closed. It'd happened in the room that served as a study in their London home, the same room his father had shut himself in for many months, buried in work, or so Benjamin had thought. It was the room where neither Benjamin nor his mother felt free to enter, and even when they did, they felt unwelcome, so that they mostly stood at the doorpost, calling him out to tea, to lunch, to receive the mail. Benjamin still remembered the pen stationed on his father's desk, the smell of his father's aftershave crowding the room. He did not remember why he had gone searching for his father on that particular day, only that it was urgent. But his old man was not in the room, and Benjamin's calls of "Father, Father?" were met with silence. For some reason—he had not meant to—Benjamin looked at his father's desk. He'd leafed through the papers, through a magazine, until he found something else on the table. By the time his father returned to the study, surprised to find Benjamin there, it was too late. Benjamin now held in his hand evidence that could not be erased. Pictures of his father with another woman. The woman in the picture appeared to be in her mid-thirties and had low-cut Afro hair. She was dark-skinned. African. She was smiling at the camera. Standing beside her in the black-and-white picture, Benjamin's father held a cigarette to his mouth; he, too, was smiling, his face turned to the woman. In the second picture, he held the woman against his body, his shirt unbuttoned at the neckline.

"What is this?" Benjamin asked. He did not notice himself sit down when he'd first seen the picture, and now that his father had entered the room, he stood sharply.

"What are you doing here?" his father asked. His father had gone to take a shower; his hair was still wet, the curls still tightly wound, the mass of dark brown hair crowning his head like a curl cap fitted just for him. Benjamin had never peered closely at his father's hair up until that moment, having been obsessed instead by the hue of his skin. Now, looking at the woman in the picture and watching his father, all he could see was the texture of his old man's hair.

"Who is she?" Benjamin asked, rephrasing his earlier question.

"You were not supposed to see that," his father started, moving toward Benjamin. He made to snatch the pictures from his hand, but Benjamin moved his hands out of reach. "Can a man not have some privacy in his own home?" his father had muttered, irritated.

"Does Mother know?"

"Of course not," he replied. "And you mustn't tell her. You know how sickly she gets when she is worried."

Benjamin tried to move, willed his muscles to lift themselves and step away from his father's desk, but he found that he could not. So he sat down again.

"Tell me," Benjamin said.

"There's nothing to tell," his father replied, gesturing to the door.

"Tell me now," Benjamin shouted, surprising himself.

This was the way Benjamin came to learn about his father's secret life. There'd been a woman in Ghana, though his father described it as the Gold Coast back then, despite their independence. She was a widow with two daughters, both of whom were under ten. She ran an orphanage that doubled as a learning center for teens, and she'd been working in collaboration with the church missions. They'd met in Birmingham during an exchange program championed by the British council. After two years of writing letters, Benjamin's father had gone to Ghana himself, unable to continue with the charade. It was not serious at first, his father explained, a part of him was largely curious, wondering in midlife what his life would have been like if he had not left Africa as an infant, if he'd been left there to grow, to build a life among his mother's people. She understood him, this woman, and she made him feel connected to a part of himself he didn't know he had.

"Is it over?" Benjamin asked.

His father had not replied. He'd instead pulled out a chair across from Benjamin.

They'd both sat there, man-to-man, in silence. After a while, his father said, "Yes. She called it off. She found a suitor from her clan."

"You still care for her?"

"Does it matter?"

"It does to me—to Mother. "

"Well, it is quite over now. You need not worry."

Benjamin had been stunned at what he termed his father's pretense, how his old man kept telling him for years how to court women, while he was himself secretly yearning for someone else. Benjamin kept the conversation to himself, until three weeks later, when his old man slumped in that same study and subsequently died in the hospital. This was December 1960. Afterward, Benjamin ransacked his father's bedroom, his study, spent hours with his mother, leafing through paperwork, searching for the pictures; it was his attempt to protect his mother from that betrayal. For months, he wondered if his father loved his mother, if his father loved him, if he regretted the life he came to have as a Black man in London, however light-skinned he appeared. And then the other side of the questions—had his father been drawn to the woman because she reminded him of a part of himself that had been taken from him?

It was now, after all these years, while still sitting in that hospital examination room, that Benjamin finally admitted to himself why he had packed his bags and gone to Nigeria in 1962. It was not merely to connect with his roots or from a sense of responsibility to the past. No. It was because he was his father's son. Because there was something about the soil and the people that would always call to him no matter where he was in the world. Now, after many years, the country had not forgotten him. It was calling again.

Very well, he decided, as he stepped into the hospital hallway. He would get into his car, stop at the gas station, then at the local pharmacy, where he would pick up the same aftershave cream that he had used for the last twenty years. Then he would go home and call Nwando. He was going back to Nigeria.

17

The Lovers

Lagos, 1960s

Y ou're awake?" Benjamin asked, toweling his hair. He'd come out of the bathroom to find Margaret standing in the hallway. In the months since they'd learned of the pregnancy, Margaret had started sleeping more, and Benjamin had by now gotten used to leaving for work while she was still in bed. So finding her in the hallway this morning surprised him.

"I don't think you should go to the office today," Margaret said.

"Why?" Benjamin asked, distracted.

She was five months along, her tummy bulging beneath her nightgown. Benjamin went into their bedroom and came out in his shirt and underpants. "Where is my pocket watch?" he muttered more to himself than to her. "I shall be sorry if I turn up late again." He paused and saw that Margaret had moved to the living room, where she was now crying, one hand resting on the dining table, the other on her belly. This also startled him. The sudden drama of the scene. It was so unlike the stability of the past few months. Margaret had grown more tired as her pregnancy progressed; the baby slowed her down in a way that put off her plans for work, for school. They had initially planned to make the trip to the village early in December, where they would play on the pregnancy and have a hurried traditional wedding. But Margaret no longer felt up to the trip, so they also put it off. They would wait until March, when the baby was due to arrive; then they would go shortly after Easter to get Ma Adaora's blessing. Her pregnancy-induced lethargy had brought a quiet settling into their life. Their love, their routines, their small disagreements—there was a rhythm to it. But now, what was he to make of this sudden crying?

"They are not happy," Margaret said through tears. She pulled out a chair and sat. Benjamin should have walked to her, comforted her. The thought was in his head, in his fingers. But he did not move.

"They are not happy," Margaret said again. She looked up, her eyes now clear. "If you leave for work, they will come for me." She sniffed. "They will come for our child," she added.

She sounded so sure of what she was saying, so matter-of-fact, so troubled. This was the reason why Benjamin left for work anyway. He would show her that it was all nonsense when he returned alive and unharmed. He would also point out that she, too, was unharmed. He would say to her, "There now, do you see there was nothing to worry about?"

And so he'd left for work in a taxi—a short drive, less than fifteen minutes. Distracted, he did not, as he usually did, take in the view of the city during the drive, watching the people charge into their day, his mind wholly occupied with coming back and showing Margaret that she was wrong. When he arrived at the building and stepped out of the taxi, he was surprised to find Cynthia in the compound. She was about to leave when she saw him. "Ben?" she said.

He lowered his head instinctively, then realized there was no point in pretending he could not see her.

She laughed. "Oyibo, you want to hide?"

"Cynthia," he said, trying to sound cordial. "You look well."

"Thank you. Are you surprised?"

"Not at all."

"You look like you've lost some weight." She walked over, touched his collar.

"Not this again," Benjamin said, his face straight. Cynthia always had a sense about correcting things only after she declared them faulty. When they were together, she'd comment on his hair, his collar, the iron lines on his trousers.

"Oyibo, calm down, I'm just playing with you. I came to see the director."

"I'll leave you to it, then." He made to turn into the reception area.

"How is she?" Cynthia called from behind.

"Who?"

"Your wife."

"Maggie? She's very well," Benjamin said, walking away.

"Hope she's not giving you any problems."

He stopped—he knew he would regret this conversation, but he could not help himself.

"What do you mean?"

Cynthia chuckled; she walked toward the entrance to the office now. Toward Benjamin. "I hope you understand what you bargained for—"

"What I bargained for?"

"A woman like that; no family, living alone, so headstrong, I hear."

"Not unlike you, then," Benjamin said.

Cynthia's face fell. "There's talk about her in the office, you know. Very moody, that girl. Very stubborn. Did the director not say anything to you? I even hear she sometimes talks to herself."

"I don't have time for this, Cynthia. Have a good day." He nodded and walked off.

Benjamin spent the rest of that day watching the clock, waiting to get back home to Margaret, to lay his hand on her thigh while they listened to the radio together. He would even tell her about the exchange with Cynthia. Margaret was not the sort of woman to get jealous. To her, Cynthia was a fact of his past, like his boarding school days, or his time at the broadcast network. He knew that the exchange with Cynthia was something they could talk about freely, laugh about, so he bought some ice cream on his way home, taking a longer route to the store she liked to shop at. He knew that she would complain that it was too sweet, too much sugar, but she would not put it away until she was at least halfway done. He found himself whistling on the trip back home. Once he arrived, he alighted from his taxi, reaching for his keys, taking the stairs two at a time.

Their flat was quiet when he finally got in. He did not find Margaret in the bedroom, or in the living room, or in the bathroom. He felt a momentary confusion, as though he had opened the door to another family's apartment. Then he gathered himself and rushed out of the house. He walked to the local mart where they did their grocery shopping; then he walked to the ends of the street, twice. When he still did not find her, he went home, got into their car, and drove around their neighborhood. He returned home to their compound, and he could see that the flat was still dark. Has she left me? he thought quietly. No. He shook the idea out of his head. There's no way she would have left me. Should I involve the police? The neighbors? he wondered. No, not right away. Perhaps he would wait till morning. He was confused, but still in the car, waiting. Eventually, in a daze, he returned to their flat, unaware that three hours had passed. He found the door open. Had he left it open when he rushed out earlier? He walked in and closed it behind him. He moved to the other side of the living room to shut the barricade to the veranda, wondering again how he could leave the apartment with all the doors open. This was when he found Margaret lying on the sofa, in the dark.

"Where have you been?" His voice was loud. Exasperated.

"You're back?" She sounded like she might have just woken from sleep.

"Where have you been?" Benjamin asked again. He was pacing, running his fingers over his hair.

"I went out. I was just around the area."

"What do you mean? I searched everywhere."

He turned on the light switch; he wanted to look at her while she gave her answer. He saw that she was wearing rubber slippers, that her feet were dusty; there was some dirt smeared around her elbows. She followed his gaze to her feet, and her eyes flared as though she, too, was just now seeing herself.

"I'll go wash up," she said, and went into the bathroom.

Benjamin reminded himself that it was the pregnancy, that he would find a way to suggest a visit to the doctor again. Perhaps there was something they could give her at the hospital. She seemed to be forgetting things—days, time. He thought about writing to his mother—she might understand such things; perhaps she could say something to Margaret, give some useful tips about pregnancy-related stress. But he shook himself out of the idea. Then he thought about what Cynthia had said. *Moody.* This was the word Cynthia used. Now he wondered: Had Margaret done something like this before in the office? But who could he ask? Not Ma Adaora, who did not even know that they had wed. Not his own mother. Certainly not the office workers itching for gossip.

The next day, when Benjamin returned from work, Margaret was not at home. Again. He sat in the living room until about ten p.m., when she returned. He tried to calm himself when he asked her where she had gone this time. But she'd simply refused to respond. The day after that it was the same thing. Finally, she explained on that third day that she got tired of sitting around the house waiting for him, that she wanted to walk, here and there, be outside, smell the air.

"But you come back so late," Benjamin said.

"I come back when I'm ready."

He stepped back. "But your hair?"

"My hair?"

"I mean, you don't style it; you wear your house slippers."

"Excuse me, I didn't know I was going on a fashion parade."

Things continued like this until the Friday of that week, when Benjamin returned from work and found her at home, waiting for him. She'd prepared jollof rice with fried chicken. She'd cleaned out their bedroom, the bathroom. She'd even picked out some of Benjamin's shirts and ironed them—for work next week, she said, beaming.

"No outing today?" Benjamin asked, eyeing the pot of rice.

"I wanted to make you dinner."

"What is the occasion?"

"Do I need a reason to cook for my husband?"

He looked at her, at the food, but he did not sit.

"Very well," she said, rubbing her belly. "The occasion is that our daughter wants her father to have dinner."

Benjamin laughed. He knew she said it to draw a reaction from him. In their earlier discussions, Benjamin had joked that he was a proper Igbo man and so expected a male child first.

"A girl?" he now said to Margaret. He could feel his muscles relax. "And how do you know this?"

"Never worry about that." Margaret smiled. She rubbed his back, then served a plate for both of them.

By the next week, their routine returned to normal, almost as if the disappearances of the previous week never happened. He'd return from work, and they would have dinner together, sharing the same plates. However, even this resumed intimacy was fated to be short-lived.

It was a Thursday evening. They had just finished having dinner; Benjamin was sitting, reading a newspaper. Margaret lay against him, her face pensive.

After a moment, she asked, "Do you think I'm crazy?"

"How do you mean?" Benjamin said. He rested his hand on her shoulder, squeezed gently.

"I mean like a lunatic. What if you came to Nigeria and married a crazy woman?"

Benjamin laughed nervously but said nothing.

Margaret sat up.

"Tell me, Benni. You think I'm crazy?"

"I shall say no such thing."

"Very well, if you won't say it, I will say it."

She paused.

"You will say what?" Benjamin asked.

"Never mind."

She got up, took the plates to the sink, and started to wash them.

"You're just going to sit there like a king, abi? Let your pregnant wife do all the cleaning?"

"You know we can get somebody to do this work," Benjamin said. He patted the sofa beside him. "Come sit with me."

"I think it was a mistake, Benni," she said as she rinsed off the dishes.

Benjamin sighed. He did not need to hear another word to know where she was going.

"What were we thinking? How could we have been so reckless?"

"You think being with me is a mistake?" Benjamin said.

"Think what they will do to us—to our daughter."

"You keep saying 'they.' Who do you mean?"

Silence.

"C'mon, Maggie, we can't keep having these conversations. You are a smart woman. How can you believe these things? It must be wearisome."

Margaret walked to the door, checked that it was closed. Then she closed the curtains, then checked the door again.

"What are you doing?" Benjamin asked.

"Stop asking me questions," she hissed. "Can't you see? I'm trying to protect our child."

She looked about the room as she cleaned out the kitchen. For the third time, she went to the door and checked the latch again. Benjamin closed the papers, walked toward her, and tried to hug her. She slapped his hand away.

"We should never have married," she whispered. "We should never have married."

"It's all right. It's all going to be all right, Maggie." Benjamin held her again. She'd stopped slapping his hands away. They stood there for a few minutes, lightly swaying.

"Perhaps we should go to London," Benjamin said after a few minutes.

"No," came Margaret's charged response.

"No?"

"I won't allow you to harm my baby," Margaret replied sternly. She wiggled out of his grip and went to their bedroom.

▼▲▼

By December, Margaret, who was now six months along, announced that she would go to Umumilo.

"You're in no condition to travel," Benjamin said.

She was on the bed, folding cloth diapers they'd received as a gift for the baby.

"I don't want to quarrel. This is important, please," she said.

"I suppose I can arrange for private transport to take us down," Benjamin said. "I don't like this at all," he added.

"I think I should go alone."

"You don't want me to come along?" He got up from the bed, walked to the living room, then came back. "Maggie, you can't be serious."

"I have a feeling about Ma. I feel like I need to talk to her." She was still fixated on the diapers, but her voice was pleading.

"I reckon you want to talk to her about this—mistake," Benjamin said, gesturing at himself.

"Don't say it like that," Margaret said. She walked to him and took his hand. Then she leaned in, wrapped herself around him, her stomach wedging them apart.

"Think about it. If I speak with Ma directly, if I allow her to see me in my condition," she said, gesturing to her tummy, "she'd be more open to our union. Your presence will only complicate things."

"Why now? We agreed to go after the baby comes."

"I am doing it for this baby, for her safety. Should we not try to appease the dibia before she is born?"

He scowled.

"At least promise me you'll think about it?" Margaret said.

"I will think for a very long time," Benjamin said, still scowling.

▼▲▼

Two weeks after their exchange, news reached Margaret that Ma Adaora was dead. It was Benjamin who'd opened the letter, as he did with all their correspondence. And it was he—his face damp with sweat—who held Margaret as she scanned through its contents.

In January, while Margaret was seven months pregnant, they made their way back to Umumilo for the burial, a solemn and abbreviated affair since they only arrived on the day Ma Adaora was laid in the ground, and left the next day. One of Margaret's cousins—one of Ma Adaora's other grandchildren—had visited Margaret's old flat and gotten her new address from a neighbor; this was how they came to find her living with Benjamin. They were surprised that she could do such a thing—have a quiet wedding as she had said, if indeed she had had this claimed wedding. It was a betrayal. An abomination. The fact that she had married against the counsel of the elders. And worse, that Ma Adaora had not been around to sanction it. For this reason, the wider family had sidelined Margaret in the burial plans. She, who was Ma Adaora's closest grandchild, and named after Ma Adaora herself, had become second-class offspring, only learning about decisions after they were made. They returned quietly to Lagos after the burial, despite the gossip and silence from her communal peers. Margaret told Benjamin that it did not matter. That she had never been close to these people anyway. Yet, more of her other cousins and kinsmen visited her in their Lagos flat, almost as though propelled by the news of her pregnancy. Some of them congratulated her on the baby. We wish you had told us; we assumed it was just an affair, we assumed you would outgrow him, they explained. On the other hand, Benjamin had started to move with extreme caution around Margaret since the news of Ma Adaora's death. It was as if he was waiting for Margaret to fall apart. But she did not. He worried about her condition, about their baby, especially since Margaret's behavior had been a little unsettling just weeks before. In any case, he at least made sure to be home an hour earlier than usual. He made their dinners. He washed their clothes. If Margaret coughed or sniffed, he was by her side. Occasionally he would think about their conversation in December, how emphatic Margaret had been about visiting Ma Adaora. But was he not right to protect his wife? He wondered if Margaret blamed him for robbing her of that final goodbye. He wanted to bring it up with Margaret—his concerns, his feelings of guilt. But she seemed to sense it and push it away. In the immediate weeks after they returned, she became very practical, preparing for their new arrival, arranging furniture, shopping. And any other free time she had, she spent entertaining distant relatives. By the first week in March, their baby was born. Nwando Priscilla Fletcher. They'd named her Nwando because it meant child of peace, or a child of consolation—a blessing that followed a bereavement or disaster. They'd also chosen Priscilla to honor Benjamin's grandmother. The infant brought new demands to their routines. If there was a right time to talk about Ma Adaora, it was now long gone. Once the child arrived, everything changed.

▼▲▼

The last time Margaret and Benjamin were together, Margaret had not combed her hair for a full week. She'd not taken a bath for almost three days, and she had stopped breastfeeding the baby, who was only seven months old. Benjamin had arranged for a domestic helper—a middle-aged matron who came to the house daily. She cooked and cleaned; she made formula and akamu for the baby. When Benjamin returned home in the evenings, he would take over Nwando's care from the matron, as he often found Margaret still in bed, her face unwashed, her shirts sometimes smeared with soup or stew. He learned from the matron how to strap the baby across his back with a wrapper. Sometimes he sang. He made faces. He read to her.

It was grief, Benjamin reasoned, thinking about Margaret. It was all the emotion she had bottled up in the weeks following Ma Adaora's death. Sometimes, when he returned, the housekeeper would explain to him—Madam did not allow me inside; madam slammed the door shut. Sometimes he would think about Cynthia, about what she had said about Margaret being moody, the talk around the office. Then he would think about his mother. She'd finally wanted to come to Nigeria after the baby arrived, but Benjamin convinced her it was not the right time. Margaret was sick; maybe with depression, since her grandmother died, Benjamin said in his letter. His mother had written back. "Well, she has a child of her own now. Tell her to come out of it."

One day, after Benjamin returned from work, the housekeeper nudged him toward the veranda; she wanted to talk. Benjamin nodded. But first, he went to their bedroom to check in on Margaret. She was still in her nightwear, but Nwando was beside her, giggling. Margaret had her hand on the child, tickling her, making sounds. Mummy loves you, she'd said. Then she tickled again. It was the most tender image he'd had of Margaret and Nwando in many months. He turned and followed the housekeeper to the veranda.

"Oga, don't be angry by what I say," the matron began.

"Is everything all right?"

"It's your wife, my madam. I think she needs to be in a special place for people like her."

"People like her?"

"Yes. People in her condition."

"Her condition?" It occurred to Benjamin that he was repeating her words.

"Yes, don't be angry, oga. I mean like psychiatric hospital."

Benjamin felt like he'd been slapped.

"Psychiatry?"

"What I mean is she needs to be with people like her," the matron said again.

There was a weight in his stomach. A tremor in his left palm.

"Oga, are you understanding me?" the woman pressed.

"I think you've made your point," Benjamin hissed. He excused himself and went to the bathroom.

They had circled this mountain too many times. There had been signs. Her dreams. The abrupt disappearances. Even the rumors at the office. Benjamin asked himself why it took the conversation with the housekeeper to make him place the dots in a single line. He'd always known that something was not quite right, but he thought it was just women's trouble.

What would his mother say? How would they cope—how would Margaret ever be able to go to school, accomplish her goals? He had not agreed to this, he thought that night, barely able to sleep.

The next day, in the middle of a conversation with the director, Benjamin was suddenly struck with a vision of his father from years ago. Love had to be practical, his father would say. Think, boy, think. His head was heavy, his mind in a fog. Now what? he wondered. He'd been thinking about the best thing to do. But for whom? The image of his father struck him again, and he suddenly felt as though he was choking. He excused himself, went to the loo, loosened his tie. His hands were shaking. He was sweating. Think, boy, think. Of course his father's advice had not stopped his father from having an affair with the Ghanaian woman. Benjamin had merely followed in the footsteps of his father, and his grandfather—falling for these African women, walking into love that was cursed from the beginning. He sat on the floor in the bathroom, the smell of urine filling his nostrils. Think, boy, think. He tried to calm his breathing, willed his hands to stop shaking. He was a man—he would think things through. Of course he would figure things out.

On that last day together, Benjamin had come home from work with a bag of groceries. He had gone shopping and so had a full bag of smoked fish and cabbage and tomatoes; three packs of peanuts, roasted just the way Margaret liked them. The television was off, the flat quiet, which surprised him; Margaret liked the background noise. He knew the housekeeper would have left, so he went to the bedroom in search of Margaret. When he did not find her, he unbuttoned his shirt, already sensing the familiar fear building in his chest. He looked in the bathroom, on the veranda. There was no sign of Margaret or the baby. He felt his hands begin to shake again. His head throbbed; he leaned against the wall and inhaled. He felt for his watch in his pocket—it had not been too long since the housekeeper left. Surely they were close by. He tried to move but found that he could not. Could not breathe. His hands were cold, jittering. He clasped both hands together and willed himself not to think of his father. Seconds passed, and he heard a cry from behind him. It was at this point that he moved to the kitchen. He found them both on the kitchen floor. Margaret sat on the bare brown tiles, resting against the fridge, mumbling beneath her breath. Except for her black brassiere, she was topless, her wrapper tied around her waist. The baby was at the other end of the kitchen, next to the dustbin, a smeared diaper in a heap beside her. Benjamin tried to reach for the child, but he found he could not move. He stood there, as though glued to the kitchen entrance. Think, boy, think. His father's image resurfaced in his mind against his own will. His chest. Why did it feel like he had been running? He took in the sight of his wife and child. Once again, he willed himself to move toward the child. But he could not. The room smelled of defecation. The child cried louder. Margaret looked at him. His heart screamed inside his chest. Think, boy, think. He could see his own father now, in the hospital where he'd been pronounced dead. Was this going to be his fate too? He could not breathe. He closed his eyes. He opened them and the child was still there, though she had stopped crying. Think, boy, think.

Finally, he turned into their bedroom and began to pack his bags.

18

Margaret

Umumilo, 2005

The room was lit by the soft yellow glow of the ceiling bulb. The damp air smelled of tobacco and palm wine and mouth odor, a musty mix that made Margaret exhale sharply. The dibia began to speak; he sat close enough to Margaret that his saliva landed on her upper lip, her left ear, the edge of an eyelash. Still, she did her best to sit quietly on the mat laid out on the ground, her legs crossed into each other; pain stabbed at her knees from the effort. She would not allow temporary discomfort to cloud the purpose of this meeting, she thought. Alongside Margaret and the dibia were Matthias and five of her cousins—her kinsmen; all eight of them crammed against one another so that their shoulders touched and one person's breath carried to the next. The dibia was an older man, two years shy of eighty, but strong enough to perform his duties without any concerns. On this day, he hosted the meeting in his personal obi, with his elderly wife and grandchildren in the vicinity. Usually, these affairs were conducted at designated shrines tucked away at the edge of the village, in parts of the city that were as much forgotten as the customs of the people. But over the years, the Gods, too, had evolved. They now dwelt in homes, occupying alternative spaces that the people assigned to them.

Initially, Margaret tried to fix the cleansing into a single event. She wanted to have one central ceremony with her entire family where the solution to her problems would be announced or performed. But the dibia told her things did not work that way. She would need to come for the consultation before the final cleansing. It was during this consultation that she would be told the specific requirements of the cleansing. Margaret listened and wondered if Benjamin would remember the last time, when they had both visited a dibia those many years ago. She wondered if he still thought of it as nonsense.

The dibia explained something else, but she'd missed his last two sentences, so he nudged her with his elbow. She looked at him now with the same muffled silence that made her ignore the smell of the room. She was here on his terms; she would do everything they wanted. Her cousin Matthias explained to her that the dibia would provide a list of the items that were needed. Sometimes a goat, a ram, chickens, tubers of yam. In rare cases, some unreachable exotic item like the tusk of an elephant, the skin of a snake. These days, it was mostly monetary equivalents. Margaret nodded at Matthias vigorously, of course, grateful that she could write a check and measure up with what was needed. She felt adequate to these demands even though she was alone in the village, having arrived ahead of Nwando. Soon she would be surrounded by Nwando, Chuka, Nosa. And even him—Benjamin. Soon, in a matter of hours, she would reunite with the man she once thought she would grow old with.

She tried to keep the reason for her visit quiet—admonishing Matthias and the others to be discreet. It was nobody's business; they would conduct their affairs and be done with it. Although Margaret had not returned to Umumilo in many years, she was not surprised that news about her affairs still found its way to the people. The village had a way of extracting the private details of her life. It started during the war years with a small rumor by the kinsfolk who described her as Nwa Okolo—the descendant of Okolo whose senses had escaped her. In short, the rumors about her health swept through the townspeople in hushed whispers, and her absence did not do much to help her reputation.

In fact, the village was still reeling from the last rumors it had heard about Margaret, even though the event happened fifteen years ago. It was right when Nwando and Nosa had just married. Months before then, mother and daughter had locked horns over certain decisions about the wedding—the venue, the drinks to serve, which caterers to use, if Nwando should be marrying Nosa at all. As the wedding drew closer, Margaret insisted that they had to keep a low profile, being the private person that she was. She had said to her daughter, "You should do something small. Why call all that attention to yourself, to the family?"

"Mummy, who knows us? What attention are we calling? You are not even thinking what Nosa might want, what his family might want," Nwando said.

Margaret decided to share the particular incident that fueled her caution. Early that February, she explained to Nwando, when the oil company she worked for was about to launch its pilot leadership training program in Warri, they'd set up a press conference. During the press conference, one of the journalists—he was wearing a green coat, Margaret was sure of this, and he was wearing an adire hat, Margaret was also sure of this. The said journalist raised a hand to ask Margaret what he could do to ensure that his sixteen-year-old daughter got into this leadership training program.

"Can you imagine?" Margaret had said to Nwando as she narrated the incident.

"What's not to imagine, Mama? Everybody wants the best for their child; no one believes they can get anything by merit alone. Can you blame him?"

"That's not what I am saying, Nwando. Listen to me, let me finish," Margaret answered. She leaned toward her daughter, motioning her over with her right hand in a conspiratorial gesture.

"This man has not dropped the matter. He has been following me for some time now. He has not given up. I act like I don't know, but he has been lurking around in the office," Margaret explained.

"Following you how, Mummy?" Nwando asked, her eyes sharp and questioning. "Are you sure you are not imagining this? Should I be worried?"

"Don't be silly, you know I'm fine," Margaret replied, irritated. "Anyway, I don't want anyone to think we are using the company's money to fund your wedding."

"What do you mean? Nosa is paying for everything."

"Yes, but people don't know that. Besides, I am not comfortable with the way you go on about his paying. We can carry our weight too."

Neither Nwando nor Margaret had discussed the journalist incident again. The wedding came and passed, and everything seemed to have settled.

However, one evening, a few weeks later, while returning from work, Margaret had asked her driver to stop by the market so she could buy fresh fish. It was Friday, and Margaret knew that her house help would come around the next day, that she could send her to get the fish when she came, but she also wanted to be in the market herself, feel her hand deep inside the freezer as she rubbed the scales of all the fish frozen together. She had just made the purchase, and the seller had brought out his knife to cut off the heads—she never could stand fish heads. She reached her clean left hand into her purse to count out the money in crisp ten-naira notes. As she raised her head to face the seller, she caught a glimpse of the journalist outside the shop. He was standing on the street, wearing his green coat and adire hat. Their eyes locked. Startled, the journalist turned around and began to run. Margaret, wanting to put an end to the harassment, began to chase him.

And so it was that she removed her shoes, her jacket, her wig—and she ran. She jumped over the potholes and the gutters, vaguely aware of young men rushing out of their shops, of her own driver shouting, "Madam, wait, wait, what is the matter?" All she knew was that she was tired of hiding, tired of avoiding this man and his dirty green coat. She had to give him a talking-to today, once and for all. Eventually, what stopped her was a nail in her foot. She stepped on it and there was blood; then she tripped and fell into the gutter. By the time she fully recovered from her two-day admission at the hospital, her cousin who had arrived in the city from the village came to pay her a visit. He said he wanted to check if she was all right, if the rumors were true. When she asked what rumors, he shrugged. The one everybody is talking about, he said finally. They are saying that Mama Margaret ran mad in the marketplace.

Now that she had returned to the village, she could almost feel the weight of the people's collective memory. The eyes boring into her. This was why she did not want to pose any resistance or engage in any negotiations. Whatever the dibia asked, she would do. Whatever they wanted, she would give. And if somehow word got around that she had returned to find a cure—that all her money could not treat the sickness in her head—then so be it. She would face a thousand rumors, a thousand pointed fingers, if it all meant there was a possibility that Chuka would be free of the curse. She was grateful that she'd prevailed on Nwando and that Chuka would be present for the cleansing, but it was a close call, since her daughter repeatedly tried to change her mind.

"You can't be serious," Nwando said to Margaret when she revealed that even Chuka had to be present for the cleansing. "This is the middle of the school term; he needs to concentrate."

"It's only one week at the most," Margaret replied.

They were speaking on the landline connection, and it was raining, and the sound seemed muffled so both Margaret and Nwando spoke in raised voices.

"What will I tell him?" Nwando shouted. "I'm not going to fill his head with your stories."

"Tell him it's a family reunion," Margaret shouted back, feeling the strain of a headache. "His grandfather is coming, isn't he?"

"Yes—but why does Chuka have to come? I don't understand," Nwando said again.

Margaret moved the phone away from her ear, looked at it, and pulled it close again. "What do you mean you don't understand—have you forgotten what happened the other day?"

"How will this ritual change what happened?"

"They are angry. We have to appease them. Have you not heard anything I have said to you?"

"Okay—so, if they are no longer angry, Chuka will start to behave better. Is that what you are saying, Mama?"

"Exactly."

"And what about you? Will you also start to feel better?"

"This is not about me. You must find a way for the boy to be here; otherwise, it will all be for nothing." Margaret dropped the phone without saying goodbye.

In the end, it was the boy himself, Chuka, who decided. Nwando called his boarding school mistress from her home landline. She'd said to him, Grandma wants you to come to the village for a week.

"The village," he repeated.

"Yes, there's bad electricity and no cable service," she mentioned, trying not to sound obvious. She heard Chuka laugh at something another boy said in the background.

"You know what? Don't worry about it. I'll tell Grandma you have your mock exams for graduating year."

"Will you be in the village?" Chuka asked, still distracted.

"Yes."

"And Grandma will be there?"

"Yes, but it's just us grown-ups."

"But Grandma wants me to be there," Chuka suddenly said, serious.

"Yes, but I can come up with an excuse, we can say that—"

"It's okay, I'll go," he finished.

After a quick pause he asked if he could bring his friends.

"No, Chuka. What part of family reunion did you not understand?"

Nwando had called Margaret that night to say, "I guess you have won. Chuka has agreed to come with us." Then she added, "But, Mama, it's just for a few days. He needs to concentrate on his studies."

This was how they concluded the matter. Now Margaret sat at the dibia's obi, from where she could only anticipate the coming resolution of things. As of early that morning, Nwando and Chuka were already in the city and would no doubt be in the hotel by now. Benjamin was supposed to arrive with Nosa much later in the day.

Margaret looked at the dibia as he moved through his collection of totems. A short broom made of dried raffia, some tobacco powder spread in a small wooden bowl, water that appeared stale but was in fact meant for prayers, a tray of familiar spices. He muttered some ancient Igbo incantations that were heavily rhythmic to Margaret's ears, so that she briefly thought it was a shame that there were no

English translations to the chants. She thought about her Christian faith again, her church before she stopped going to church altogether—the idea of a virgin birth; a God who became flesh; the sweeping adventures of the patriarchs; the Red Sea parting, a man in the belly of a fish. She did not have a problem believing the Bible. What she did not understand was why Nwando would believe those things but refuse to believe Margaret when she said that the voices in her head were aggrieved spirits seeking compensation. How was it not clear that reality had no boundaries—that life and spirit were as inextricable as life and death?

"Maggie, the message has arrived," the dibia said, interrupting Margaret's thoughts. He gestured to Margaret.

"Take this bowl—jiri nwayo—be careful, there is no rush," the dibia said, as though speaking to a child. "Now—take a breath and think about what you desire for your family. The reason that you have come all this way."

Margaret collected the bowl, held it with both of her hands, placed it on her thigh. She'd arrived at the dibia's at about noon, but the ritual, which was a mix of incantations and silence, entailed long periods of waiting. They were now surrounded by night, with nothing but the sound of crickets and the whispers of the dibia's wives and grandchildren in the air. It had not occurred to Margaret that she could arrive in this moment and feel even slight hesitation. She knew what had brought her here—her desire was clear: to end the curse once and for all, to ensure that her grandson, Chuka, was protected from all this. Still, when the dibia asked her to think about her desire, she paused. What happens if the curse is lifted? Would she then be well, like Nwando had asked earlier? And if so, would it erase the years she had lost? What exactly would change about her life?

It occurred to her that she could erase the curse, but she could not erase the life it had already given her. Or erase what it had already taken from her. She held the bowl and found herself speaking to her Christian God, asking him to take control. Then she prayed to her ancestors, asking them to bless her mission.

I want to clean out this scourge on my family. This sickness ends with me, she thought. She returned the bowl to the dibia.

He took the bowl from her, peered into it. Then he turned his face away, as though he had been exposed to something unsightly.

"Nna anyi, what is it?" Matthias asked.

"We will do the mixture again; perhaps there was an error. This is a hard bargain," he replied.

"No, nna anyi, tell us what it is, we can take it. We would not have come here unless we were ready."

The dibia turned to Margaret and asked, "Are you sure this is what you want? There can be no going back. Once I pronounce it, it cannot be taken back."

"I am sure," Margaret said.

"Very well. This is the verdict of Agwu and the judgment of the ancestors," the dibia announced. "Life in exchange for life. The only way to correct this is the equivalent return of one of you."

"What do you mean?"

Margaret searched the dibia's face silently, suddenly aware of the strands of hair dangling from his nostrils, of his thin grayed eyebrows.

"Since your ancestor Olisa never got the death that was due to him, one of his descendants must die to account for his sins."

"You mean his direct descendants," one of the cousins said.

"By blood or by marriage," the dibia finished.

"But he is long dead. Surely his sin should be atoned for by his death," Margaret said.

"That is true—but he did not die at the hands of the Gods and therefore his crime has not been avenged. The blood of one of the defiled virgins still speaks."

"Forgive us, nna anyi, it appears you must spell it out for us, so that we do not leave with confusion," Matthias interjected.

"The matter is already concluded," the dibia said. He settled the bowl by his side, some of its contents spilling on the ground. Matthias peeked at the container as though he might see what the dibia had seen.

"But I thought the curse—I thought it was about my marriage to the foreigner."

"And?"

"And we have not been married for many years now. We have since parted ways." Margaret was scrambling for solutions.

He shook his head. "Perhaps my uncle whom you saw those years ago was not precise. It is about the foreigner, but it is also about you. It is about the sin of your father's father. It must be avenged."

"Is there another way?" Margaret said now. "I can triple the amount for the ritual."

The dibia shook his head and began to adjust his wrapper.

"The verdict is clear," he said again. "One member of the family will have to pay. It will happen before the year runs out," he finished.

▼▲▼

"You know this makes no sense, Mama," Nwando said.

They were at the hotel Nwando had booked in Ekwulobia; Chuka was downstairs swimming in the pool even though his mother had asked him not to. Nwando faced the window, peering out at the dusty red streets. There was a man dressed in dirty clothes, standing before a roasted corn seller. The man scratched his groin, then placed the same hand on the corn, turning it around. From where she stood, Nwando could hear their banter in Igbo. The man was asking to get some cobs of corn for free—after all, no one had stopped to purchase one all afternoon. The seller called him a drunk, then waved him off. But he stood there, unrelenting, looking at the corn, his eyes wide with hunger. As Nwando watched, transfixed by the exchange, she remembered an incident from her undergraduate days when her roommate had died while away on holiday. It was now this image of that roommate that suddenly consumed Nwando as she thought about the dibia's verdict of death.

It is true that Nwando's life was filled with absences—the father who was never there, a mother who was only half in her mind. She had grown up with the absence of siblings, outliving the phase where she relentlessly pursued the idea of sisterhood. But death? The idea that her life could be marked by a loss that was that permanent? She felt a chill.

"It makes absolutely no sense," she repeated, turning away from the window, closing the blinds.

"How much of my life has made any sense?" Margaret asked.

It was a simple question, softly spoken from where she sat at the edge of the bed, holding the pillow in her hands. But it sounded like a slap.

"How can you say that, Mama? What about me? Do I not make any sense? What about Chuka? Have we not made any sense?"

Even as she uttered the words, Nwando knew that there was no point, that her mother had created a story in which she was both the villain and the hero, the source of the problem and the one who would correct it.

"I have made my decision, Nwando. If somebody will die, it will be me. If somebody must go, it has to be me; I am doing it for you and Chuka."

"This is ridiculous; you are not a martyr. That old man is not God, he does not get to decide who lives and who dies."

"I want to discuss my burial plans when we return to Lagos."

"I will have no such discussion," Nwando said. She laughed a small laugh as the absurdity became even more apparent. "In fact, the moment my father gets here, we are leaving."

They sat silently beside each other, the sides of their thighs touching. It was just another phase, another hurdle, Nwando was sure of it. They had been at this junction time and time again, trying to solve a problem that they both knew was unsolvable.

Nwando got up, walked back to the window, tugged at the blinds, disappointed that the spectacle between the roasted corn seller and the man had come to an end. Soon she would meet Benjamin, the stranger with whom she had been speaking, whom she had accused of betraying her. His flight had been delayed. She had thought, at first, that it was him making excuses, an attempt to wring himself out of the commitment. But he'd also kept asking about Margaret, not always directly, but always leading the conversation there. Yes, yes, he was coming down at Margaret's request. Still, he wanted to know what time she would arrive, if they would all ride to the village together, what Margaret did in her leisure time these days, if she was seeing anyone. He did not ask the last question so directly. He asked instead if she had many friends, and then, if her friends were men. Nwando shook her head at the memory of that question. Nwando might have been amused if she wasn't so distracted. Now Benjamin would arrive and listen to Margaret speak about this so-called verdict. And Nwando would have to look him in the face and say that the woman he had come all this way to save has volunteered to die. Or worse, that if she did not volunteer herself, some member of the family would die instead. Can you even believe this! she'd declare to him. Of course, they would laugh about it. Then they would return to Lagos, where they would talk about his life; he would spend time with Chuka, and then he would return to America, and that would be the end of this whole thing. Unless, unless . . . No, it made no sense. Her mother was getting worse despite taking her medicines; it was time to commit her to the hospital, try something else. Nwando saw it now, clear as the sand on the streets, there was absolutely nothing to worry about; she would play along until Benjamin arrived. Perhaps even until the cleansing, and then she would see that Margaret got the help she needed.

19

The Kinsmen

Umumilo, 1906

In his first few weeks, the baby could barely suckle. When Priscilla held him up to her breasts, he'd turn his head away, his face twisted in distress. He'd come earlier than he was supposed to and was, therefore, too small, too pale. Priscilla did not think he would live, not if he continued to reject her milk, and not now with his father gone, along with those profuse promises about life in Europe. In the face of Derek's death, their courtship had become, to Priscilla, a lie, all their plans unraveled by his absence. Priscilla would have to revise those plans; this time around, she wanted to create a life that felt fixed and dependable, sturdy enough to hold up her son. In this world, Priscilla thought, one could live either at its center or as an outsider—a stranger watching from the margins. This had become her reality. An unmarried woman with a bastard son was an outsider. With the realization of her new status in society came a sudden and intense hunger—a hunger to belong, to be welcomed back among her people, perhaps even the hunger to carry a man's name, to come under the protection of his social standing. She, who had once secretly enjoyed the sense of alienation she felt from her people, who had loved a man so devastatingly different from her people, now wanted only to return home.

They started their lives—mother and infant son—at the outskirts of the village, in the small hut where Derek had lived, where their son had been conceived. This forgotten place was close enough to the church, where a distressed Father Patrick had insisted she should remain. But there was only so much the morning mass she still attended could do to protect Priscilla from the pointing fingers of her people. The villagers had made it clear; she was not to be seen—the child who defecated at the feast of his brothers surely could not be allowed to dine with them. No. They had to remain outcasts. They refrained from being seen in public, from trips to the market, the farms; Priscilla only went to the river early, before the village awoke. Yet, Priscilla wanted to protect her fussing infant son from that same hunger, from the pain of needing for his life to matter in a way that society said it did not. But she also knew that the extent of a mother's power was to provide nourishment. The choice to eat was not up to her. She could provide the breast, the milk, but she could never regulate his appetite.

Priscilla's days became increasingly smaller, moving from hunger to contemplation, tightening around the struggle to feed her child, to shake him awake with life. Her suffering was severe and yet so simple, the pattern unchanging until one unsuspecting evening when she came upon the vagabond himself. The boy—for he was to her eyes but a boy—had forced himself on the two other women, maybe more, but not on her. She had lost nothing to him. If anything, it was she who had taken from him, she thought. It was she who had wrapped her pregnancy around his shadow. Yet, Priscilla could not explain the instant hatred she felt for him initially. Perhaps it was the fact that he took from those women their most prized possession; perhaps it was the sting of her own loss, sharp as a fresh burn. When her son was but two weeks old, she had gone to the church through the back bushes, hoping to get some yams and cooked food from Father Patrick. In truth, she merely wanted some company, for she had not seen her brother Okolo in all that time. But the atmosphere was stilted; even the leaves of the bushes seemed to sway with malice. Umumilo had become a grave site, a village haunted by its ghosts. On her way to the church that Sunday morning, she did not expect to see Adaora, whose stomach was fully blown, whose face had become nearly twice its usual size. They saw each other at the same time. The bush was dense with trees, but the day was bright enough for the sun to fall through the small forest.

"And what are you looking at?" Adaora hissed.

"Nothing. Forgive me," Priscilla answered in dialect. She made to turn to the other side but remembered she was heading to the church.

"Did you hear that Nneka died last week?" Adaora said to her back.

Priscilla stilled for a moment but continued walking, so Adaora picked up a small branch and threw it at her. Priscilla's son cried out, and it startled both Priscilla and Adaora.

"Her baby came early. Like yours. But her body was not ready," Adaora continued.

Priscilla did not know what to say, how to relate to these women. It was not her body that had been violated.

"Is that your boy?" Adaora asked, walking to Priscilla. "Let me see." She unwrapped the cloth that covered the baby, then shook her head.

"What is it?" Priscilla asked.

"Nothing," Adaora said. After a small pause, she added, "At least you wanted it."

It was then Priscilla saw that Adaora had been crying, that the swell of her cheeks was not just from pregnancy but from tears.

"When he comes," Priscilla said, looking at Adaora's stomach, "it will not matter whether you wanted it or not; you will only see that you must care for it, that you will fear for its life; and when that happens you will see that you love it."

Even as she said it, she could sense the falsehood of her words, but she had wanted to comfort Adaora somehow. Standing in her own guilt, the best she could offer was the lie she had told herself—that something good could come out of such loss.

Adaora stepped back, almost startled by the statement. She looked at Priscilla, then laughed. "I could never love this child," she said, and she turned around and walked away.

Over the next few weeks, Priscilla recalled this encounter with Adaora, the platitude she had offered, her own silence when she heard of Nneka's death. Nneka—only a child.

Was some of the blame on her?

▽△▽

Before Bassey's demise, he had returned to Okolo with news that Mr. Walter wanted to see him again.

"Have you thought about our offer?" Mr. Walter said, speaking through Bassey.

"I know what you want," Okolo began. "I know what you will get, you and your people—but you have not told me what I or my family will get in exchange."

"Your sister, of course. She has been shunned, has she not? We can bring her back to society." After a pause, he added, "In the process we can also make you a very rich man."

Okolo laughed. "Your money is of no use to me. What would my people get?"

Bassey interpreted. He went into a spasm of coughs, then sat down.

"What about influence? You will be well respected if you work with us."

"Respect?" He laughed again. "Of what use is your respect to me? I have a title among my people, one that I won with my own bare hands."

"Ah, but you're mistaken. This is a small village; the respect you have is only within these circles. There are men outside your village with power—real power. And they do not know you, my friend." Mr. Walter walked up to Okolo, touched him on the shoulder. "Think of the life you could afford your family, your children. Think about Priscilla."

There were few things as honorable as a good name, a good reputation. And he, Okolo, had a good name. But his good name had become redundant in the shadow of the white man's presence. Okolo thought about Priscilla then, hiding away in the village, her baby sickly. These men could send her off, and then what? What would become of her?

"What do I have to do?" Okolo asked.

"If you take this offer, you will become our mouthpiece—intervening between the Crown and your people," Mr. Walter said.

"I may work with you," Okolo grunted, "but I do not submit to any Crown except Agwu and my ancestors."

"Very well. We can arrange something."

"And I will do nothing to harm my people," Okolo added.

Bassey interpreted, and Mr. Walter laughed. "As you wish," he said. "We have an assignment already. If you pass this test, we have an agreement."

"Hmm," he grunted. "What is it?"

"Your sister—we will leave her be. I hear she speaks English. She can take work with the school; she will have a modest but respectable life."

Okolo nodded.

"However, we received an urgent telegraph recently. The boy's relatives have sent for the child."

"And?"

"This is your mission. You must deliver the child to his relatives."

"My sister's child? My own nephew?"

"Your sister may have birthed him, but he is a son of the Crown."

Okolo looked at Bassey, then at Mr. Walter. He shook his head, but he did not leave.

He had barely agreed to their treaty, and already they had tasked him with the impossible.

⩔⩓⩔

"So, you are well?"

"I am well, my brother."

"And the baby, he is well? He has all that he needs?"

"We are fine, nna anyi—the baby is fine; a little quiet, but I am sure with time he will grow into himself."

"The child, he looks sick, he is too thin," Okolo said, holding the boy in his hands.

It was a tender image to Priscilla's eyes, her brother holding the child.

In the weeks that followed the death of Derek, after the guns had been fired, and Thomas and Boko had dropped to the ground, Priscilla thought that she would never see Okolo again, that she would never watch him pace the ground searching his thoughts for the solution to a problem, that she would not hear him whistle that flute sound that he liked so much, or complain about young men who had grown too soft, who squirmed at the first sign of a fight. She'd thought that with her betrayal, she had lost her brother, too, and she'd grieved this loss.

Indeed, Okolo was nearly a man when Priscilla was born, and by the time she was old enough to talk and run, he had killed his first antelope. As a child in her father's house, Priscilla had sat on the mat at Okolo's feet while he ate his garri and onugbu soup. She'd waited for him to clear his throat, for any sign that suggested he might need something: a cup of water, a washbowl, extra food. She made sure she was available to run such errands, to serve him in that unstained, wholehearted manner. Even after he married and moved out of their father's compound to start his own life, Okolo had still been the most interesting thing about Priscilla. For while she did not have any striking features, while she stood at the margins and watched the other virgins dance at the village festivals, she, at least, was the youngest sister of the revered Okolo.

Although they did not share the same mother, Okolo had surprised everyone with his keen interest in Priscilla. It was not that he was a particularly emotional man; as his mother's only child, he had grown up playing in the compound alone, chasing chickens and rats. By the time his father married his second and third wives, and their yard sprawled with infant brothers and sisters, Okolo was already fighting in the market, at the roadside; he had no need for the consuming distractions of siblings. And yet, there was that keenness for Priscilla. There were some who said it was because, of all the thirteen children of their father's household, it was Priscilla who most resembled Okolo—that shared flat nose, their eyebrows bushy, arched in the same slant, their two front teeth broken apart by a small space. He permitted Priscilla in his presence even on the nights he refused to see his mother. He answered her endless questions. Once, moved by an unusual dream in which Priscilla was accosted by village hoodlums, Okolo had accompanied Priscilla to the stream and on all the errands that she had to run that day. And so no one was surprised that it was Okolo who opened his household to Priscilla after their father had chased her off. They were not shocked, even when she did the unpardonable and got with child right under his roof. Another man would have been less tolerant, would have distanced himself from the stench of her. Another man would have stopped her from going to the white man's church, from thinking that she could forge—for herself—a life apart from her fathers. Still, Okolo had indulged, and indulged. At the time, Priscilla had been grateful. She had even pitied him when the news of the pregnancies first came out, when the villagers began to mount pressure, when the rumors began that their cherished warrior had a sister who had been spoiled in such an open way. But then, it was also this Okolo who had pushed Father Patrick aside. It was Okolo's outrage that the villagers had followed. It was his dignity they sought to protect, to defend, as they raised those stones to Derek. How was it that she, Priscilla, could love a person so dearly and yet despise him so much?

The first time Okolo came into the hut, two market weeks after she had the child, after Derek had died, she had felt the spit forming in her mouth, a strange dread settling in her stomach. The baby, still very frail, had been on the ground, asleep. She could not look at her brother, this man who had snatched and torn her life to pieces. At first, willing to defy the elders, he had asked her to return home with him; he would care for the child. As a wrestler, he had surmounted greater obstacles; he had torn the flesh of tigers and danced with snakes. Surely raising this baby would be no different. His voice was strong, gruff, his chest taut and tight, but his eyes betrayed his guilt. She had asked him if moving into his place would bring back Derek from the dead, if it would bring back Thomas and Boko. She had asked him if it would make him sleep better at night, knowing that everything rested on his shoulders. She did not expect the blow from him that landed on her face, the way her mouth cracked open under it, the thickness of her own blood. She charged at Okolo, attempting to push, to pull, to exert herself against him in some way. But he struck her again, so that she fell away from him, hitting the ground.

"You will never speak to me this way again," he barked.

"Is it not your fault?" he continued. "If you had not brought this disgrace, hidden your shame under the suffering of other women—it is you who brought this tragedy upon our village." Then he had stomped out, still enraged, but his words remained after he left. Priscilla would not fully come to associate his accusations with herself until the day the vagabond clobbered away at the food in her hands. Maybe it was true; maybe all this was her fault. She had stolen from the village through her deceit. She had dismissed Derek every time he'd brought up the idea of making their relationship known, insisting that she needed the time to be right, that no one would be the wiser. But the baby had been a surprise.

One week after their quarrel, Okolo returned. He brought supplies: Yams. Spices. Parts of a butchered goat. Wood to set up a fire. They did not discuss what happened the last time; it was not the way either of them was predisposed to handle situations. Priscilla offered Okolo the baby, but he refused, saying it was her job to hold the child; it was his to provide. They continued this dance, week after week, Okolo showing up at her doorstep with supplies. Asking questions about the baby, about both of their well-being. Occasionally he sat, offering snippets of information about the village—a new superintendent, another school, a larger parish (he kept from her the details of his own arrest).

However, on this latest visit, Okolo arrived without supplies. This was not an immediate problem because Priscilla had an overflow. But her brother lurked, pacing about the small room so that he covered its breadth in three swift strides, before finally saying:

"Achalugo, you can't go on like this, things may get bad." His words alarmed her; he had not called her by her native name in a long time.

"Is anything the problem, brother? Is there anything you are not telling me?"

"Y-y-your Derek's people, they are coming for the child," he replied.

Priscilla did not hear the rest of what he said. She had spent so much time fearing for the boy's life, and now she saw it was futile; he, too, would be taken away from her, like his father.

"When?" she asked.

"We don't know yet, but someone is coming."

"I will not," Priscilla started. "I will not give up my son."

"The decision is not yours to make."

"And it is yours?" she screamed.

"Yes, sister. Yes, it is mine," Okolo screamed back. "What do you think will happen if we say no? Have you not heard about Thomas and the rest, dead in their prime?"

"I will not allow it; they will have to kill me first," she said.

"They will kill you and they will take the boy," Okolo said.

He made to leave but stopped at the door, turned, and said softly, "You do not fight a battle you cannot win; this is the right thing to do."

20

Margaret

London, 1970–1975

Margaret arrived in Bromley with one agenda—to find Benjamin, to bring him back to his senses. To bring him home. At first she'd been hurt by his abandonment, then confused. Finally, the anger came. It was the kind of anger that settled squarely in her belly and from which she had forged the resilience to continue with her life. The war came months after he left, and she'd put off thoughts about him even then. She'd even found a way to accept the accusations of her people. She had become a proverb to them—the woman who ignored her elders' counsel will eventually be abandoned by her untested allies. Yet, the pain of his abandonment had dulled quite unexpectedly, just as the war ended and families counted their survivors, eager to build their lives afresh. In any case, the idea of reconciliation eased itself into her mind ever so gently. After all, she was raising a child. They had not quarreled. He was not unfaithful. She had to be sensible. She would go to London and show him that things were better with her. They had to try again. It was against the backdrop of these self-made promises that Margaret arrived in London late in June of 1970, alongside her toddler, Nwando.

Before they'd left Nigeria, while packing their belongings, Margaret tried to explain the enormity of her trip to Nwando. "We are going to see your father—and then we will be together as a family." The child did not understand, but it did not matter; once the mission was complete and Benjamin was back with them, the rest would be sorted out.

Shortly after they arrived in London, Margaret had carefully braided Nwando's hair and laid out her pretty green dress, along with her red ribbons, her white knee-high socks, her black moccasin shoes. When Margaret was done, she'd held Nwando away from her and inspected the child—satisfied. They arrived at Benjamin's family home on Windsor Road and knocked on the door. But there was no answer. Margaret knocked again, and continued knocking, each time a little louder, certain that she heard movement, the rustling of curtains, the clinking of a jammed lock. But no one came to them. She looked around the neighborhood, getting a bit nervous. Finally, she squatted toward Nwando and said, "Let's go, we'll come back."

"What about Father?" Nwando had asked.

"And what about him?" Margaret replied. She was already holding Nwando's hand, walking away from the house.

That evening at the hotel, Margaret found the yellow pages phone directory and traced the phone number assigned to the Fletcher address. The next morning, without bathing Nwando or brushing her teeth, she'd pulled the girl by the hand and said, Hurry! We are going to speak to your father on the phone. It was not clear to Margaret why she said these things to Nwando, as if building anticipation in the child's heart would somehow change her fortunes, but she continued to tell those little lies: Your father will come on the call; we will be a family again, see? You might start school here in London. Yet Nwando had seemed detached, almost indifferent—she was a child raised in the shell of a war that had eaten the men. She did not yet know that she wanted a father.

They reached the phone booth, and Margaret inserted the coins, dialed Benjamin's mother's home. Then she waited.

"Fletcher residence?" a shrill voice answered.

"Hallo," Margaret replied. Clearing her throat, she continued. "May I be on to Benjamin, please?"

"And who might I say is calling?"

"Margaret. Tell him it's Margaret." After a short pause, she added, "It's his wife."

The line went still for a long moment.

Margaret used her left hand to smooth her skirt, to smooth Nwando's hair; she put her thumb to her mouth and wet it with spit, then lowered it to Nwando's face, where the child's own saliva had dried against her cheek. Finally, the person on the other end of the line replied.

"Maggie, correct?" the woman at the other end said. "I'm afraid Benjamin no longer lives here."

Margaret did not know what to say; she had not anticipated a situation in which she would arrive at the threshold and find Benjamin, once again, beyond her reach.

"All right," she replied as soon as she gathered herself. "Can you have him reach me at the hotel where I'm staying? You can tell him I'm there with his daughter."

"I'm afraid that's no longer possible," came the reply. "Benjamin now lives in the United States with his wife."

His wife. Margaret felt her chest tighten.

"Ma Fletcher?" Margaret said tentatively. She paused, breathing heavily, then continued. "Ma Fletcher, would you like to meet your granddaughter?"

"Oh, child, I'm afraid you have me mistaken. Benjamin is my

nephew. My sister, his mother, died months ago," the reply came. And then, without any warning, the line went dead.

Margaret had been to London once before. At the time, she was all but a child herself, barely eighteen and one of the three people in her village to have a European education. Two of those three were from the Okolo household. She was the only one who had won a scholarship from her secondary school; the village had raised money for the other two. She'd been there all of fourteen months attending secretary school, and when that long year was done, she'd concluded that this London was not a city for her. She did not like what the cold did to her knees, her hair. She did not like the way that people looked at her when she spoke, strained their ears—the way she had to constantly repeat herself. Moreover, there were better opportunities back home at that time; houses were cheaper, pupils had more respect for teachers, and no one asked her stupid questions about life in the village. Now, over a decade after her last stay in London, and with a small child of her own, Margaret wished she'd been a little more intentional in maintaining her old contacts. Since she'd learned of Benjamin's absence, she was not sure what to do, whom to turn to, how to manage her life in this space that was both strange and familiar. It occurred to her to try again—to visit the Fletcher residence and insist on speaking to the aunt. Was she not her relation by marriage? Was the woman not a little bit curious about Nwando? She could have called back, given the aunt a message for Benjamin; but there was something about learning that Benjamin had a wife. In America. They were not even properly divorced, and already he had a wife. She was not hurt by the news, or confused, or angry; she was embarrassed. In any case, Benjamin was now long gone from her life, and she had to move on.

The Nigeria she left this time was not as eager, or as welcoming, as the Nigeria she'd longed for a decade before. She was not sure what she would be returning to since the Igbos were still licking the wounds inflicted by the war. There were no opportunities. She had no husband. No plans. She therefore decided she would stay in London a little while, work a little bit. It was also at this point that Margaret made the move to rent a room within a two-bedroom flat, occupied already by two other women. She'd found the listing in the newspaper and without thinking, she'd taken the train to the address and signed the subtenancy agreement. When she showed up the next day with Nwando, having not mentioned that she had a child, neither of her flatmates seemed eager to protest.

The room was smaller than the room in the hostel Margaret stayed in during her secretarial studies. There was only one window, which opened to the back of the yard, so that the view outside was simply the row of buildings down the street, and below it, a pile of rubbish. For furniture, Margaret and Nwando had a single bed, which Nwando slept on alone, while Margaret slept on the floor. It was early November when they moved in, which meant the afternoons were already shortened and the city could no longer shake off the grip of coming winter. In spite of the chill, Margaret had, every morning, woken up at precisely five o'clock and opened the window to air out the mold from the room.

Her flatmates hosted dinners a couple times a week with their cliques of hotheaded intellectuals. They watched films and argued loudly, smoked, and discussed the state of women in society. Margaret did everything she could to avoid them. How could she possibly explain to them that she had no quarrel with men, or with the state of society; that her daughter simply needed a father, and that she herself wanted a husband who was now married in America? She admired their devotion but also thought that their protests did not feel practical to her in that moment. What she wanted—needed—was a kind of useful intervention, a way to remain in London. She needed a job to sustain her child and herself—and for God's sake, she would like to have a simple night of dreamless sleep. She'd told the women that she'd come to visit relatives but that there were some complications; she was not sure how long she would stay, though she had already inquired about a school nearby for Nwando. After Margaret enrolled Nwando, she came to her own decision. She would take the examination to get her law degree, and once she was done, she and Nwando would return home.

And so their lives in London began.

In those early months, Margaret's routine had been simple. Wake up before her flatmates, sneak into the kitchen and pack lunch, which was often slices of bread with cheese and tomatoes—it was all Margaret could afford, and for many years after, neither Margaret nor Nwando would see a sandwich and not feel their stomach tighten, their hunger suppressed. As soon as Margaret was finished packing the lunch, she'd sneak into the bathroom, leaving the lights in the hallway off. Then she'd shower with near military precision. It was only then, after she was clean and dressed, her hair braided into cornrows, or sometimes left in an Afro, that she would wake Nwando. It was an efficient system. She and Nwando would leave the house before the first flatmate woke, and they would return too late, too tired, for meaningful conversation.

There was one additional thing Margaret had taken to doing in these quiet months—sweep through the yard with a flashlight before dawn. The first time it happened, it was because she'd quietly carried a feeling that she was being watched through the night. That first morning, she had told Nwando to go back to sleep because she wanted a moment to check something outside. Nwando asked her, What is it, Mummy, what is it? But Margaret told her to shush, to go back to sleep, it was nothing. It was that same night that Nwando began to pee in the bed.

On one particular morning, after Margaret had opened the windows, packed lunch, and taken her shower, she returned to the room to wake Nwando.

"It's time to get up," she said, softly at first, tapping Nwando on her shoulder. But her gentleness, it appeared, was wasteful caution. Nwando, in this regard, was like her father—she could sleep through anything.

"It's time to get up," Margaret said again, this time hurried, impatient. She remembered her own mother waking her from sleep when she was a child, singing to her with a voice that reached Margaret in her dreams, and she felt a pang of guilt. She had never sung to Nwando. But her mother, admittedly, did not need to wake her as frequently as she had to wake Nwando. As a child it was mostly Margaret who started the day in her household, waking before her mother and father, before the chickens.

Without meaning to, Margaret liked to think of her relationship with Nwando through the lens of her relationship with her own mother. It was her way of keeping score of the things she was doing right, the things she wanted to do differently, or better. But no matter how many items she ticked on her list—feed the child, wash the child's hair, comfort her when she cries—Margaret still felt that there was something unusual about her relationship with Nwando. There was one more impulse she could not quite put into words—she only referred to Nwando as the child, even during conversation with other people. The first time it struck Margaret was at the one-week mark of her stay at the apartment, when her London flatmates casually apologized for the cramped room, its peeling walls, the small bed. Margaret responded, "It's okay, the child sleeps on the bed, and I sleep on the floor."

"The child?" her flatmate responded.

"Yes, the child; her name is Nwando," Margaret said with a polite smile.

Naturally, on that morning in London, while stirring Nwando awake, Margaret's mind was filled with one thought. The child. I must wake the child now. She did not know why she felt the impulse, or what made it so urgent, only that she must shake, shake the child awake.

"Get up now, we have to go," she said. In the same breath, she pressed her hand softly against Nwando's cheek. Moments later, as they made their way to the train station, heading first to Nwando's school, and then to the campus library where Margaret studied and worked, she felt the brush of an inexplicable instinct and she remembered why she had woken the child with such fervency. She stopped, squatted until she was at eye level with her daughter.

"Did you see him?"

"Is it the man you asked me about yesterday?" Nwando replied, looking at her black moccasin shoes, already beginning to scuff at the toes.

"Yes. Have you seen him now? Tell me."

"No, Mama. I haven't seen him."

"Are you sure?"

Silence.

"Tell me if you have seen him."

"I have not seen Grandpa Okolo," Nwando muttered. She raised her hand to touch Margaret's earring.

"Okay, that's good. Thank God. Remember—if he appears to you, or if somebody else appears to you, you must tell me at once," Margaret said in a whisper.

When Nwando did not say anything, she continued. "Do you understand me?"

"Yes, Mummy, if I see him, I will tell you," Nwando said.

"And what does he look like?"

"He is tall and dark, and his eyes are angry."

"And what must you do when you see him?"

"Tell my mummy."

"Good girl," Margaret said, pulling Nwando to her chest in a hug. She held her like that, first against her stomach, then by her side, the child firmly pressed against her hip.

▼▲▼

"I can't remember the first time I saw him," Margaret said in a whisper.

It had become her habit during her sessions with Dr. Mary Pryce to lean over and speak as quietly as she could. This was in 1975, a year before Margaret returned to Nigeria, two years before she bought the duplexes in Festac and got the job at the oil company.

"You mean the first time he appeared in your dream?" Dr. Pryce asked.

"Yes, the first time I saw him," Margaret said.

"All right."

"Is this a bad thing, that I can't remember the first time I saw him?" Margaret touched her head as if trying to remember.

"It depends."

"On what?"

"On why you think you need to remember him."

"I think he wants me to remember him."

"Who?"

"My grandfather," she said, feeling desperate. The woman wasn't listening.

"Which of your paternal grandfathers? You said you have two of them."

"My real grandfather—Okolo. He's the only grandfather I know."

"And he's the one who comes to you in your dreams?"

"Yes. I mean—no."

"So it is more than one person you see?"

"Exactly. It is my people—the village. They don't want me to forget."

"And when you forget, they punish you?"

Margaret was quiet, chewing on her bottom lip.

"Have you asked them what they want?" Dr. Pryce asked.

Margaret looked at her, suspicious. "You are not getting me. They don't want anything; they are just angry."

This was their regular session together—Margaret and the psychiatrist, Mary Pryce.

Margaret had made it clear in their first meeting that she was not mad. Or sick. That she did not understand what the fuss was about. If it was not for the incident at the library, she would not even be here.

Dr. Pryce had listened quietly.

"It says here in your file that you have occasional episodes of hysteria," she finally said.

"I have bad dreams," Margaret said.

"And these dreams—they only occur in your sleep?"

"Sometimes they bother me when I think of them."

"Tell me about the dreams."

It was here that a reluctant Margaret, for the first time, began to share her dreams with someone other than Benjamin. What did she see, what did the characters look like—what did they want? Dr. Pryce's questions had forced Margaret to look deeper, as though she was close reading one of her legal texts. She'd begun to describe the limbs and eyes, journaling them down in a notebook. Perhaps someday she would share it with Nwando, so she'd know what to look out for. But the questions became bolder, more intrusive. The doctor asked her what the dreams meant—what her grandfather wanted, which elders she saw. She asked her to write down their names, to give them a point of reference to help her remember that they were long dead. "Just because you see a thing does not make it real," Dr. Pryce had told her on that first visit. Meanwhile, as Margaret spent her days with the doctor, her flatmates—whom she had tried so hard to avoid—had taken to watching Nwando. They picked her up from school, made her lunch, did her homework with her, starting the same day that Margaret was locked away in the hospital.

This is what happened. Margaret was at her workstation at the law school library, where she'd taken part-time employment. One of the students walked up to her, wanting to check out a book. She remembered the student placing the book on the counter; she remembered the student tapping her hands on the counter as though in a hurry. And then the next thing she remembered was being restrained by other students. There was a small crowd by the counter at this point. One of the students or visitors—she was not sure which—had slapped Margaret in the face; another spat on her. She remembered feeling like the boundaries of reality were somehow blurring—and then the world went blank. When she woke up, she was in a hospital room with bright fluorescent lights, surrounded by nurses who did not smile. Her hands were chained to the sides of the bed. She had been found out. It was the first time a name was given to her condition—hysteria—although the name would take on many forms during the course of that year: dementia, mania, and, finally, schizophrenia.

Over the years she would think about her condition, for that's what it was to her doctors—a condition, a diagnosis. Not a history or a past. Such a diagnosis, it seemed, was a self-contained unit, complete with symptoms and treatments, and thoroughly defined in the language of science and rationality. A woman's temperament was a result of her hormones. A man's cancer was either genetic or environmental. Every material thing was rooted in another form of material reality. Perhaps this is why she had been stunned by the questions Dr. Mary Pryce had asked her.

"Have you asked them what they want?"

She knew that Dr. Pryce meant this metaphorically. That this question was merely a way for her to say something else.

"You don't understand. They are angry because I married my husband. My grandfather also did something terrible."

"Have you considered that you might be wrong?"

"What do you mean? The events I described are true; this is a history told to me by my grandmother. I'm not imagining it," she argued.

"I understand. But what if your interpretation is wrong? Is it possible that no one is watching you?"

"What do you mean?"

"Perhaps you only think you're being watched. Perhaps this is your way to grieve going against your grandmother's wish. To deal with your guilt."

"But they are watching me!" Margaret was exasperated.

"And you see them watching you?"

"In my dreams, yes."

"And when you wake up?"

"Yes—"

"You see them when you are awake?"

"I feel them. I can feel their eyes."

Dr. Pryce scribbled in her notes. She looked up, adjusted her glasses.

"Look, just because you see something does not mean it is real."

"Humph," Margaret said.

Dr. Pryce prescribed some medications for her, referred her for some tests, and invited her to counseling.

It was in this season—newly introduced to medical treatment and psych counseling—that Margaret gained some control over her life. She finished law school with distinction, saved money, raised Nwando without incident or mishap. It was also in this period that she understood that Benjamin was not coming back at all. The wait had been in vain.

21

Benjamin

Umumilo, 2005

Benjamin was scheduled to travel to Umumilo with Nosa. They'd decided to route his flight through Abuja because Nosa was already in the city for a meeting with a few government officials. It was from Abuja that, together, they would make the trip to the village where Nwando would be waiting with Chuka and Margaret. Benjamin's job was simple—to make it there, to not disappoint. Nwando did not use those exact words, but it was there in the clip of her voice. There were a few updates about Nigeria that Benjamin had gathered while preparing for this trip—news of the rising cases of kidnapping; bandits who targeted people from international flights right outside the airport; in a nation that had enriched some of its citizens and deprived so many at the same time, wealth and poverty living as neighbors. He allowed his mind to walk through old anxieties—the last time he was accosted in Lagos, stories he'd heard through the years about coups and assassinations. He told himself that it was smart to remember that he did not want to be here; that if it were not for Nwando, for his need to connect, repair what was broken, he would not be here at all. He reminded himself that he was here for Chuka, whose picture he had stared at for hours the night before his flight.

Even now, he could still remember seeing Nwando as a baby, on that floor, the dirty diaper with the pile of banana peels and paper wrappers about her. He remembered Margaret, oblivious to their daughter's tears, muttering to herself from where she sat. He reminded himself all through the flight that there was a reason why he left the first time—and that he wanted to keep this reason clear in his mind. He was so close now. So close to being in the same room with them again. But this time around, when it was time to leave, he would do it properly. He reminded himself that he was not coming back to stay. This was not a reconciliation. It was not.

However, he also remembered that he had once come very close to righting his actions with Margaret. It was in 1976. His aunt—his mother's only surviving relative—had taken violently ill, so Benjamin, though not a man to say goodbye, had returned to London with his American wife to pay his final respects. It was supposed to be an easy week. But the day before he was to return to the States, his aunt called him to her bedside.

"There's something you must know, Benni," she said.

She lay on her bed, weak though her fever and cough had abated. Her face glowed, damp with sweat, her eyes sunken with disease.

"You're tired, you should rest," Benjamin said, trying to ease her discomfort.

"The woman from Nigeria—she was here. I thought about writing you," his aunt wheezed.

"The woman from Nigeria?" Benjamin asked.

"Margaret? She was here with a little girl—she claims she brought your daughter."

Benjamin felt his hands go cold.

"When was this? What did you say to them?"

"The truth," his aunt rasped. She tried to sit up but fell back against her pillow.

"What truth?"

"I told her that your mother had died, that you were off in America. Married."

"What is she talking about?" Benjamin's then wife had asked from the doorway. He ignored her.

"When? Where is she now? Tell me," Benjamin said to his aunt.

"Was I wrong? I told her the truth, Benni."

"Do you remember what she said? Where she is staying?"

"I think she mentioned a hotel. Give me a moment to recall," his aunt said.

Benjamin had rushed out of the house as soon as his aunt had named the place—it was two streets away. When he arrived at the hotel, he stopped at the lobby and looked at the hotel clerk—the people checking in and out; he wasn't sure whom to speak to, what question to ask. He wasn't sure if he was ready for any answers. What was it his aunt had said—she was here with a little girl? That she called six years ago? He'd known even then that they could not have stayed in a hotel for six years; that he had missed them; that there was no way to explain what had happened in Lagos. But he also found himself following the pull of his aunt's words. Margaret had been here. She had come. She'd come with Nwando. What if life had given him a second chance? What if he'd missed it? He sat on the floor of the lobby now, willing his hands to stop shaking. The image of Nwando on the floor of that kitchen filled his head again. After waiting for hours, his explanation indecipherable to the hotel workers, he got up from the floor and went home. It was the last time he spoke to his aunt, and it was the final blow to his first American marriage, since the woman was surprised to learn that he had been married before, and that he had a daughter. When she finally filed for divorce years later, she'd explained that it was not so much that he'd kept this former life from her, but that he was the kind of person who could abandon a family in the first place. He had left no clues, given her no reason to suspect. What she meant was that he did not carry any remorse, or if he did, he did not show it.

▼▲▼

"We finally meet, ehn, my father-in-law," Nosa said, laughing.

Nosa had come into the executive airport lounge with the confidence of a man who knew exactly what he was looking for. Benjamin was seated at the end of the bar. Beside him was a couple—seated in the same row—the woman looked Asian, the man was Black, but it seemed not Nigerian; both of them were middle-aged. They were smoking and drinking at this VIP lounge. Benjamin fought the urge to ask for a cigarette. Instead he willed himself to focus on the bland tea he ordered. His eyes were already beginning to pepper in the way they usually did whenever he was tired. He'd barely slept, never been one to nod off in an aircraft. And so, when Nosa's voice boomed from the entrance, Benjamin looked up with unfeigned annoyance. This was his daughter's husband. This loud man with his boisterous public persona whose cologne was so strong it almost drowned out the smell of fresh coffee and cigarettes. He squinted now, trying to read Nosa's body the way he often did others. Nosa was handsome enough, but in a way that was not remarkable. His good looks were born of the fortune of not having any facial mishap. His face was clean—no beard, not even an errant chin hair. He was almost tall, five foot ten, dark-toned—darker than his pictures, and darker, it seemed, on his face than his arms. Then there were his eyebrows, scant; what did the man do with all his hair?

"You are Nosa?" Benjamin said. His voice came out gruff, tired. He winced, hating the sound of it.

"That I am, that I am, my in-law," Nosa said, beaming.

He reached out and hugged Benjamin. It had no bone to it—the hug—as awkward as two schoolboys forced to make up after throwing punches, their chests barely touching. Benjamin decided in that moment that he did not like this man; that perhaps, if he had been around, Nwando would have found someone more suitable. As they exchanged their stifled pleasantries, Nosa raised his hands and two heavy-built men appeared at his side, both of them in dark T-shirts and sunglasses. They turned out to be the security detail that Nosa had arranged. The man moved around with private security. Benjamin was both relieved and amused. You can't be too safe, Nosa had said, reading Benjamin's face. I only use them when I have to make certain trips.

"How was your flight?" Nosa asked.

They'd come out of the lounge and were exiting the terminal. Benjamin could see now that the two men had on their sides what appeared to be guns. There was a slight commotion just outside the airport, nothing too serious, but with these things, one could never tell.

"It was good, long—we didn't expect the delay in Frankfurt."

"Ah, that's one thing with these airlines; they are full of unexplained delays." Nosa laughed. Benjamin grimaced. Then they drove off. It was not until they were inside the vehicle that Benjamin allowed himself to exhale. And it was not until they were speeding out of the airport that he looked out at the landscape. His mind drifted as he watched the stretch of tarred road, the small hills of the city spread on both sides, the greenery, that baked golden filter of the Abuja sun. His mind drifted.

That fateful day after Benjamin abandoned Margaret in their

Lagos home, he'd spent the night with his friend Kunle. The man had taken a long look at him when he arrived at his door and said he hoped there was no problem, how was his wife, and so on. But his questions were brief enough, and soon the conversation turned to other things. The next day Benjamin moved to a hotel since there was only so much he could explain about spending two nights in a row away from his family. Three days later, he took a bus to Ghana. He'd told himself that he was merely taking a break. A man needed his breaks. Once his head was clear, he would go back to Maggie, apologize. He had not planned to leave. After all, leaving required extensive calculation—did it not? And he had barely taken a few shirts in a small bag. Yes, he had left the note for Margaret, but how many times in their quarrels and arguments did she herself say she was tired of him, that she needed a break?

Once Benjamin arrived in Ghana, he decided that he had to see the woman with whom his father had an affair. His father's own secret. He was not sure where he would search, and he did not have many details except her name and that of the organization she worked for. He made inquiries about the woman, surprised to learn that she still worked there. His own father was dead, but her life seemed unchanged. He made a request to see her and arrived at her office on the agreed date. The woman was about forty-five now. She'd remarried and she'd shown no surprise at the mention of his father's death.

"You knew he was married, and you went ahead?" Benjamin asked her when they met.

She looked away from him. "We tried to stop. It's not that simple."

"But you didn't stop."

"Why did you come here?" she asked. "Your father is dead; it was over before he died."

"I had to see for myself."

"I am a married woman." She looked around the room. "You shouldn't contact me again."

He looked at her—trying to see her through his father's eyes. What was so special about this woman that made the old man break his vows to his mother? He decided in that moment that it was enough. This obsession that he shared with his father and grandfather, the need to pursue forbidden love. It would end with him. Benjamin realized he would never look back. Perhaps he had known all along, but it was after meeting with that woman, watching her leave the canteen while he sat back to gather his thoughts, that he felt the decision now harden in his heart. He was not going back to Lagos.

22

The Kinsmen

Umumilo, 1906

"Your trip. How did it go?" the visitor asked.

"It went the way it was supposed to go," Okolo answered.

Okolo was in no mood to talk about the trip. What was he to say, that he had trekked a full day's journey with his sister and her child? That they had reached the banks of Ekwulobia? That he had stopped on many occasions during the journey to allow his sister's crying to abate, only for that of the baby to erupt? That, with all his strength and authority, all the goodwill he had accumulated, all those years fighting, his name sung on the lips of the women of the village, he could get neither his sister nor her child to cease with their tears? He had known many blows in his life, but this was by far the worst, having to witness the separation of a child from its mother. And yet what was the alternative? To lose his sister to exile? To lose the opportunity he now held to foster the advancement of his people? No, he had thought. The child was a small price to pay for the changes that had now become necessary, for which he now saw clearly that he was best positioned to champion for his people. You see, in addition to being a warrior, Okolo prided himself on being a competent negotiator. He understood a good deal when he saw one, and surely, this situation—a child given in exchange for freedom—would benefit everyone. Priscilla was young. She could still marry. She would have other sons—a quiverful of them if she desired. It was a fair trade.

Okolo was sure about his decision because he had learned the secrets to negotiations while serving his father's cousin Mazi Mbafo. His uncle Mbafo was an excellent trader, known across the villages for his diligent enterprise. It was a commonly held opinion across Umumilo that there was nothing that Mbafo could not sell. When Okolo was just six years old, his uncle Mbafo took him into his care, and thus into the craft of his trade. It was in this world that Okolo came to learn where the yams at the farms go. It was also the first place he'd seen the bark of trees trimmed and polished for use. By the time Okolo turned twelve, he'd started going as far as four villages away to speak to other traders on behalf of his uncle. When he did not run the smaller errands, he accompanied the servants to the more serious negotiations. Incidentally, around this time Okolo had also begun to fight, so that as he sold items village by village, he fought in the marketplace and by the streams—sometimes at only the slightest provocation. At sixteen, he had won two wrestling matches, earning for himself the status of a local champion. He had also become old enough to set up his own shop. It was, therefore, no surprise to him when his uncle called him into his obi one evening to discuss his plans.

"My son, you have served me well," Mbafo said to the young Okolo. "You have served me better than ten servants," he continued. "What would you say if I asked you to take over my shops instead of starting out on your own?" Mbafo said, surprising Okolo greatly. "Don't respond too quickly. Speak to your father first, then come back to me on the next market day."

Okolo thought hard about this opportunity. He'd even spoken to his father about the issue. In the end, Okolo had to reach the decision on his own. It had become clear to Okolo after ten years serving Mbafo that there is nothing you cannot get if you have the right item to exchange for it. It was the way he came to understand the world—everybody wanted something. If you learned what a person wanted and gave it to them, you would gain an ally. And if you learned what your enemy wanted, you could turn them into a friend, even if only momentarily. This was the secret to happiness, perhaps even power. Yet, Okolo also knew that to get something of value, one in turn had to part with something of value. There is a cost to every desire, a price that must be paid. It was with this clear-eyed practicality that Okolo came to negotiate his life. It was also these ruminations that led him to choose the life of a wrestler despite his uncle's offer. In trading, he reasoned that he would always be Mbafo's boy—the nephew who was brought in; his fame would be secondhand, existing in the shadow of his great uncle. Wrestling, on the other hand, was completely his own. It was the gift that his chi had given to him, the path decided by the Gods. And in this, at least, the glory would be his; the fame would bear his own name. And so Okolo had chosen wrestling because in this area he could best forge the future he wanted. And when Mr. Walter's offer came, it was this same future that Okolo considered when he made his decision—a small child in exchange for freedom, he thought again and grunted. Yes, of course he had made the right decision.

▼▲▼

The woman who came to receive the baby looked like them and spoke their language. It was a fact that outraged Okolo, who himself had been expecting to meet a milk-colored woman from London. He almost stomped out of the church they'd agreed to meet in, demanding to know where the boy's so-called grand-aunt was—insisting that he would not hand over his nephew to this strange woman. But his anger abated when he learned that the child's grand-aunt was awaiting their arrival in Lagos, that she had sent this woman who spoke Igbo but lived in Yorubaland to retrieve the child. It was not wise for a frail, middle-aged woman to make such a trip down herself, the officer who escorted the woman had explained.

The woman who was sent walked up to Priscilla and made a gesture to receive the child.

"He does not like to feed very early in the morning," Priscilla said, holding the baby to her chest.

"Pardon?" the woman said.

"He is not much of an eater. If he has any foods in the morning, before the sun reaches full strength, he will vomit. It is not good for him," Priscilla said, clarifying each part while holding back a sob.

"I will keep that in mind," the woman responded.

"I have named him Lotanna—it means remember father. It is good for him to bear the memories of his own father," Priscilla explained. She took a step back, still holding the baby to her chest. She turned her face to Okolo, who was standing by the door.

"I will let his people know," the woman replied again.

"But I am his people," Priscilla said.

"You must hand the boy over to me now," the woman said, impatient.

Priscilla did not budge. She continued to hold her child to her chest but moved toward the window. She held the curtain and peeked out.

"How will he nurse? Who will hold him at night when his fevers rise?" Priscilla said to no one in particular.

"That's enough. Let me have the boy." The woman's tone had become firm, commanding. She turned toward the door, addressing Okolo this time, in Igbo, "Tell your sister what she needs to do. Evening is coming. I must leave soon."

Okolo looked up at Priscilla, full of hopeless pity. Then he turned back to the woman, ready to say something cutting. Who was she to speak about evening coming? The church was hosting her; she had a place where she and the boy would pass the night. Was it not Okolo and Priscilla who made the long tiresome trip? She did not even have the goodwill to offer them water.

"Give her some time. You know this must be difficult," he said instead, swallowing his anger. Eventually, he went to Priscilla and gently pried the baby from her arms. There was no struggle. She did not resist or hurl insults at him. She simply allowed the baby to be taken.

Up until that moment, Okolo had held the boy with a carefully erected shield, keeping a safe distance. Now, as he was about to release him to this stranger, Okolo looked the child in the face for the first time and realized that the boy had Priscilla's nose. It was unmistakable. It was a nose he spotted on his own two young sons. A nose so renowned in his family that people recognized his clan as far off as three villages away. There was a strange irony to this moment. To—finally—see the beauty of a thing only on the cusp of losing it. Yet, he did what he knew must be done. He handed the child to the woman. His first assignment for the British thoroughly completed.

"So have you heard?" the visitor asked.

"Heard what?"

"You mean you have not heard?"

"Eche, I wish you would stop dancing about in circles and say what you mean to say," Okolo replied.

"Hmm, perhaps you should hear it from somebody else."

"Mister man," Okolo called, "speak your mind or leave my home."

"Have you spoken to your friends at the secretariat? Have you heard from your master Walter?" the visitor continued.

"I have no master besides Agwu and my ancestors," Okolo replied.

"Indeed," the visitor said.

"When is the next council meeting? We have canceled the last two rotations; we must make up for those at once," Okolo said.

The visitor said nothing; he began to whistle and walk away.

"What is it?" Okolo said loudly.

"We held the meeting in your absence, and we had a vote too. Mazi Diri, he will be taking your place."

Okolo laughed. "Nonsense," he said. "Is that what you could not say to me?"

"It is not that," the visitor said. "Look, my friend, you have helped me; that is why I came here today, I wanted you to know that the chiefs think you have taken sides. They say you are a traitor. I wanted you to know."

After his guest left, Okolo sent his servant to summon the chiefs. He was calling for another meeting. He said it was urgent. Following his requests, the chiefs showed up, one after another, until all eleven of them were gathered in his obi.

"My people," Okolo began. "There is talk from the birds that a vacancy has been announced in the seat I rightfully occupy. I know this cannot be true," he said. "Not after everything I have done for the village."

"It is only momentarily," one of the chiefs said, "until we are sure where you stand."

"What does this mean?" Okolo said.

"We hear that your sister has given up the boy. That it is you who oversaw this exchange."

"Yes. And what is that to you?" Okolo asked.

"We suppose that you plan to bring her back into the village," the man continued.

Okolo was surprised. "Of course I plan to bring her back," he said. "It is the reasonable thing to do."

"In that case, you can no longer have a seat among the council chiefs," the man finished.

"You cannot be serious. What do you mean?"

"We are saying what you already know to be true. A child cannot smear his shit in his mother's stall without some punishment. She disrespected the village, and she must stay out of it."

"But she is to take a job at the school; Mr. Walter has pardoned her."

"Well, we have not. You can either work for the white man or you can honor our customs, but we cannot allow you to do both," the man continued.

"B-but she is my sister," Okolo stuttered. "She is our daughter."

"She stopped being our daughter the moment she lied about her pregnancy," the chief continued. "Her lie has cost us the lives of our kinsmen."

"She is but a child. How will she survive?"

"Like every other person who has brought shame to their people."

"My home people, you are being unreasonable."

"Yes, the situation has always been beyond reason."

"So you ask me to choose—between the council and the foreigners; yet if I choose the council and our customs, my sister will remain punished?"

"It is the way of our people, my brother. You must not think this to be personal."

▼▲▼

Priscilla had refused to speak to Okolo once they handed over the boy. Okolo had gone to visit her early that morning, before his own guest arrived. He had entered her yard expecting the worst, convinced that she would have done something as utterly unforgiving as the situation warranted. He found her sitting on the floor of her shed, holding the baby's old wrapper to her chest. She was not crying, not speaking; he could barely even hear her breathe. He tried to convince her to return to his place, but she still refused. Even his talk of her getting work at the school did not entice her. He told her that she would have more children, that he, Okolo, was a man of influence, and there were men he could persuade to marry her, men who owed him favors. She was, after all, still young and beautiful. Above all, she was his sister; he would do anything for her. Indeed, it was the precise mission to reinstate Priscilla back into society that had compelled Okolo to call for the village council meeting, but he had not known about the plans for his so-called replacement.

Okolo told the men that he needed time to ruminate, that he would make his decision before the sun set the next day. In his mind, he made his plan to go to Mr. Walter, to ask for some of the solidarity that was promised him, the so-called respect. Perhaps Priscilla could be taken in by the secretariat, given work in a different province. It was the least they could do, after taking her child. If that failed, he had another plan—Bassey. The young interpreter would have to do as a husband for Priscilla. They both spoke English and were keen on the white man's ways. Yes. He would send for Bassey and let him know he needed his help—man-to-man. He needed him to marry his sister.

The next day, Okolo went in search of Mr. Walter but found him in a foul mood. He stood in the room, waiting for Mr. Walter to raise his hand, the gesture that summoned him into his presence. Okolo realized then that Bassey was not in the room, which he thought strange. Mr. Walter got up from where he was perched, then walked outside and summoned a young girl that Okolo had seen in their quarters on occasion.

"Good afternoon, Okolo. I hear your trip went well," she said.

Okolo was surprised to hear her speak to him directly, having collected the words from Mr. Walter. It dawned on him that she was there to interpret.

"Where is Bassey?" Okolo asked.

"This is what Mr. Walter wishes to inform you," the young girl said, moving aside to give Mr. Walter more room for his pacing. "We found him the day that you left for the city. He has died."

"You found who?" Okolo asked.

"It was a fever," the girl answered.

"What do you mean it was a fever?" Okolo said. "Who did you find?"

"We found Bassey in his sleeping quarters. It appears he died while he slept."

"You are telling lies." Okolo was now shouting at the girl. Mr. Walter smoked a cigarette, his left hand in his pocket, looking out the entrance.

"Please keep your voice down, Okolo. We are handling the matter quietly."

"Where is he now? You must take me to him at once," Okolo barked.

"He was buried that very morning," the girl finished.

Okolo sat down on the bench in the room, unable to stand any longer.

"What happens now?" Okolo finally asked.

"Nothing. He has been buried."

"This is not what I speak of. What happens to Priscilla—to my sister?"

"Oh right, the girl. We have to be patient. I will need to do some paperwork once the school is ready to run. We will of course need your help to convince the villagers to attend."

"And for now—where does she stay for now?"

"We have nothing to do with where she lives," Mr. Walter said. He smoked his cigarette. "We leave the domestic arrangements to you."

"But my people—" Okolo stood up. He sat again.

"My people have refused to reinstate her back to society."

"Is that right?"

"She cannot survive alone on the edges of town. All by herself now that her son is gone. She must be among her people."

"I'm sorry to hear about your concerns." Mr. Walter inhaled his cigarette.

Okolo thought again about Bassey, the compelled marriage, then almost immediately he remembered that Bassey was dead. Who would marry Priscilla now? The child was gone, and he was no longer sure how he would keep his promises to his sister.

He sprang up.

"You made me promises. You told me you would take care of her." He was shouting, but the interpreter was no longer speaking. She left the room and returned with two officers. Okolo looked at them. He tried again.

"My sister needs a place to stay. Can your people not help?"

Mr. Walter had his back turned to Okolo by now. He raised his hand to gesture to the interpreter that he would return. When he came back into the room moments later, he placed a single manilla on the bench beside Okolo.

"For your trouble," he said.

As Okolo watched Mr. Walter walk away, he wondered what he would do now that the chiefs had given him an ultimatum. He could bring Priscilla into his household—dare them to challenge him. Yet, he also knew that if he made such a move, he would lose his standing with the village once and for all.

Okolo thought about the custom of his people; if it rains, you do not leave your neighbor's pots unattended. When trouble comes, you do not throw your face the other way. Except they were turning away now from Priscilla. His own people. They were turning away from his blood.

23

Margaret

Ekwulobia, 2005

Benjamin and Nosa arrived in the village the evening before, but even when Nwando scurried to meet them, Margaret stayed in her room. Later that night, Chuka knocked on her door, a little before midnight, smug as ever. He'd been frustrated to learn the previous day that he was supposed to share a hotel room with both of his parents.

"And what is wrong with that?" Margaret teased.

"But it's just one bed," he'd said. It was uncomfortable, he added and shuddered. Margaret laughed. She'd wanted to tell him that it was just one bed in her room, too, but he had already plopped himself on the mattress, playing one of his games. She took a blanket and laid it on the floor, thinking to herself—Benjamin is actually here.

"Will you show me where you grew up?" Chuka asked.

"Of course, my darling. After our family cleansing."

"Oh, is it a family cleansing? Mummy said it's a family reunion."

"Well, it is also that."

"Okay. But what is the cleansing for?"

Margaret's gaze moved to the door, as though she was expecting someone. She started to scratch—and Chuka, stubborn but also sensitive, moved to the floor beside her and held her hand.

"Don't worry about it," Margaret answered.

"But Grandpa will be there?" Chuka added now, his voice softened.

"Yes," Margaret replied.

"He doesn't have to come; he's not a part of this family," Chuka said.

Margaret moved her eyes from the door and looked at Chuka. "That's not very nice!" she said, jabbing him lightly on his shoulder. Her voice was stern, but her eyes danced with laughter.

Finally, morning arrived. Margaret stood in front of the mirror, clipping her hair in pins and trying to decide if she would go without powder. She had never been the kind to put on makeup, even though Nwando asked her to try—once in a while. She saw a piece of clothing on the corner of the bed now and smiled, recalling that it belonged to Chuka. He'd left his shirt while running off to get ready. She looked at her face in the mirror, checked her hair, and exhaled. It was time to go.

▽ △ ▽

When Nosa and Benjamin arrived at the table, Chuka stood up stiffly. He hesitated, then hugged his father. He looked at Benjamin and muttered—Good morning, sir. Benjamin smiled, raised his hand to brush his hair in that uncertain way of his that Margaret still recognized.

Nosa smiled. "Chuka, give your grandfather a hug."

The boy went in, hugged Benjamin lightly, turning to look at Margaret as he did so. But if Margaret felt any pulse of his loyalty, she did not show it. Her eyes were fixed on Benjamin.

His face had grown soft. She observed now how his skin drooped in places that had once held firm. He'd never been a particularly handsome man, her Benni, but she had always liked the contours of his face, the edge of his jawline, the tilt in his upper lip, his nose. By now, he had traded a full head of hair for thin strands of white. When they were younger, there was something about the way his hair fell over his face, slanting against his eyebrow. She still remembered the softness of it against her fingers. Margaret had teased him in the months leading up to their wedding, saying that his hair was the only reason she agreed to marry him, because she would have the opportunity to see it all fall away.

"I have not seen an onye ocha over thirty who does not have a bald spot—what do you people do with your hair?" she'd joked.

Now, watching him, all Margaret could think was that she'd missed it—the gentle shedding of his hair, that widening patch of baldness, the certain panic that would have accompanied the loss. She imagined him waking up, facing the mirror with a kind of obsessive self-interest as he monitored the ways that time was changing him. In fact, the only time Benjamin had seriously considered giving up cigarettes was when he heard that it would help him avoid early signs of aging. Margaret had loved that hair, those plain-looking features, that nose sitting displaced on his face.

Margaret continued to look at Benjamin, even though he'd barely looked at her since he entered the hall, except for that quick instant when her eyes lifted from the table and caught his as he walked in. She took in his striped cotton shirt, his plain trousers, the light pink of his big toe pushing through the brown strap of his sandals, his slight fatigued limp from sitting too long in the aircraft, the soft bulge of his stomach. There were, also, the freckles she once knew, tiny dots that had now deepened into age spots, marking his hands and face with time. She wondered if this was how he saw her, too; fragile, eaten up by the years.

"You look well," Benjamin finally said to Margaret.

Margaret could tell by the twitch of his lower lip that he'd struggled to say those words. It was the same look of consternation he had when he'd asked her to marry him. She should have appreciated the effort, and maybe a part of her did.

"You mean I do not look crazy?" Margaret replied.

She did not know why she said it, or why her voice sounded angry, scalded.

"That's not what I meant, Maggie," he said. He looked at her this time. When she matched his gaze, he moved his eyes to the table.

"Of course that's not what he meant, Mama," Nwando interjected, her eyes beginning to water. Chuka stopped eating; he now kept his eyes on Benjamin, following the exchange. Nosa was chewing on the cashews placed as appetizers in the center of the table, hiding a small smile on his face.

"But it is what he is thinking," Margaret continued. "Is it not what you are thinking, Benni?" She raised her hand in the air as though she'd suddenly come up with an idea. "In fact, it is what you are all thinking," Margaret added now, more emphatic.

"Chuka," Nwando suddenly said, "can you excuse us, please?"

"But I haven't started eating," he protested.

"You will eat later. Give us a moment."

Chuka looked at Margaret, at his father. "Why did I even come?"

Margaret tried to remember why her grandson was leaving the table. Did she say something, or were they sending him away so they could finish their plans? She was tired. Perhaps she should take a break from her medicines now that Nwando was not monitoring her so closely. The fogginess from the drugs dulled her, and she needed to be alert precisely for occasions like this, so she could sense when they connived against her. She knew it now. This was the reason Benjamin came—to distract her. And then what? They'd bundle her off to some remote location in the name of treatment.

"Mummy, you need to calm down. Nobody is thinking anything," Nwando said when Chuka was out of the scene. Her face had grown surprisingly calm and controlled.

"I will calm down when I'm dead," Margaret shouted. "Is that not what you want? You think I don't know you are working with them? You want to get rid of me."

"Mama, lower your voice. Are you tired? Do you want to go upstairs?" Nwando asked.

"Is that where you put the trap? Upstairs?" Margaret's eyes searched the room, the windows, the door.

"Okay, let's not go upstairs, then. Let's eat, please."

"Where was this food made?" Margaret asked. "I will not eat it until I know where it's come from."

Nosa straightened up; the two escorts moved toward him, but he waved them away. Margaret glanced at them from the side of her eyes.

"I demand a release," she said. "I demand a release immediately—where is my taster? I will not have this poison. Give me the release before I call my lawyers," Margaret continued.

"Mama, it's okay. It's me, Nwando. It's just me."

The hotel manager paced about three tables away from them, trying to decide when to intervene. Nosa had dropped his cutlery and was looking at Nwando.

"I know that code," Margaret hissed at him. "That's your secret sign to call them. You think I don't know what you've been planning? I know that code."

What happened next surprised them all. Benjamin scooted his chair close to Margaret, then he scooped up a piece of yam with eggs from her plate with his fork and brought it to his mouth. The table stilled. Margaret grew quiet. He repeated the action two more times, then spoke softly to Margaret.

"I am your taster; the food is okay. See—it is safe. You can eat it now."

Moments passed before Margaret replied.

"Don't be silly, Benni. You are not my taster." Then she picked up her fork and began to eat.

They continued to eat and drink, wine for Benjamin and Nosa, a malt drink for Nwando, water for Margaret, their forks clicking away at the plates. They sent food up to Chuka, whom Nwando said was better off away to allow the adults to speak freely. Toward the end of their meal, Margaret raised her head and announced, "Benni, I really want to thank you for being here despite our—history."

"Ah, Mum, let's finish eating first, please."

"It will be over soon—I assure you," Margaret continued, brushing off Nwando.

"What will be over?" Benjamin asked, looking at her.

"All of this," Margaret said. She waved her hand, gesturing between herself and Nwando and Nosa. "My sickness—the curse. It will all be over."

His eyes widened in surprise, but he was nodding.

"They have not told you, have they?" Margaret's voice had become clear, more controlled. "We've had the pre-cleansing meeting with the dibia—the native doctor," she said. "It was supposed to be the usual instructions, that is what I assumed, what we all assumed," Margaret explained. She cleared her throat. "But he has given the verdict. I mean, we still need to go for the cleansing itself, so your trip is not completely wasted, Benni," Margaret said, her voice apologetic.

"I don't mind being here, Maggie," Benjamin said. "I know it's not in vain."

"You still don't understand—the verdict has been given."

"What is the verdict? Tell me," Benjamin said, leaning in.

Nwando coughed in the background. Nosa's phone rang.

"In less than three months," Margaret whispered. She leaned in to Benjamin too. "In less than three months, I will pay the price, and then everything will be right again." She leaned back into her seat.

"The price—?" Benjamin asked.

"Remember my grandfather, the one in your uncle's journal, the one who did those horrible things?"

"I remember everything," Benjamin replied. He moved his hand close to Margaret's on the table so that their elbows were now touching.

"Yes, exactly. Someone in the family has to die the death that was assigned to him, and I've decided it will be me," Margaret explained, grateful for his understanding.

Nosa laughed. "Let's not get carried away, Mama. Nothing is decided." He looked at his phone as it quieted down, then declared, "I will have a serious talk with the dibia tomorrow. I'm sure he can find a more amenable option."

Benjamin did not take his eyes off Margaret, so she continued, stopping only briefly when the waiter returned to ask if they needed anything else.

"You understand, don't you?" she said to Benjamin. "You know why I have to do this."

"What does he know?" Nwando cut in. "Is there something you are not telling us? What exactly is he supposed to know?"

"Is this what they said?" Benjamin continued, his eyes still on Margaret.

"Not them," she whispered. "The priest. The village priest at the shrine. I gave my word to him that I would pay the price, so that this—" She stopped. "I did it to save all of us."

Nwando was tapping her foot under the table, her heart racing.

Benjamin asked, "Did they say how it will happen?"

"No." Margaret sighed. "Maybe it will happen in my sleep, who knows?" she said, feigning indifference.

"Mama, did you have any wine?" Nwando asked, looking at her husband. "Did you give her alcohol?"

"What if nothing happens?" Benjamin continued.

"That's not possible. The dibia has passed the verdict; look what happened the last time we dismissed it."

"All right," Benjamin said quietly.

After a short moment, he asked again, "But what if nothing happens?"

"Something will happen."

The next day, Margaret and her cousins gathered at the dibia's obi again. This time around, Nwando joined them, along with Chuka, Nosa, and Benjamin. The demons had returned, and Margaret watched as they trudged about the small room as if conjured by the potential of the cleansing. The ritual itself was simple—an evening under the moon, a concoction of herbs and fermented rice in a calabash passed around, from which everyone had to drink. They were to all come dressed in a cotton fabric, their necklines and faces bare. The dibia would smear a mixture of herbs on their necks and shoulders, so that they became visible in the land of the spirits. His youngest son served with him that night, hummed with him, prayed with him—called on the ancestors, on the spirits, on all the unknowable mysteries of the Gods. Margaret and her family watched silently, as spectators, having no real part in the ceremony except to drink what they were told. When the ritual itself was over, the dibia moved toward each of them, gently patting their shoulders. When he got to Margaret, who was last, he declared, "It is settled, then," his voice a low hum across the room. It was a question, not a statement.

"Yes, nna anyi, we know that," Margaret said.

"And your people, they agree with you?" he asked, looking around.

"Yes, they are all agreed," Margaret said.

"Let them say it, then. It is good for me to hear them say it," the dibia continued.

"Well—" Margaret said, looking at Nwando. "Are you not agreed on me getting well?" she asked.

Nwando tried to speak but decided it was better to hear the verdict for herself first. She could contradict the verdict when the dibia mentioned it directly.

When there was no response, the dibia continued. "Your mother here," he said, looking at Nwando. "Your sister"—he turned to look at Matthias and the other kinsmen—"she has chosen to return home to her roots. You all know about the trouble that has followed her all her life. You all know that when an odor travels with you from house to house, it is not the world that stinks, but your own armpit.

"Are you all aware of this?" the dibia then asked again. "Are you aware and agreed that a problem that began on the soil must be treated on the soil?"

They nodded.

"It is concluded, then," the dibia remarked. "You must all return home and prepare yourselves. Each of you must set your house in order."

Nwando nudged Nosa.

"Each of us?" Nosa asked. "What do you mean by we must all set our house in order?"

"It means there is no way to tell which of you the Gods will take. The ancestors have decided not to reveal."

"I'm sure there is another solution," Nosa said, a nervous laugh escaping his mouth. Nwando shook her head and clutched Chuka's arm. "Don't listen to him," she whispered to her son.

"There must be a mistake," Margaret intervened. "I'm sure there's a mix-up somewhere. Remember that I offered myself, that I said it is me who will pay the price, since I am the source of the problem?"

"What price?" Chuka asked. "Price for what?"

"Oho, so now you want to negotiate with the Gods. You think you will speak, and they will listen? No one tells them what to do, no one," the dibia responded to Margaret.

Confusion settled across the room.

"Just to be clear—this affects only the direct members of the family, akwa ya?" It was Matthias who was asking now, his hands on his head. "You know that we are umunna, we are just kinsmen. We are just distant relatives; we are not even connected by blood," he continued. The dibia had begun packing his things, whistling a low tune. He ignored the question from Matthias; he looked at Chuka, at Margaret. Then he looked at Chuka again.

"If you are still here when it is done, send word to me," he said to Margaret, and then he walked away.

▼▲▼

On the way back to Lagos, Margaret had gotten into another argument with Nwando, who now came up with all kinds of accusations. She said that Margaret was getting worse, that coming to Umumilo, getting the family involved, was a mistake; she should never have agreed to it. She should never have agreed for Chuka to be in that room; she did not want to be there, but Benjamin had persuaded her to see the whole thing through. She regretted that she had listened. In any case, this was purely medical. The only way to move forward was for Margaret to get a new treatment plan. But Margaret refused, argued, pleaded. She reminded Nwando that they'd had an agreement and she had stuck to the medicines all this time. She threatened that if she was taken into the hospital against her will, they might as well forget the dibia's verdict since Margaret herself would jump off a building.

"You will do no such thing," Nwando shouted.

Margaret decided she would prove to Nwando that she did not need a new treatment. She would keep to her routines, tend to her small garden. She would pray. And she would wait. Back to that old friend—time.

"Madam, welcome; how was the trip?" her new housekeeper, Bayo, asked when Nosa's driver pulled in that evening.

"What trip?" Margaret replied.

"The trip to the village," the housekeeper said, following behind Margaret with her bags in his hands as he made his way through the kitchen.

Margaret stopped by the staircase, as though searching for something.

"Oh, that trip? It went well. How are your parents doing these days?" she asked earnestly.

"My parents are well," Bayo replied. However, his parents had not been well in a long time. In fact, his parents were dead.

"Good. That is good." Margaret climbed the stairs to her bedroom; then she turned around and came back down. "Tell your mother to come see me. We need to finish our plans," Margaret continued. "Do you understand me? Is that clear?" She held his eyes.

"Yes, ma, it is clear. What would you like to discuss with her, ma?" Bayo asked.

"Don't worry about that. Just tell her we need to talk. She will understand."

"Yes, ma. I will pass across your message. Are you ready to eat now?"

"Wait, Bayo—come closer," Margaret whispered. "I don't want people hearing about this, okay? Come closer—tell your mother the child is doing fine," she said, then yawned.

"Okay, ma, I will tell her," Bayo said.

When Margaret retired to her bedroom, the housekeeper walked to the landline phone stationed beside the kitchen counter. After the call, he dropped the phone back onto the receiver with a satisfied smile. Nwando and her husband were on their way, but Bayo had to wait until they arrived. The evening passed. His shift had ended an hour and thirty minutes ago and he was a little nervous about traveling back to his place that late at night. Still, he agreed, knowing that any attempt at being less than amenable might cost him the work altogether.

"What are you still doing here?"

Startled, Bayo jerked up, surprised to see Margaret down in the living room, her stockinged feet peeking out of her boubou.

"The road is blocked, ma. I said let me wait a little before I start to go home," he explained, feeling flustered. To cement his ruse, he quickly added, "I already called my mother and delivered your message."

"Which mother? Your mother is dead," Margaret replied, eyeing him.

"Yes, ma, I mean, no, ma. Ma, you asked me to deliver her a message," he muttered.

"And why would I ask that?" Margaret replied. She had the vague recollection of chatting with him, but was it not about cleaning? About some errand she'd asked him to run? In any case, she'd come down to clear her head. She'd just had a dream that revealed the answer to her. The dream had been a simple voice in the darkness. What if you die before anybody else can, before they lock you away with the doctors? And then she woke up. It was still night. She'd felt such a sense of control. Indeed, a life was a life, and hers was no less valuable. If she died before they snatched one of her own, would a debt paid not still be a debt paid?

She suddenly understood exactly what she had to do.

The doorbell rang.

"Who is that?" Margaret asked in alarm, rushing to hide behind the curtain.

"Have you taken your medicine, Mama?" Bayo asked. He rushed to the door and unlatched the lock.

Even before seeing anyone come in, Margaret knew. Then she saw Nwando, and she saw the men walking toward her. Her eyes filled with tears.

"Mama, we agreed, you promised me," Nwando said, as if in explanation.

"Agreed what? Who are these people?" Margaret shouted. When there was no response, she turned to Bayo.

"Help me, Bayo, please. Please help me. Don't let them take me away," she said, desperate. "Bayo, won't you help me? I have a plan. I have a plan that will work," she cried.

24

Benjamin

Umumilo, 2005

It was a little past midnight; Benjamin felt the weight of the day in his knees and knuckles. He had not stopped thinking about his trip—about Margaret's words, about his own reaction to her. He'd taken off his shoes, wanting to feel the cold of the tile against his feet. The hotel staff had already knocked on the door to his room twice. He'd assured them that no, he didn't need a change of towels, and yes, the hot water was working just fine. When he was finally alone, he sat on the bed and looked at his hands; he could feel them tremble, but they appeared still to his eyes. He had done what he came here to do, he thought. He had boarded the flight with a heart condition; he had shown the contrition that was expected of him. He was not naive; he had not come seeking forgiveness; he'd come as a kind of mission, an assignment he needed to see through. Now that he had come, and seen her, and touched her, it was time to go. It was time to leave Margaret and her God and the priest and their verdicts. After all, they had lived separate lives for decades. Margaret had done fine without him. Yet, there was Nwando, and there was Chuka. He wanted from them what he had refused to give Margaret—an assumption of duty, loyalty—the sense that he was their blood and that they had to create room in their world for him. He wanted to not be by himself the next time he found himself in a hospital. However, the boy, Chuka, would not even look at him, and Nwando would not be alone with him, and Nosa talked too much, and Margaret—well, he did not want to think about her. It was too much for his heart to think about Margaret, to see her as she was now but also as she was during their time together. He looked at his hands again; this time he saw them trembling. He thought about his mother, and he thought about his own relationship to God, a convenient memory that had been discarded over the years.

Once as a young boy, Benjamin believed that he had found God. His own father, Mathew Fletcher, had never been religious, which meant that both men considered the idea of faith not only elusive but also impractical. To the Fletchers, the logic was simple—a God who wanted to be seen or felt would make himself a bit more apparent. It was therefore pointless to pursue a God who had no serious intention of being found. Benjamin's mother, on the other hand, was a devout Catholic who said her novenas and went to confession weekly. When the time came for Benjamin's secondary school education, he ended up in a Catholic school. This Catholic education was his mother's only true consolation; the idea that her son would, at least, find God within the hallowed walls of the school chapel, with their compulsory prayers and devout reverend teachers. But Benjamin did not find God in that first year in boarding school, and he would not need to try again until he reached his fifth year, when his mother had taken ill. Benjamin had been away at school when it all transpired; he'd been neck-deep in preparation for his A-level exams. One afternoon, he met his father at the quadrangle.

"Your mother is sick; the doctors have tried everything; you must come say goodbye."

And so Benjamin, age sixteen, had taken two long trains and a coach ride home. Upon arrival, he'd found his mother in the parlor, propped up by pillows so that she sat upright and faced the window, her skin ashen, her voice stretched and faint. She'd grown thinner, a third of her size since the last time Benjamin saw her. She said she wanted to be near the light, that she wanted the world around her to stay bright and clear when her time came. She'd been wearing her sleepwear, with blankets draped over her legs. My poor boy, she cried quietly when she saw Benjamin, raising her hand to touch his face but too weak to succeed. Benjamin tried to hold her, tell her she would be all right, but he'd seen the blood from when she'd coughed, folded away in her handkerchief. He watched how, even in that sickly state, his mother held her rosary in her hand. In his mind, he could not understand how she could hold the rosary but be too weak to touch his face, or how she seemed to hold on to a God who seemed bent on taking her life. He was upset. It was unfair. The one time his mother needed God to save her—to help her—he refused. That night, Benjamin went up to his room determined to do the one thing his mother had failed to do—challenge God. He would roll up his sleeves and have a proper discussion, not that it would do much good; his mother's condition was enough evidence that his father's sentiments and his own suspicions were correct. God was either not real or not interested. However, when the moment came for Benjamin to tackle this unseen being with his own pious accusations, he'd found himself on the floor, his chest racking from crying, heavy with defeat and desperation. Instead of anger, he asked God for his mother's life. He begged God to take him instead. It was the first time in his life that he prayed earnestly. Then, by the end of the week, Benjamin's mother's health had taken a turn for the better, a fact that confounded the doctors. Even back then, Benjamin had been sure that his mother's recovery was the result of his bargain with God, that at any moment now the Lord would come to ask for his payment—Benjamin's life.

He'd returned to school, after giving his father a severe hug, after crying on his mother's chest. He told them it was because he was happy, but in his heart, he felt it was the last time they would see him. He had made a bargain with God, and surely God would collect. But that was Benjamin at sixteen—naive and desperate. He had not thought about his faith for decades. He'd grown into adulthood and into a stubborn secularity. But now, in his hotel room, he thought about Margaret, about the verdict, the clear-eyed certainty of the dibia. He got up, moved to put on a sweater. Then, surprising himself, he went down on his knees and began to pray.

25

The Kinsmen

Umumilo, 1905–1908

The man known as the vagabond had taken to living in the bush just north of Priscilla's hut. The cave he stayed in had ancient markings inscribed on its walls—the stories went that they were carved by a different clan, men of the same tribe who did not wrestle like their fathers; they played the flutes and wooed their women with song. Priscilla knew this because she had been there with Derek, holding his hand as she traced the inscriptions, translating to him in fragments of English.

The first time Priscilla sighted the vagabond, it occurred to her to reach out to Father Patrick, or perhaps to mention it to her brother Okolo—the rumors were that the vagabond had escaped. That the villagers were seeking him out. Indeed, she, too, wanted him removed at once; she did not want her infant son breathing the same air that he did. It also occurred to her that she, too, was now at risk. Not only could he invade this peace she had constructed for herself, but he could also take from her what he had taken from the other women—the right to refuse. She thought again about what she said to Adaora, that it did not matter how the child came, but as she looked at the vagabond she wondered how she thought that anything good could come from him.

Weeks had passed since Priscilla first noticed that the vagabond moved on the pathway to her shed. One evening, she'd cooked a pot of yam porridge, then eaten a large portion of it, wanting to save the rest for the next morning. She did not know why she did this, but she stood up, tightened her wrapper, and walked out of her hut, toward the cave where the vagabond was staying. This was the first of many times she presented him with food. He snatched it from her hand, nearly half of its contents spilling on the floor. He picked it up in clumps, waving off a chicken attracted by the food. The vagabond had said nothing to her, merely sat there, throwing the sand-coated food from the ground to his mouth. She watched him though his face was shrouded by the night. There was something ironic about it. Her own son, whom she desperately wanted to shake alive, for both their sakes, rejected her milk. And yet, here was this boy desperate for food.

The next day, Priscilla brought rice. And then she brought bitter leaf soup. And then she brought more yam porridge. She told herself that it was not kindness she was showing him. They were entering into a kind of bargain. She would nourish him, and in exchange he would keep away from her, from the village. Priscilla had tried to talk to him on occasion. She wanted to ask him if he knew about Nneka. And why did he choose Nneka knowing her age, her innocence. Not that any woman deserved to be violated that way, but Nneka was a child. And now she was a dead child. But her prodding was met with silence, and his silence stirred up the anger she thought she had forgotten. He was the one who was supposed to die, she'd reminded herself as she stirred the soup or beans. He was the convicted—awaiting execution. And her poor Derek had been the Christ whom the people had traded in exchange. She was angry at everything—her son for refusing her milk, the vagabond for surviving while her Derek died, and the white man's God whom she no longer felt she knew. Yet, day after day, in spite of herself and her questions, she took food to the vagabond. They continued in this quiet relationship—the provider and the provided for.

Unknown to her, they would live like this for three more years. Priscilla would learn from the village whispers that the vagabond's escape was an abomination. That the verdict of the Gods could not be allowed to hang in the air, unfulfilled. Yet, she kept his presence a secret. It was only when the vagabond died that she sent word to the village to come for his body. It was then that news of her harboring him came out, and it was then that she was told that the sins of his crimes must rest on her head. She had harbored a man wanted by the Gods. She had robbed the village of vengeance and robbed Nneka of justice.

Okolo, who had by now married Adaora, asked how she could do such a thing.

"And you—you would keep such a thing from me. But why, sister? You know what this boy cost our people."

She said nothing.

The elders had taken Olisa's body, but they had set up a trial for Priscilla at once. They had taken her through the customary court, which now existed in collaboration with the white men. She had spent two nights there before her judgment was passed. Exile. She was to leave Umumilo and never return.

In the morning before Priscilla was to set out, Adaora snuck through the village with her toddler son—the child that the vagabond put in her. She'd told one of the guards that she had brought a message from her husband, Okolo. That she had to speak to Priscilla in private.

"I want to know why," she said while they were alone.

"I'm not sure. I did not mean to cause any trouble," Priscilla said, meaning every word.

"It is just like the last time. You and your lies—your secrets."

Priscilla looked at the child squirming at Adaora's hip.

"You have a healthy boy," she said to Adaora.

"And you have nothing," Adaora replied.

There was no need for more words. Adaora had been so wounded by the idea that Olisa had been in the village all along and by Priscilla's betrayal. She had come because she wanted to hurt Priscilla as much as her actions had hurt the village. And she had no weapon, except what she called the truth. Her own bastard child would grow up with a mother. But Priscilla's—wherever the boy might be—was already paying the price for her sins.

"You are correct," Priscilla said, looking at Adaora's child. "I have nothing." She thought of her son; a vision of him walking flashed through her mind. A vision in which he seemed happy. She turned to the guards and said, "I am ready."

26

Margaret

Lagos, 2005

God was punishing her, Margaret explained. This was all punishment for her sins—for going to the dibia, for not having enough faith. The cane on her back, the throbbing in her head, the screech-screech sounds of her ancestors hiding in the walls, could they not hear, not see? The walls shone with the eyes of dead men watching. Ghosts everywhere, watching. How could they not see? she asked, laughing. How could they become as blind as the tables and chairs and cups? She continued laughing, mimicking the voice in her head. I am right, you know? God is good. God is good because even if he slipped on banana peels, God was too big and too kind to fall, but the last time he fell, he caught everybody. God is a great catcher but sometimes his hands are used for punishment—how is all this not obvious by now? Look at his hands, she continued—his precious big hands moving like snakes, crawling through her back, holding her neck. Is God not a snake? she stopped to ask. She would stomp him out, snuff out the life in him, she declared. After all, she had outsmarted God the last time. This was the real reason they came for her—because women are not supposed to be in power. Nobody likes that. Especially the ancestors. Especially Pa Okolo. And yet, she was not a woman—not really. She had stolen God and put him in her pocket. Now he was frantically reaching for her hairpins. The banana peels are in the bathroom sink. She must not let him know that she has found him. She has found God—who is laughing now?

"Mama, that's enough!" Nwando said, a little more loudly than she intended. She stretched her hands to Margaret's thigh and pinned down her arms there, to keep her from moving. They were in a small room with a small man whose name was Dr. Manuel. His hair peeked out of his shirt and rolled-up sleeves. For nineteen days, Margaret had been sleeping, rambling, barely eating.

Now this Dr. Manuel, a frail-looking man in his seventies with a gray crown of Afro, looked at Margaret, smiling.

"Easy, madam, be gentle for me, okay?" Dr. Manuel said, as one might address a four-year-old. Nwando and Nosa had found the doctor three years ago. They'd met him at a dinner party organized by Nigeria's ambassador to Turkey, and though they had said nothing at the time in response to his clinical successes on people who lived with schizophrenia, they had been quietly relieved to note that he was setting up a consultancy in Lagos for a few private clients who did not want to travel far.

"She appears to be getting worse," Nwando said, still holding down Margaret's hands.

"I see," Dr. Manuel responded, still smiling. The air conditioner whistled in the room and the sound of the nurses in the next room filtered to their ears.

"Is it normal?" Nwando asked.

"Well," the doctor replied, moving his face from Margaret to Nwando, "*normal* is not really language we use with our patients."

"What I mean is that it has never been this bad before," Nwando continued, feeling chided. "Her medicines have always worked."

"The medicines are not always an exact science—there are external triggers too. Life disruptions, age-related fatigue, those kinds of things that make the medicines seem to lose their potency," Dr. Manuel explained. "I will place her on a new treatment plan once our assessment is finished."

"And how long will this treatment plan last?" Nwando asked, though what she meant to ask was, How long before Mama is well enough again?

"These things vary," he replied. "Is there anything you would like to tell me?" he asked, addressing Margaret.

"Go on, Mama, is there something you want to say to the doctor?" Nwando encouraged her.

Margaret scratched her neck, looking straight ahead.

Nwando tapped her again. "Mama, won't you tell Doctor about the dreams, at least?"

Margaret did not respond. Nwando turned to the doctor. "I suppose we'll see you at the next appointment." Nwando made to get up.

"Why am I here?" Margaret asked.

"We came for your checkup," Nwando replied, settling back down.

"Interesting painting," Margaret continued, ignoring her daughter.

"What makes it interesting?" Dr. Manuel asked, his eyes sparking with interest. He had brought out his pen from his breast pocket and reopened the notepad he had closed earlier.

"How about you answer my question, and I answer yours," Margaret replied. Dr. Manuel's right leg stopped jerking.

"You are here because your family is worried about you. They want you to get help," he replied.

"Get help from who?"

"From me. It is my job to help people like you."

Margaret began to laugh. "Do you believe, Doctor? Are you a believer?"

"It depends. There are all kinds of things to believe in, or not to believe in."

"I mean this work that you claim to do. Do you believe that you help people? Do you believe that it is in your power to fix what is unfixable?"

"I believe it is my job to try—to learn."

"But would you try if there was no money attached?" Her eyes were clear now.

"Mama, you are being rude to the doctor," Nwando exclaimed.

"No, it's okay," Dr. Manuel said, raising his hand. "I don't mind her questions at all." Then he turned to look at Margaret. "It seems you are more concerned about money than about getting well."

"Are we not all more concerned about money than about anything else? If my family had not paid you, would I be here now? Would you be interested in people who cannot pay you?"

"Please ignore her. She likes to tell people off," Nwando said, apologetic.

Dr. Manuel laughed a small laugh. "How do you feel, Margaret? Tell me how you feel."

"Like we are both wasting our time. I already know how this will end," she said, and then she slapped her neck.

"And how will it end?" Dr. Manuel asked, scribbling faster in his notepad.

"The way that all things end."

"And how is that exactly?"

"The eventuality of all life is death—is it not?"

"Mama, please, don't even start this here," Nwando said, riffling through her purse, searching for nothing.

"You're correct. That does not mean that the point of life is death." The doctor paused a little, then continued. "You know, as sober as the notion of death is, it is not necessarily what gives meaning to life."

"Oh, so you are a philosopher too?" Margaret said wryly.

"I am only answering your question. Tell me how that makes you feel," Dr. Manuel continued.

"What?"

"Death," the doctor said.

"I think it should follow the right order," Margaret answered thoughtfully. "The old first. Always the old first. A child should not have to go before their parent."

"Is that what you are afraid of? That you will lose your daughter?"

"This is what will happen if I remain here, if nothing is done."

"Who told you this?"

"I have to go for her and my grandson to remain."

"I'm sure you believe this," Dr. Manuel said. "We can talk about it, if you want."

"You are a detestable man; do you know that?" Margaret said, surprising both Nwando and Dr. Manuel.

"Okay, that's enough," Nwando said. "We must leave now." She had barely finished speaking the words when Margaret turned around and smacked her on her face.

Nwando held her other cheek, as if the pain planted on one side could only be felt on the other.

"Dr. Manuel, we'll be seeing you next week, thank you," Nwando said. Then she walked to the reception area, where she signaled for the two private security guards who had been cleared by the hospital and were responsible for moving Margaret between facilities.

▼▲▼

What am I doing here? Margaret thought one morning. Have I died and somehow remained unaware of it?

It was her sixth week at the private psychiatric ward where she had been locked away—eating, sleeping, waiting. As though to remind her that she was still among the living, Margaret made a friend, another patient named Nkoli.

Nkoli was fair-skinned and tall. She sported a low haircut. Although she was clearly younger than Margaret, her eyes seemed much older. She had thick strands of chin hair, and a few shave bumps on her jawline, which is to say that it was a hard face, softened only by a dimple in her left cheek.

Both women—Margaret and Nkoli—had their breakfast in the section of the dining hall reserved for people of certain economic means. Initially, Margaret used to eat alone, every day at exactly 8:50 a.m. But one morning, while she sat eating breakfast, the door flung open, and a nurse ushered Nkoli in. The woman moved toward Margaret and took the seat next to her. Margaret had felt insulted by the proximity. She continued to eat in silence, and the other woman did not say a word to her. Instead, she opened a magazine the nurse offered her and began to read. Rough as her face appeared, there was a casual elegance about Nkoli, her small fingers, her clean and trimmed nails, the way she gently placed the table napkin on her thigh. It may have been the sense of quiet decorum Nkoli displayed, or the fact that she seemed to have her own personal nurse assigned to her, but Margaret decided to break the silence.

"How long?" Margaret asked.

It was one of those presumptuous questions, open-ended.

"Fourteen," Nkoli answered in a thick accent. She forked a roll of spaghettini into a small lump of chicken.

"Fourteen?" Margaret asked.

"Fourteen years," Nkoli said. She did not look up from her meal.

"Hmm." Margaret responded. "What for?"

Nkoli glanced at her magazine, ate some more. Then she laughed.

"The man I married says I have anger issues." She stopped, looked at Margaret now. "He says that I don't like people."

Margaret nodded.

They sat in that shared silence the rest of that morning, surrounded by the hum of bathroom slippers and faux-leather shoes pattering on the concrete.

The next day, they had another exchange. It was their first real conversation.

"How did we get here?" Margaret asked as they sat down to breakfast.

"Are you asking me?" Nkoli replied. "My youngest son has taken over as CEO of my farming business. He is just twenty-three—barely out of school."

Margaret raised a teacup to her mouth, pausing to inhale the steam. She did not drink. Instead, she kept her face toward Nkoli as she considered how mild the woman's problems appeared to be, how trivial compared to hers.

"I have a theory," Margaret now said.

There was a long pause as both women continued eating.

"What is it?" Nkoli finally asked.

"The obvious one. We are cursed."

"You believe in that kind of thing?" Nkoli eyed Margaret.

"I don't see why not."

"Hmm," Nkoli said. "By whom?"

Margaret raised her fingers to touch her head as if thinking. "I suppose I can't speak for everybody," she finally said.

"Anyway," Margaret started again. "I can't speak for everybody, but I can speak for myself. You see, my grandfather—he did some very bad things."

"And?"

"You know what they say about the sins of the fathers?"

Nkoli laughed.

"You are laughing? You think it's funny?" Margaret asked. She wanted to leave. She wanted to stay. She did not think she would be this desperate for the company of another human.

"I'm not laughing at you, my friend. They have you on medication, right?" Nkoli asked.

Margaret felt slapped.

"This sins-of-the-father thing," Nkoli said. She laughed again. "I won't ask what your grandfather did. But tell me, do you really think he committed the worst sin on earth? Do you know what secrets people's families hide? I won't bother you with my own family skeletons. Going by this theory, the whole world should be mad!"

"You don't know what my grandfather did," Margaret said.

"And you don't know what the pope's grandfather did. Yet the pope is the pope, and you and I are here," Nkoli continued.

"I merely provided my own theory," Margaret said.

"It is a silly theory, but I want to hear more about it."

"My family and I recently went to a priest."

"You are Catholic?"

"No—interdenominational. But I mean a local priest—in my village."

"I see," Nkoli said, nodding. "What did the priest say?"

"He said the sins of the fathers have to be atoned for."

"You believe him?"

"I believe in answers," Margaret replied. "I am a woman of solutions."

"And your being here—it is not a solution?" Nkoli asked.

"It is not the solution I need," Margaret replied.

Nkoli laughed.

The nurse stood by the door, watching. She had come to get Margaret for her morning pills, but she was still eating, by herself, and she carried on quietly with the conversation she had with herself. Some days, the nurse observed that Margaret was more earnest, more animated, even gesticulating. But she'd never gotten close enough to hear what she was saying. In this moment, however, she was speaking quietly. Perhaps she should leave the woman be, the nurse thought. She would make her rounds and then come back for Margaret. Her medicines could wait another hour or two.

▼▲▼

Nwando knew her husband's smell, that musky fragrance that hung in the bathroom hours after he had showered, the deep floral tones that clung to his shirts. She knew his smell, fresh from sleep, saliva dried at the edges of his mouth. He was the kind of man with loose pores, sweating easily even when he was in an air-conditioned room, the sweat itself evidence of some distress, or nervousness or anger or fear. On many days, she could not stand it. Yet she knew two solid truths about their marriage. One was that Nosa was a good man; his kindness had been one of the first traits that endeared him to her. Two, she was lucky to have married him, a man who had grown to match every expectation she'd had as a young woman. She'd never had cause to suspect an incident of indiscretion on his part, and even though there were seasons when they were more distant, they always found their way back to the intimacy of their early years. Nosa was loyal. He'd stood beside her after their first child, and when two years passed without another conception. He'd stood beside her through three miscarriages after that. When the doctors finally made their decree, that she would not be able to have another child naturally, he'd made a decree of his own—one son was enough. As a wife, Nwando had lacked for nothing. She had equal access to his resources, the freedom to work a job at her convenience, knowing that she did not need to. Still, there were times when she wondered if this man was not too weak. If another man would not have been more fitting to her own dispositions toward life. Beneath his wealth and worldliness, Nosa was almost like her mother. Deeply suspicious. There was always someone at the office who conspired against him. Or always a pain in his thigh or his back that signaled a medical emergency. It was as if he expected to turn around one day and find that the world was going to break. He tried to do good, live right, shelter himself from the ill will of other people. And where he could not control these outcomes, he avoided certain people completely. It was similar in pattern to her mother's lifestyle, except that he was well while her mother was not.

Now they had entered this season of their marriage again. Nosa, reeking of fear; she, completely nauseated by it. Therefore, she was not surprised when he came home the other evening and said they had to talk. It had been three months since they returned from the village, but the verdict still hung over them. The night after the cleansing, she'd been so unsettled by the dibia's verdict. How did she go from not believing to a fear that completely overpowered her? It made no sense. But she could already sense Nosa considering their options. She needed someone with whom she could discuss the issue. Someone who saw the world through her eyes. Nosa was not going to be that person, so she had gone to Benjamin's room, knowing how late it was. She did not consider herself too emotional; life with her mother had hardened her. But once she saw his bag on his bed, the memory from a lifetime of his absence rushed through her. She began to sob. Eventually she stopped after he convinced her that it wasn't what she thought. She knew it was a lie, but she accepted it. They talked about Margaret's health, about Nwando's plan to have her hospitalized; they even talked about the years, how odd it was to be raised by a mother who was so accomplished and yet unpredictable. Benjamin had told her then that he wanted to help in his own way; he did not want her to feel that the burden was hers to carry alone. He would stay, at least until Margaret was back to being on the mend.

In the months that passed, Nosa seemed happy. She was relieved. Even Chuka seemed less apprehensive. But somehow the dibia's words, which they had all put away, began to grow louder. It was through Nosa, her beloved husband; it was through the man closest to her that the Gods found their outlet in her home.

The first night Nosa brought up the verdict, they had quarreled loud into the night. She could not believe she would have to deal with her mother in the hospital, and now her husband, over a verdict that she'd long concluded was a sham. A ploy to get money from city people. On the evening of their most recent quarrel, Nosa had announced to her during dinner, "I think we should take a trip abroad, three of us, just a year, until things settle." She had laughed because it was typical of him. His instinct was to run, and he was simple enough to think that the curse could be real but that he could distance himself from it with a passport. Now, arriving home from the supermarket and thinking so clearly about that argument, she decided she needed to have an urgent talk with Nosa. She would square things between them. Enough of this nonsense plan to travel. Chuka was about to write his mock exams; he needed to focus. She and her husband could at least try to offer him stability in the coming months. Besides, her father was still in town—what were they supposed to do with him?

"Honey, I'm back," she announced when she entered their home.

Silence.

Martina, their housekeeper, rushed out and explained that Nosa had been upstairs all day. Nwando could see that his car was parked in the compound. She went upstairs into their bedroom, but there was no sign of him. She came back downstairs, calling. There was no response, so she'd assumed he perhaps went out on a walk. Nosa and his walks. She decided she would go to the bathroom and freshen up, then wait for his return. What she did not expect was to find Nosa lying on the bathroom floor, conscious but dazed, his head bleeding.

She fell to her knees beside him, shaking him, screaming. He turned to her, writhing in pain. Her Nosa. Her darling, precious husband. She ran downstairs to fetch Martina and Joseph, their driver. All through the trip to the hospital, her hands would not stop shaking. A year in London, he had said. She would call Chuka's school; she would make plans. She would explain to Benjamin once he returned from his outing. She picked up her phone to call him, but his phone was switched off. She felt her face wet with tears. A year in London was not bad at all.

27

The Lovers

Lagos, 2005

He would see her one more time. He would hold her hand and say what she deserved to hear: He was sorry; he should never have left; he truly loved her. Already Benjamin had stayed in Nigeria far longer than he anticipated—almost three months now. His days were quiet—reading, talking with Nosa, Nwando; in the evenings they'd all gather together at the dining table to eat and banter over Nigerian politics. Nosa introduced him to his friends, insisting Benjamin accompany him to clubs, to events, sometimes to work. Each time these invitations came, Nwando sent him off, happy for both men to get along. The boy, Chuka, was still distant—still guarded; Benjamin could see his grandmother in him; Margaret had been the exact same way. Yet even his detachment seemed to wane as the weeks passed. He came home every two weekends or so from boarding school, and Nwando was often eager to impose on him a trip that involved Benjamin and her and Chuka. They were not exactly relating like family, but the boy had begun to ask him questions and respond to him in full sentences.

The time the dibia assigned for the execution of the curse had passed. Benjamin was in the best shape of his life, with the contentment of a man who had everything he needed. Now it was time to return to the States. He would do things properly this time; he would say his goodbyes.

In truth, he'd tried to leave earlier, on the night of the ceremony, after he spent almost two hours in prayer. He'd gotten up and packed his bags. His plan was to leave the trouble behind. But Nwando had knocked on his hotel door very early the next morning and seen his bags packed, then looked at him and started to cry. She'd sat on his bed and wept, and he'd sat beside her. He had tried to console her, but he did not have the words. Eventually, he'd patted her gently on the back and said, "It's not what you think."

The months flew by, and Margaret had, in all that time, been secluded at the hospital. Every week, Benjamin told himself that it was good that she was getting the care that she needed. And every week he convinced himself that Nosa had been right to worry, to show concern for his family. Benjamin had wanted to stay until Margaret was out of the hospital, or at least well enough to see him leave. And now that time had come. He spoke to Nwando about needing to visit Margaret in the hospital before he returned to America; he explained that it was long in coming, that they had things to clear up. It was the third Saturday of the month, which meant that Margaret was scheduled to go on her drive around the city, Nwando explained, so she made plans for her and Benjamin to make the trip to the hospital. She was surprised when she realized that Benjamin wanted to visit Margaret on his own.

"But where will you take her?" she asked.

"Around—there's a park your husband mentioned."

"And what will you say?"

"Never mind two old chaps—we can manage a discussion."

"But what if—" She stopped.

Benjamin smiled, knowing what she meant but did not say.

"The park is not that far from the hospital," he said. "Try not to worry."

▼▲▼

Benjamin found Margaret at the waiting area in the clinic.

"It's you," Margaret said when he walked in through the doorway.

"It's me," Benjamin replied.

He was tired, but he felt energized by the sight of her, as if he was twenty-four again. He'd rehearsed the conversation they would have, the right cues he would give—hold her hand, look her in the face when he announced his decision to return. He would be the man she expected him to be.

Benjamin smiled at the nurse who led him to the reception area, where he signed some papers. He'd come to visit Margaret a few times, always with Nwando. But she hardly spoke with their daughter during those visits, and even worse, she never acknowledged him. So he'd stayed away after the first few times, receiving Nwando's update on how she was faring, how she had miraculously taken a turn for the better.

He sat beside Margaret. "So where do you want to go?" he asked. He looked at a painting on a wall, trying not to sound too eager.

"Home," she replied.

He turned to look at her; they both laughed. He helped her up.

"Nwando would have my head if I took you home," he explained once they were outside, the sun stinging their eyes. They decided to go to a small private resort that Benjamin suggested, one of the options

Nosa had presented to him the night before, though he did not say this to Margaret. They entered Ikoyi, the driver moving along the back streets that led to the resort. There was a small sign that read MACAULAY; it was where Benjamin had his first apartment after he left Cynthia—the living room was huge, but the bedroom was tiny and suffocating, so that the first time Margaret visited she'd referred to it as a prison cell. Now when they passed it again, they looked at the sign, then at each other. For the second time that afternoon, they laughed. Benjamin's phone rang then. It was Nwando on her way home from the supermarket, calling to check about the drive; she was just heading home herself.

"We've just left the clinic," Benjamin said with a smile.

"How is she? Is she upset I didn't come with you?" Nwando asked, concerned.

"Not to worry. I'll call you if we need anything," Benjamin continued. Then he turned off his phone.

They arrived at the resort, and Benjamin moved to open her car door from outside. Margaret hesitated.

"I don't feel comfortable; let's go back," she said, still sitting.

"No, please. It's quiet here," he added—desperate. "Look, I've switched off my mobile; we don't have to hear from Nwando again."

"It's not Nwando," Margaret said, shaking her head.

"Please. Please, there's something we need to talk about."

Margaret looked at him from the car seat, squinting at the sun. "Just talk? That's all?"

"What else can it be?" Benjamin laughed. "Yes, just talk," he added.

They walked into the resort and took a table by the waterfront, where they ordered malt drinks and finger foods and sat watching the ducks. There was a breeze on her face as she sipped her malt. Margaret found herself starting to relax.

"So what do you want to talk about?" Margaret started.

"What do you want me to talk about?" he joked. He was losing his nerve. Perhaps this was a bad idea.

"When are you leaving?" Margaret asked after a moment.

"Right after the New Year."

"I see."

"You've always known how to go straight to things."

"One of us has to," Margaret replied.

"And I've always been the sort to avoid things." He held her eyes until she looked away.

"At least you bothered to say goodbye—you may be losing your edge for surprise," she said dryly.

Silence.

"I never learned what happened to her—you know. I never learned what happened to Priscilla. It seemed so unfair," Benjamin said.

"What do you mean?"

"She just dropped off the face of the earth—vanished. She never got her own ending, not in the journal, not even in my uncle's letters."

"It is typical for people sent off in exile," Margaret answered.

"Yes. But she did nothing. She should not have been punished for doing nothing."

"Why are you telling me this, Benni?"

"Because . . ." He allowed the words to trail off.

"You want my pity?"

"I did not take the dibia's words seriously about our marriage, but I should have thought about Priscilla. She did nothing wrong, and still things ended badly for her."

They allowed a short silence to pass between them, then Margaret said, "So you agree that this all happened because we disobeyed. You agree that the curse is real?"

"I don't believe in curses, Maggie. You know this," he said.

Margaret turned away.

"I believe that people sometimes punish others for things they do not understand."

He leaned closer, touched her hand on the table. "There were things I did not understand back then, and I punished you for it. I punished you and our daughter."

"You've gotten sentimental," Margaret said. She turned to him but withdrew her hand.

"I loved you, Maggie," he said.

"Liar."

Another silence passed.

"I will not forgive you," Margaret said. "And don't tell me what you believe. You left because you were weak—spoiled. You were selfish and could not take it. You could not take my condition. It was too much for you."

Benjamin sighed, stung by her words.

"So what now?" he asked.

"Well," Margaret said, adjusting her boubou. "What has happened has already happened. Now we find a way to move forward."

She looked refreshed, youthful—the new medication was clearly working. He wanted to reserve this moment, allow her the recovery she truly deserved. She said she would not forgive him, not now anyway, and that was fine. Forgiveness would have been too much; he did not want such an easy absolution. What he wanted was a chance to be heard—to explain. He felt a slight tremor in his hands. It must be the chill of the early evening, the serenity of reconciliation in the making, he thought.

"It's getting late," Margaret said.

"It's so peaceful here," Benjamin said.

"So peaceful." She nodded.

He signaled the driver, who went out to get the car. They walked to the entrance of the resort to meet him, Margaret's hand in Benjamin's. There was a young couple in their late twenties observing them from a distance, thinking to themselves how sweet and intimate Margaret and Benjamin looked.

Benjamin let go of Margaret's hand only when they reached the car. He opened the door for her and waited to see her settled. The peace of the waterfront seemed to leave with them; she smiled at him once he was seated. Could it be that she was happy with him, or that she was feeling better? Could it be both? It was more than he could ask for—it was more than his father or grandfather got.

Benjamin turned on his phone once the driver pulled out of the resort. He saw a text from Nwando. He dialed her number.

"You switched off your phone?" she said, upset.

"No," he lied.

"I tried to reach you; it was urgent."

"Is everything all right?"

She started crying, softly. It was Nosa; he'd fallen in the bathroom, broke his head and leg. Nwando was now in the hospital, waiting to hear more from the doctor, but the doctor said he would be fine, that he just had a mild concussion.

"There, there; take it easy," Benjamin said. He felt his stomach tighten. Another tremor in his hands. There is quite a chill this evening, he thought.

Benjamin felt his stomach tighten again, but he assured Nwando that it was a harmless event. He would drop off Margaret and head to the hospital at once.

The call ended, and he thought about Nwando clearly; her worries had a dramatic flair, even if, like him, she held it off for as long as she could. Nosa would be fine. People fall in bathrooms all the time.

Beside him, Margaret was quietly humming. Her eyes were closed; it was hard to tell if she was awake or asleep. There was soft music coming from the radio. Their hands rested lightly against each other. Finally, they arrived back at the hospital.

"Maggie?"

She murmured but did not stir.

"We are here, Maggie," Benjamin said. He was smiling. He was still cold. She sat up, looked around. The driver was pulling into the hospital. She'd fallen asleep. She reached out and touched Benjamin's face, her eyes as tender as when they were wed.

Benjamin exhaled. "There's no rush," he said. "We can sit in here a while."

Margaret nodded. "I just need a moment." She was still looking at Benjamin. The driver stepped out of the car and left them to themselves.

"It's all right, you know," Benjamin said to Margaret.

"What is all right?"

"Us. We will be all right; I can sense it." He exhaled again.

"Oh, please—" Margaret said dryly.

Minutes passed. Margaret sat up. "I am ready."

She did not wait for Benjamin to stir but climbed out of the car and stood outside. When moments later Benjamin remained seated, she walked to his side of the car.

"Well—are you coming?"

"Yes, please. In a moment," Benjamin said.

He looked out at Margaret through the window.

"Take care of yourself—will you?"

She nodded.

He kept his eyes on her, his hand on his chest. He could smell fried eggs and baked beans. It reminded him of Sunday mornings in his childhood. Margaret opened the car door and leaned toward him. Benjamin looked up, searching her face. He opened his mouth—Mother?

"Are you all right?" Margaret asked.

He exhaled again. Margaret screamed his name; she screamed for the driver, for the nurse. She held his hand and began to cry.

She could hear the voices now—the elders, the village, the drums. She could hear the cackling of laughter and the opening of doors, the driver and nurses who were moving her aside, getting a wheelchair, struggling to lift Benjamin out of the car. Finally she heard Benjamin's voice—in her head, or in the hallway, or perhaps coming from him as he was being lifted out of the car. It's all right, you know—he'd said.

For the first time in forty years, she believed him.

Acknowledgments

To Tony Elumelu, whose kindness and humility I deeply admire—thank you. Although incredibly accomplished, he often credits his success to hard work and luck. Luck in the sense that being at the right place at the right time, meeting the right people, could transform a life. I have often reflected on this idea of luck with a bit of skepticism, but it is with this book that I feel most inclined to call myself lucky. The work we do is important, and yet, how do we account for the many fortuitous encounters that turn a vision into a realized object? In my case, I have been surrounded by an excellent network of support for which my gratitude is immense.

I am especially grateful to my agent, Allison Malecha, who believed in this project from the start and brought an enthusiasm that championed its growth in ways I could never have imagined. My wonderful editors, Lashanda Anakwah and Anita Chong, were incredibly kind and wise in directing a raw MFA thesis into the novel you now hold in your hands—I could not have asked for a better team. Thank you to my publishers, Phoebe Robinson and Stephanie Sinclair, and to the incredible team working behind the scenes at Penguin Random House, especially the editorial, marketing, and production crew at Tiny Reparations Books; as well as McClelland & Stewart. To Lemara Lindsay-Prince, whom I owe a debt of gratitude for her early championing of this work in the UK. Thank you, Joelle

Owusu, Helen Conford, Danai Denga, and the wonderful crew at Merky Books. Thanks, too, to the amazing Jane Finigan for seeing the vision for the UK.

To my thesis committee at Florida Atlantic University—Ayse Papatya Bucak, Andrew Furman, and Sika Dagbovie-Mullins—you were among the first to see this work, and it was your encouragement that gave me the boldness to take it further. I was also lucky to have the most vibrant group of readers and fellow writers at the program. To Colton from workshop whose last name I shamefully cannot remember. To the best readers, Hailey Keane, Merkin Karr, my dear friend Aaron Guile, program director Becka McKay, and all those who offered feedback and kindness, I'm so grateful for each of you.

My friends were incredibly supportive in so many ways, but I especially want to thank Remi Roy and Adebola Rayo for checking in on me through the craziness of grad school and pandemic life, and particularly for the resources they offered that enabled me to focus on finishing the early draft of this work. To Efe Paul Azino, Joy Isi Bewaji, Kemi Sade, Sylvester Ojenagbon, Esther Okonkwo, Lucia Edafioka, for those pandemic Zoom-writing sessions. As well as the many others I can't name here—thank you for all your support, seen and unseen. Thank you to my family, especially my wonderful siblings, for putting up with me; you have my love, always.

Finally, I especially honor a mentor, teacher, and friend, Pastor Taiwo Odukoya, who has since transitioned to join the ancestors. He was among the first to call me a writer even when I did not think of myself as one. I grieve that he will not get to see these pages, though in a sense, he saw them long before I did.

About the Author

Tochi Eze is a writer and lawyer from Nigeria. *Longreads* named her short story "The Americanization of Kambili," one of "Ten Outstanding Stories to Read in 2023." She has an MFA from Florida Atlantic University and is currently completing her PhD dissertation on postcolonial literary aesthetics at the University of Virginia.